PEACE AMID THE CHAOS

PEACE AMID THE CHAOS

Shannon C. Singleton

I Rise Publishing

Copyright © 2025 by Shannon C. Singleton

All rights reserved.

No part of this publication may be reproduced, distributed, or transmitted in any form or by any means, including photocopying, recording, or other electronic or mechanical methods, without the prior written permission of the publisher, except as permitted by U.S. copyright law. For permission requests, contact I Rise Publishing.

WeRise@IRisePublishing.com

https://www.irisepublishing.com/

The story, all names, characters, and incidents portrayed in this production are fictitious. No identification with actual persons (living or deceased), places, buildings, and products is intended or should be inferred.

Cover art: AI-assisted image generated using Canva, with design and editing by Shannon Singleton

1st edition 2025

ISBN: 979-8-9900501-4-3

To God—

Thank You for the gift of words and the ability to shape them into stories that carry meaning and heart. Thank You for trusting me with this calling—to create, to inspire, and to speak to the soul. May every word I write reflect the hope, strength, and grace You so freely give.

CONTENTS

Acknowledgements	IX
1. Room 98	1
2. Phone Call from the Past	12
3. Welcome to D Ville	25
4. The Welcome In-Between	37
5. The Things We Don't Know	50
6. Cold Hard Facts	62
7. Fantasy of Possibilities	74
8. It's Me	85
9. Almost Beautiful	96
10. Beneath the Surface	108
11. Lunch Date	121
12. One Simple Question	132
13. Supporting Cast	147
14. Flashback	163

15.	Victoria Rose Original	177
16.	Underneath It All	192
17.	Today, It Ends	204
18.	Just Do	218
19.	We Have to Do This	233
20.	A Way Out	246
21.	What Have You Done	255
22.	I Won't Go Back	265
23.	Why Not Start Here	278
Epilogue		287
About the Author		297
A Note from the Author		299

ACKNOWLEDGEMENTS

To my family and friends—thank you for your unwavering support and belief in me. I truly couldn't have made it this far without you. While I can't name everyone individually, please know that I am deeply grateful for every word of encouragement, every kind gesture, and every moment of your time throughout this journey.

A special thank-you to my nephew, KJ, for being the very first person to read the early pages of this book and offer thoughtful feedback. To my sister, Rah (a licensed therapist!), thank you for helping me craft the emotional and psychological layers of my characters with authenticity.

To my son, Jaylen—thank you for your honest, no-holds-barred feedback, especially on the most emotionally tense scenes.

To my siblings Deon, Kevin, and Gabby, and my nephew, Darien—thank you for answering all my random questions and helping me shape background details and dialogue with realism.

To my amazing beta readers—KJ, Rhonda, Tamara, JM, Jerry, Chas, Khalil and Kaylie—Your insight challenged me to dig deeper.

Thank you to my family, friends, the Indie Authors Group in the Atlanta Writers Club, the Loganville Legacy Lions Club, the Friends of the O'Kelly Memorial Library, and the many individuals who took time to vote or share feedback on the cover design. Your input, support, and thoughtful responses helped shape one of the most important visual elements of this book, and I'm deeply grateful.

I appreciate every single one of you. Your support means the world to me.

Chapter One

Room 98

Miriam pulled into a spot near the hospital entrance without much effort—not that she was surprised. At this hour, the lot was nearly empty, the quiet hum of the night settling over the area. Overhead lights cast a pale glow across the pavement, stretching shadows from the few scattered cars.

Lafourche Medical Center stood ahead, a simple, two-story brick structure—no towering glass windows or sprawling wings, just a no-frills square building. It was enough. In a town this size, there wasn't much need for anything bigger.

She could see her reflection in the sliding glass doors as she walked up to the entrance. Every time she saw the full length of her 5' frame, she was reminded of how desperately she wanted to be taller when she was younger. She had spent years wishing for a few more inches. Growing up, she had stretched, measured, and even willed herself taller, but nature had other plans. In the end, she figured that's why God made high heels. Slipping into a pair always gave her the height she once prayed for and, with it, a surge of confidence that made the world seem just a little more within her reach.

As she glanced at her reflection, her brows pinched together. The sight of her tennis shoes made her sigh. "I should have kept on my heels," she muttered under her breath. The doors slid open right on cue as if physically speaking her next thought, *It's too late now.*

She approached the information desk, the faint hum of a computer and the soft shuffle of papers filling the quiet space. "I need the room number for Mary Butler, please," she said, resting her hands on the counter.

The receptionist barely looked up. "Are you family?"

"Yes, she's my mom."

"She's in room ninety-eight. It's down this hall on the right."

Miriam already knew the way but nodded anyway—no need to seem dismissive. "Thank you ma'am," she said with a slight smile before turning toward the hallway.

The silence stretched around her as she walked, the only sound coming from the rhythmic squeak of her sneakers against the polished floor. Each step echoed through the empty corridor. She stopped in front of door ninety-eight.

The hospital always had a cold, sterile feel to it, and Miriam couldn't shake the discomfort that crept over her every time she walked through those sliding doors. She had lost count of how many times she and her mother had been admitted over the years. It almost felt like a second home growing up. Except it was yet another unhappy home. One where the adults gave pitiful looks, awkward stares and talked in hushed tones.

For all the giving they gave, the one thing they never gave was what her, Nathaniel and her mother needed the most: a way out. No one here ever spoke up, never offered to help her mother escape the prison that was her father. In fact, that's the one thing they seemed good at, patching them up and giving them *back* to her father.

As Miriam reached for the door knob, she felt a nauseating feeling of dread deep down inside. She quickly brought her right hand to her stomach as if to will it, command it to quiet down. With her left hand, she tried over and over again to reach for the knob, but the knob kept getting further and further away. The more it moved away, the harder it was for her to breathe. The air felt thick as mud, forcing her to draw shallow, desperate breaths. Her mind rebelled against her, conjuring an image of her father standing rigid on the other side—his eyes blazing, fists clenched at his sides, jaw tight with fury.

She made herself close her eyes and began repeating over and over in her mind, *Go my child and do my dirty work. And may the force be with you!* The phrase originated from a comical incident with her best friend Lisa and another friend during their preteen years. As the memory replayed, the world swam back into focus. Her ragged breaths slowly steadied, the familiar dance of panic receding. The doorknob—her nemesis—now stood in its rightful place, no longer warping and shifting with her racing thoughts. She drew in one last, steadying breath as her hand inched forward. Just as her fingertips brushed the cool metal of the knob, door ninety-eight swung open.

"Shiiiit!" Miriam gasped as she grabbed her chest and jumped back from the door.

A man with almond-colored skin stepped hesitantly from the room, his white doctor's coat crisp and wrinkle free as he glanced over at Miriam. He quickly stepped aside, clearing the doorway, but his eyes lingered, betraying a flicker of uncertainty. His face held a quiet blend of embarrassment and concern, yet when he spoke, his voice was calm and assured—smooth, practiced, the tone of someone who had long learned to mask any uneasiness.

"I didn't mean to startle you. You must be Miriam. I'm Dr. Crane, your mother's doctor."

Miriam patted her chest, lifting a single finger as she struggled to steady her breath. Her pulse pounded in her ears, the rush of adrenaline still coursing through her.

Dr. Crane's expression softened to concern. He shifted his weight, his grip loosening on the clipboard at his side. But he remained silent, giving her the space to recover.

After a few controlled breaths, Miriam straightened. "No problem," she said, her voice steadier.

Dr. Crane nodded. "Can I speak to you about your mother's condition before you go in? She's resting right now and your brother went down to the cafeteria to get him something from the vending machines."

Miriam reached over and grabbed her elbow without thinking. "Sure."

"Would you like to go somewhere more private?"

She glanced around the quiet hospital corridor, its familiar scent sharp in her nose. The overhead fluorescent light buzzed faintly. *It's not like anyone's around.* "We can talk right here."

Dr. Crane nodded. "Your mom came in feeling extremely fatigued. After running some tests, we admitted her-her blood sugar was dangerously high." He hesitated for a few seconds before adding, "You're aware she has type 2 diabetes, correct?"

Miriam swallowed hard, her throat suddenly dry. She gave a faint nod, her lips pressing together.

"When I asked if she was taking her medication, she admitted she wasn't," Dr. Crane said, his tone measured but concerned. "I asked why, but she didn't give me an answer. Do you have any idea why she might refuse to take it? Could she be depressed about something?"

A dozen reasons flashed through Miriam's mind-some insignificant, some deeply painful-but voicing them felt pointless. *What could this doctor do about it anyway?* She shifted her weight, arms crossing over her chest. "I don't know." It wasn't exactly a lie. She didn't know which reason, if any, was the real culprit.

Dr. Crane sighed and shifted his clipboard to his other hand. "I've seen cases like this before. Sometimes, patients get so frustrated with their illness that they convince themselves it's easier to ignore it. I had a patient a few years back—same condition, same refusal to take medication. She managed for a while, but her symptoms worsened until she collapsed at work. By the time she got to the hospital, she had suffered kidney failure. We were able to stabilize her, but she had to start dialysis." He paused allowing his words to sink in. "I don't want that to happen to your mother."

Miriam's stomach twisted at the thought. She pressed her fingertips to her temple, rubbing slow circles as she tried to think. "What happens if her levels stay high? Or get worse?"

"Type 2 diabetes can take a heavy toll on the body. The heart, kidneys, blood vessels, even the eyes-it can damage them all. Poor circulation is a major risk. In severe cases, it can lead to amputation or blindness."

Miriam's gaze dropped to the cold, linoleum floor. Blindness. Amputation. The words churned in her stomach, too big to swallow. She couldn't picture a world where her mother couldn't see or walk freely. And she prayed she'd never have to.

"I understand," she murmured.

Dr. Crane noticed the way her hands curled into fists, the tension settling into her shoulders. He wanted to say something reassuring, something to lighten the weight pressing down on her, but the words wouldn't come. Instead, he decided to focus on what he could do.

"For now, I'll adjust her insulin to stabilize her sugar levels. But once she's discharged, she'll need to make changes to her diet-lower-fat, high fiber foods like whole grains, fruits and vegetables. She has to take her medication consistently and aim for at least twenty to thirty minutes of exercise a day, three to five times per week. If she sticks to that, her glucose levels should stay under control." He paused before continuing. "It would help if you talked to her about it."

Tension seeped from Miriam's shoulders as her clenched fists slowly uncurled. The fog of uncertainty that had rolled into her thoughts began to dissipate, revealing a faint glimmer of hope. Her eyes met Dr. Crane's with newfound resolve as she gave him a determined nod. "I will. In fact, I'll go in now."

Dr. Crane gave a gentle, approving smile. "I'll see you later then."

Miriam inhaled deeply, exhaled slowly, and pushed open the door to her mother's hospital room. The dim lighting cast a soft yellow glow, stretching long shadows across the walls. The rhythmic beeping of a monitor filled the stillness. A television mounted on the wall played on mute, a long forgotten TV show flashed across the screen.

She stepped forward quietly, her pulse steadying as the hospital bed came into view. An IV pole stood beside it like a silent sentry, the fluid bag hanging motionless. To the left, a well-worn recliner sat tucked against the wall—the kind that never quite molded to comfort no matter how much you shifted.

Miriam approached with careful steps, her gaze settling on her mother's face. The scar near the upper left corner of her eye drew her in—a faded apostrophe-shaped mark, one of many permanent keepsakes from her father. She's sure he hadn't meant for it to take that shape, but somehow, it felt fitting.

Apostrophes in grammar show possession, and in his mind, that's all they had ever been—her mother, herself, Nathaniel. Possessions. Objects to control, hurt and hate. Objects to use and then discard when they no longer serve his purpose. Never having even a second thought about how they felt physically or emotionally.

She ground her teeth. A bad habit she knew she needed to get rid of. She never could understand how a person could do all these things to someone who they were supposed to protect and love. They were married in a church, for God's sake. To love and to cherish. What happened to that vow? Why did it always seem like only one person had to uphold the promise while the other got away with breaking it? Where was the empathy? Where was the putting himself in their shoes?

She knew she would never get answers. But she guessed her father was like most people. They don't really care until they are the ones being used, hated and hurt.

Miriam let out a quiet breath and refocused on her mother. Despite the weariness on her face, there was a regal beauty about her—like a warrior queen resting after battle, the scar validating the fierceness of the fight. A small smile of admiration tugged at Miriam's lips. *I hope I look half as good when I'm her age.*

Her mother's blankets were pulled up neatly to her chest, arms resting limply at her sides. Miriam stood still, watching the gentle rise and fall of her breathing, unsure if she should wake her. But she knew her mother would be upset if she came and left without saying a word.

Miriam didn't know what to say so she cleared her throat, "Uh uhm."

Her mother's eyes slowly opened, unfocused at first. Then, sensing another presence, she turned her head, her gaze searching until it landed on Miriam.

"Miriam, ya finally came!" she whispered, a smile warming her face.

"Hey momma, how you feeling?"

"Chil', I'm ok. Except fo' dese doctors always tryna fix me. I don't know why dey jus can't leave me be."

Miriam crossed her arms. "Momma, why haven't you been taking your medicine?"

Mary exhaled through her nose. "Babae, I'm jus tired, dat's all.

Miriam frowned. "It can't just be that. In fact, taking your medicine would help you not be so tired. So, please tell me what's really going on."

Mary exhaled sharply, frustration flashing in her eyes. "I'm tired a bein' sick and tired. I'm tired a havin' to prick myself all the dang on time. I'm tired a' tryna remember to take the medicine along with all da other tings I gotta remember to do or take every day and I'm sho' tired of all dese doctors and nurses comin' in here aroun' da clock, but expectin' me to get some rest!"

Miriam's shoulders slumped. She reached out and gently took her mother's hand, giving it a soft squeeze. "I'm sorry you have to go through this."

Mary opened her mouth, then hesitated before letting out a weary sigh. "Maybe I jus' need a lil pick me up."

Miriam perked up. "What would make you feel better momma?"

Mary waved a hand dismissively. "Oh, don't worry 'bout it sweetie."

"No momma, please tell me. I promise you, I'll get it for you," Hope flickered in Miriam's voice.

Mary's eyes twinkled. "I was thinkin'..," she excitedly began, but then, just as quickly, the light dimmed. "Ahh, never mind. Forget it. I don't wanna botha you."

Miriam leaned in, her voice pleading. "Momma, *please* tell me. I promise you, I will get it for you!"

And just like that, the spark returned. "Den it's settled! Ya gon' call Lisa and have her come out fo' a visit."

Miriam's mouth fell open. "Momma!" she gasped. "You tricked me! You know Nathaniel will only pick fights with her."

Mary chuckled knowingly. "Y'all two been best friends since forevah. It shouldn't be dat hard to pick up the phone and give her a call. Ya know as well as I do dat you miss her. You promised to call her and dat's what you gon' do. Don't worry 'bout your brother, I'll take care a him." Mary's voice sang.

Miriam sighed, rubbing her forehead as a weary smile tugged at the corner of her lips. She had her doubts about whether her mother could truly handle Nathaniel, but today wasn't the day to fight that battle. Letting out a groan, she shook her head.

"I was supposed to get you to promise me you'd take your medicine and eat right. How did I let you trick me?"

Mary grinned, eyes gleaming. "And ya call yoself a psychologist!" She giggled.

Miriam shook her head, laughing despite herself.

As their laughter faded, Mary let out a contented sigh, settling deeper into her pillows. A soft peace settled over her. "Thank you, babae. Fo' comin'."

Miriam squeezed her hand one more time. "Always, Momma."

Chapter Two

PHONE CALL FROM THE PAST

Lisa watched the cars go by then looked up expectantly at the light only to find it was still red. She sighed deeply and sat back in the driver's seat. She hated being late, but she really needed to finish up that report. As soon as the light turned green, her gold Acura 3.2L burst into motion. She loved its power, the way it responded immediately to her demand for speed. She smiled as it zipped and zoomed through traffic. When she needed to get somewhere, it got her there! Since earning her degree in finance and landing a job as a financial advisor at a major corporation, it was the only reward she gave herself.

She slid into a parking space at Chili's and glanced at the clock. "10 minutes late is not too bad." She jumped out of the car and headed towards the entrance. As usual on a Friday night, the place was packed. She waded through the noisy crowds standing on the outside and inside the entrance that waited to be seated.

As soon as she made it in, she started to slowly scan the seating area towards her right. When she came up with nothing, she started a new search on the left. "Where are you Josey? You've got to be around here somewhere."

About a year after Lisa moved to Atlanta, she met Josey at a party thrown by a mutual friend. From the moment Josey introduced herself, Lisa sensed a connection.

"I'm Josephine, but I'd really like it if you called me Josey," she said.

Josey's directness caught Lisa off guard. She'd always loved nicknames—the kind that felt personal, like a secret handshake between friends. To her, they were a symbol of belonging, a mark of closeness. Lisa's own name had never lent itself to a proper nickname.

"L" didn't count. It was too short, too impersonal, like an afterthought. But here was Josey, freely offering her nickname as though it came with an invitation to her inner circle. And Lisa accepted it without hesitation. In that instant, she knew their friendship would last. Just as she'd predicted, they've been inseparable ever since.

And she couldn't have asked for a better one. Josey was the kind of friend who understood Lisa without her having to say a word. More importantly, she knew what Lisa needed from a friend.

At one point, Lisa had been plagued by a recurring nightmare—a haunting memory of a time long past. For weeks, she'd wake up mid-scream, drenched in sweat, fear slicing through her like a bitter wind. Josey noticed almost immediately.

"Hey, you been getting any sleep lately? You look tired," she'd asked gently.

"Not really," Lisa admitted with a frown. "I've been having the same nightmare every night."

Josey's eyebrows lifted, but her voice stayed soft. "Oh, really? About what?"

Lisa's gaze shifted, her fingers tightening around her glass. It wasn't about trust. She trusted Josey. It was just that opening up wasn't something she did easily.

Sensing Lisa's hesitation, Josey smiled. "No worries. You don't have to tell me if you don't want to."

Relief flooded Lisa. Her shoulders relaxed as she let out a sigh. "Thanks."

To Lisa's surprise, Josey never brought it up again. Unlike her friend, though, the nightmares refused to take the hint. They continued their relentless siege, night after night.

Then, one Friday evening, there was a knock at Lisa's door. She opened it to find Josey, arms overloaded with bags. Lisa blinked in surprise, her mouth falling open.

"Don't just stand there! Help me out, these bags are heavy!" Josey huffed, shoving a handful of them into Lisa's arms.

Still reeling from the unexpected visit, Lisa carried the bags into the kitchen. Josey set her own haul on the counter with a flourish.

Lisa's eyes darted between the overflowing bags before she finally asked, "Uh, what's going on? What is all of this?"

Josey grinned, bowing dramatically. "Welcome to Poetry Reading Night. I will be your host and poetry reader for tonight's event." With a grand sweep of her hand, she pulled out bottles of wine, trays of appetizers, and a stash of snacks. "For tonight's reading, we have an assortment of fine wines and spirits to refresh ourselves as we explore the world through the words of prolific poets and poetesses. We also have a variety of savory appetizers and treats to nourish the body as the words inspire our souls."

She twirled with exaggerated grace, her hand lifted as if presenting an invisible prize.

Lisa wanted to be annoyed. Who throws a surprise event at someone else's apartment? But she knew Josey wanted her to feel better. She knew how much Lisa loved poetry, and the effort alone was enough to crack through her frustration. She couldn't help but let out a slight giggle and shake her head. Josey was never interested in poetry. So, it felt good knowing someone cared about her enough to do something like this.

Once everything was set, Lisa curled up on the sofa, a pillow wedged beneath her crossed legs. A plate of her favorite snacks balanced on her lap, and a glass of wine glistened in her hand.

Her eyes sparkled with amusement and curiosity as she watched Josey prepare.

Josey started, her voice low and mysterious. "After meticulous research and consulting with hidden masters of the field, I've curated a list of poems that will shatter the edges of your reality-revealing realms of understanding you never knew existed."

"Mmm, tell it!" Lisa cheered, snapping her fingers dramatically before taking a sip of her wine.

Josey nodded with mock seriousness and took a sip from her own glass. Closing her eyes, she inhaled deeply, then began her recital.

"A little child sits and plays
With his purple friend
They talk about adventures
And stories that never seem to end."

Lisa's head tilted, curiosity flickering as she tried to place the words. Josey continued, her voice brimming with soft wonder.

"The child learns
About friends and sharing;
About not being mean,
But caring.

His purple friend teaches
Him the important things in life
Like being polite to his elders
And doing what is right."

Lisa's eyes widened in recognition. Her hand flew to her mouth as she fought to stifle a snicker. But as Josey approached the poem's dramatic climax, the mischief in her voice was unmistakable.

"He is purple and green
His name might sound a little corny
But he is on TV everyday
And his name is Barney."

Lisa laughed so hard she snorted, struggling to breathe as she patted her chest desperately, trying to coax air back into her lungs.

"Noooo!" She cried. She took in a few more breaths as she wiped tears away from her eyes.

Josey, satisfied, simply smiled and nodded in approval.

Finally catching her breath through fading giggles, Lisa managed to shout, "Girl, where in the world did you get that?"

Without missing a beat, Josey replied with a calm, cool voice, "Now... you know I can't reveal my sources."

The night flowed onward with more comically questionable poetry selections. They drank and laughed until their sides ached, continuing long after the sun rose and birds began their morning chorus outside. After that, Lisa never had the nightmare again.

Even now, that memory brought warmth to Lisa's face. After scanning the restaurant for a few more moments, her eyes landed on a slender, dark-skinned woman sitting by a window in the non-smoking section.

"Hey girl!" Lisa shouted as she slid into the booth.

"What's up!" Josey smiled, looking up from her drink.

Josey had the greenest eyes Lisa had ever seen. The only drawback to that, Lisa thought, was she always had to explain to people that it was her real eye color.

"Sorry I'm a little late. I had something I had to finish up at the office."

"No problem. I've already ordered my dish. You better call the waiter over to give him yours 'cause you ain't eating off my plate." Josey said with a little smile on her face.

"Girl please, I never like what you order anyway." Lisa fired back, her smile matching her friend's.

Lisa called the waiter over and ordered her food.

Once the waiter left, Lisa turned and smiled expectantly at her friend. Josey, a security personnel at the bustling Atlanta Hartsfield Airport, always had a story to tell about the passengers, and Lisa loved to listen. She leaned forward, eager to hear what mess and mayhem had unfolded during Josey's shift. "So how was your day?"

"There was this fine ass guy coming into the airport to fly to New York today," Josey went on excitedly, "He had the whole package, tall, handsome, muscular and a tight little ass. He was too fine! You know what I had to do."

"You didn't!" Lisa gasped.

"Oh yes I did. I walked my fine self up to him and explained that it was security procedure to randomly search passengers and he was randomly selected. I felt all on his sexy tail. He felt like he had a big one too!"

"I can't believe you! You're gonna get caught one day. You gon' end up messing with the wrong man."

"Please, they like to get felt up like that."

"Whatever. You'll end up feeling up on a gay man and he won't appreciate that. He'll feel violated and file a complaint against you." Lisa said in a half serious, half joking tone.

"I can tell when they straight or not. All you gotta do is look at the way they walk and how their hips are shaped."

"You are impossible Josey. I can't believe you sometimes. You know you wouldn't like that if it was done to you!"

"You never know, I'd most probably enjoy it." Josey said with a smirk on her face.

Lisa pursed her lips and shook her head in disapproval.

"You know you love me!" Josey giggled.

"No comment." Lisa mumbled, as the waiter arrived with Josey's food.

"I heard that." Josey countered while she deftly shifted her silverware and glass of water to make space for her plate of juicy sirloin steak, loaded mashed potatoes and broccoli. She smiled up at the waiter and politely said, "Thank you."

He replied, "You're welcome," and turned towards Lisa. "Your food will be finished in a couple of minutes."

Lisa exhaled sharply. "I hope 'a couple of minutes' actually means two, because I'm about ten seconds away from asking for a supervisor."

The waiter forced a tight smile. "I'll see what I can do."

Josey watched the waiter disappear into the kitchen, shaking her head with a smirk. "Look at you, all hangry and shit."

Amused, she turned to Lisa-only to find her staring intently at the table, eyes wide with hope. Curious, Josey followed her gaze down to the plate in front of her.

"Oh hell, nah! Remember what you said?" Josey hollered. "I don't like what you order anyway." she mimicked in a high nasal voice. "You know what?" She pursed her lips in mock contempt, flicking her wrist as she pointed to an empty booth nearby. "Bye. You can go sit right over there in the *con-tour*!" She deliberately butchered the word "corner" with an exaggerated pronunciation to emphasize her dismissal.

"Come on, can't you hear my stomach growling? Please, I'm starving. I'm really really hungry." Lisa pouted.

With a mischievous grin, Josey delicately sliced the sirloin steak into tender sections. She speared a piece with her fork and savored it slowly, letting out a dramatic "Mm, mmm. This tastes sooooo good!"

"Can I have a bite, pleeeeaaaasssee?" Lisa begged.

"I thought I heard someone talking, but I guess I didn't." Josey responded as she took another savory bite.

Lisa made a sad face and put her head down in a dramatic gesture.

Josey looked at her and shook her head. "Ugh, alright!"

As soon as Josey finished her sentence, the waiter came bustling to the table with Lisa's plate.

"Right on time!" they both said in unison.

Lisa dug into her food. Right after her third spoonful, she let out a squeal and jumped up a little out of her seat.

Josey's eyebrows furrowed up as she cautiously, but swiftly performed a visual inspection around Lisa's area. "What's wrong with you?

"I haven't had *any* in a long time." Lisa cocked her head and nodded it to the side.

"And?" Josey said.

"Well, I have my phone on vibrate!" Lisa said with an embarrassed look on her face.

"Here I'm thinking you saw a mouse, a spider or something!" Josey laughed.

"It's not funny." Lisa said as she fished her phone out of her front jean pocket.

"Hello," Lisa answered.

"Hey, it's me," a sad voice announced.

Lisa's head shifted down as her eyes widened and her pulse quickened. Her mind raced as she wondered what could be going on. "Miriam, what's wrong?"

"Mom collapsed last night."

"Oh my God! Is she alright?" Lisa asked, her voice rising in panic.

Miriam closed her eyes, head down and elbows on her desk. One arm propped the phone to her ear while the other hand covered her eyes as she began to speak. "She's awake and talking. The doctor said he has to increase her insulin. Apparently, she hasn't been taking it for a while now. I don't think she plans on taking it once she gets out either. She's asking for you, and I don't know what to do to get her to take her medicine."

Lisa's gaze shifted to the window. Her mind buzzed with a storm of emotions. She knew she'd eventually go back, but never imagined it would happen like this—and so suddenly. Lisa's shoulders started to round and her eyes became damp as she thought about how much time had passed since she last saw them. There was no way she could refuse mom's request. "Don't worry," she said in a calm, quiet voice. "I'll talk to her. Let her know I'll be down in a couple of days."

"I will," Miriam breathed, the words emerging on a wave of relief that seemed to deflate her entire body. Her shoulders sagged, tension uncoiling like a long-held breath finally released.

Lisa hesitated, the words catching in her throat. "Are you okay?"

"I am now that I know you're on your way."

Lisa swallowed hard, her fingers tightening around the phone. "I'm glad you called. I'll call you back when I have my flight info."

The silence that followed felt heavier than the conversation itself. Lisa could hear the faint rustle of movement on the other end, like Miriam was struggling with the weight of whatever came next.

"I miss you, Lisa," Miriam said, her voice barely above a whisper.

"I miss you too." Lisa's voice softened, though the ache in her chest lingered. "Don't worry. Everything will be fine, okay?"

"Okay."

A beat passed. Neither seemed willing to be the first to end the call.

"I'll call you soon."

"Bye."

"Bye."

Lisa lowered the phone, the screen darkening in her hand. The echo of Miriam's voice lingered, stirring memories she wasn't sure she was ready to face.

Josey's brows furrowed as she set her fork down. "Something's wrong with your mom?" she asked, confusion flickering across her face. From what she remembered, Lisa's mom had passed away years ago.

Lisa's fingers traced the rim of her glass, her gaze distant. "No, not my mom. It's my best friend's mom," she said, her voice barely above a whisper, like the words might crumble if she said them too loud. "She's in the hospital, and she's asking for me. I'm gonna use my vacation time to go down there for a week."

Josey's face brightened. "I've never been to Louisiana before! I can get us some discounted airline tickets. That's if you don't mind me coming."

Lisa forced a small smile, the weight of the call still pressing against her chest. "Not at all. I can introduce you to Miriam, her mom, and especially my brother, Devan."

"I can't wait!" Josey clapped her hands, practically vibrating with excitement. "I gotta buy some new clothes, get my hair and nails done. And definitely a bikini wax. You should never travel unprepared. You never know when you might have to dazzle the men in a bikini!" She giggled, her voice taking on a sing-song tone. "Ooh, maybe I should finally splurge on that new suitcase I've been eyeing!"

Lisa shook her head, a sigh slipping past her lips. "Can we at least finish our food before you start making plans?"

Josey grinned, unfazed. "Fine, but after that, all bets are off."

Lisa tried to smile back, but the lingering ache in her chest wouldn't let her. Meanwhile, Josey dove back into her plate, already plotting outfits and travel essentials. Lisa couldn't help but feel a twinge of envy. She wished she could see the trip through Josey's eyes — full of excitement and possibility — instead of the worry that weighed her down.

Chapter Three

WELCOME TO D VILLE

Two days later, Lisa and Josey were on a plane headed for New Orleans. Lisa sat by the window, gazing out as the tarmac sped by, while Josey occupied the aisle seat. The hum of the engines filled the cabin as the flight attendants completed the safety checks and emergency instructions. Soon, the plane lifted off, climbing steadily into the sky.

"What's the name of your town again?" Josey asked, breaking the silence.

"Donaldsonville. But us natives like to call it D Ville."

Josey giggled. "It doesn't sound like it's very big."

Lisa smiled. "Well, let's just say we measure our towns by what stores we have."

Josey's curiosity piqued. "Give me an example."

"Donaldsonville has a McDonald's, a Sonic, a Winn-Dixie and a Walmart. The residents of a neighboring city, say St. James, have to come to our town to use these stores."

"Oh, I get it. So you consider that town to be smaller than yours."

"That's right. Now take the town of Gonzales. It has everything our town has plus Cato's, Payless Shoe Store, Sally's Beauty Supply and their Walmart is a super Walmart."

"That town is bigger than yours."

"Exactly." Lisa grinned, satisfied with her lesson in small-town geography.

Josey returned her smile. "I'm getting the hang of it." She shifted in her seat, sensing an opportunity to steer the conversation in a different direction. Curiosity danced behind her eyes. "Why did you leave from there?"

Lisa's expression grew distant as she focused on the sea of fluffy white clouds stretching endlessly below. "I just needed to break the monotony."

Josey nodded slowly, recognizing the reluctance in Lisa's tone. But there was something else—something unspoken. She decided to press gently.

"I'm really glad you let me come with you and all," Josey began, her voice soft. "But I was wondering why you never really talked about your friend Miriam. You've mentioned her before, but not like a person would normally talk about their best friend."

As usual, Josey possessed an uncanny ability to detect the unspoken—a gift that was both a blessing and a curse. Lisa treasured how Josey offered care and support right when needed, without Lisa uttering a single word. But this same talent meant that when Lisa wanted certain things to remain buried, Josey unearthed those too—as if equipped with some emotional metal detector specifically calibrated to Lisa's deepest secrets. The very things Lisa would rather not think about, let alone discuss.

If left to her, these feelings would remain forever buried, sealed away in the corners of her mind. In truth, she really didn't know how to describe her and Miriam's relationship at the moment. They orbited each other like distant acquaintances who were once really close—like running into someone you knew in second grade who had reappeared in your adult life. You carried all these vivid memories of them, yet they don't behave the way they used to. She couldn't even describe it clearly in her own mind. Where would she even begin to explain? On top of that, she was afraid her emotions would betray her the moment she attempted to put words to her feelings.

"It's not like I left on bad terms with her. It's just that when you bring up good memories, the bad ones always like to tag along."

"I totally get that. No one likes to remember bad memories. But you also have to remember that they both make you who you are today. And I think today's you is pretty awesome!"

Lisa caught Josey's ear-to-ear grin as she glanced over, then back out the window. She tried to suppress a soft smile but knew it was too late.

Josey sensed whatever Lisa was hiding must be very traumatic, yet the walls of silence still stung. Six years of friendship, and still this wall remained. She'd seen those fleeting moments when Lisa teetered on the edge of confiding in her—her eyes brimming with unspoken pleas, desperate for release—only to retreat at the last second, swallowed by fear and uncertainty. The pattern was all too familiar now. Josey knew Lisa cared for her and valued their friendship, but that made it all the more frustrating to watch her friend struggle alone when there really was no need to.

Drawing a steady breath, Josey decided to press just a little further. Her voice was a delicate mix of sweetness and wounded concern. "Besides, how can you call me one of your best friends if you can't lean on me when you need to?"

Lisa let out a defeated sigh, the tension in her shoulders visible as she turned to face Josey. There was no use fighting it—Josey's persistence always found its way through.

"Miriam and I have been best friends for a long time," Lisa began, her voice low. "Ever since I've known her, her father was abusive—to her, her mom, and her little brother. There wasn't a day that went by without him hurting them, either physically or verbally. Every time I think of the times we spent together, I have no choice but to think of the bad."

Josey's brows knitted with concern. "Where's her father now?"

Lisa's response was quiet but firm. "He's dead."

Josey blinked, her expression shifting from concern to surprise, mixed with a flicker of relief. "Oh. I hope I don't come off sounding mean, but I know you all were glad when he passed."

Lisa gazed out the airplane window, her reflection faintly visible against the clouds beyond, careful to keep her expression neutral. Her mind drifted back to that moment when it happened. Relief had coursed through her then—a warm sensation that flooded every cell, every hollow space within her—yet accompanied by a persistent disbelief. As if reality might suddenly snap back, revealing a cruel trick, and he would still be alive after all. Even now, the thought sent an icy shiver racing down her spine, her body's instinctive memory more honest than her mind's careful narratives.

She inhaled deeply, then deliberately emptied her lungs completely, as though she could physically expel the thought with her breath. Turning back to Josey, Lisa's expression shifted—her vulnerability receding behind her customary wall. Her voice emerged quiet but matter-of-fact, laced with a subtle undercurrent of amusement.

"Your ass is some nosey. You're lucky I needed a discount on my ticket."

Josey blinked, momentarily caught off guard before laughter bubbled up, a mix of shock and amusement. She knew this was a lot for Lisa, and the playful jab meant she had given her all she could for now. It was her way of signaling the conversation's end without closing herself off completely. Josey respected that and decided to follow her lead.

"You are so stupid!" she teased, her grin widening. "So, how do the men look in Louisiana?"

Lisa smirked, the tension finally easing. The shift in mood was welcome, and as the hum of the plane carried them forward, the weight of the past momentarily lifted.

After about 45 more minutes of conversation, the plane finally landed. They rented a car from Enterprise and headed out on I-10 West toward Donaldsonville.

Lisa spotted the familiar Welcome to Donaldsonville sign about a half a mile or so up the road. "We are about to enter Donaldsonville," Lisa proclaimed. "Look around while you have a chance. We'll stop by Devan's apartment first, unpack and settle in."

"You're sure your brother won't mind me staying with y'all?" Josey teased, her eyes gleaming with mischief.

"What, you finally have a conscience? Of course he won't mind."

"The only reason why I asked is because men can't resist me and I don't want him to embarrass himself trying to impress me."

Lisa shot her a dramatic side-eye glance, then shook her head, fighting the smirk threatening her lips. Just as she was about to reply, a flash of red and blue in the rearview mirror caught her attention.

Lisa gasped. "Josey, there's a cop behind us. I know I wasn't speeding!"

Josey twisted in her seat, peeking through the back window. The sharp glare of the flashing lights made her stomach tighten.

"We should be fine since you weren't speeding and we have our seat belts on. Maybe he just made a mistake."

Lisa reluctantly eased the car to the shoulder, her fingers gripping the steering wheel as the patrol car rolled to a stop behind them. The rhythmic thud of boots against asphalt echoed as the officer approached.

Josey squinted, trying to get a better look. From what she could see, he was tall—easily around 6'2"—with a broad chest that filled out his uniform. His low-cut fade gleamed in the sunlight, and his smooth brown skin seemed to radiate authority. Despite the nerves prickling at her, she couldn't help but notice his confident stride. His eyes were concealed behind a pair of dark aviator shades, making him all the more mysterious.

He walked up to Lisa, his commanding presence underscored by the deep, no-nonsense tone of his voice. "License and registration, please."

Lisa silently handed over the required documents, her hands steady but her jaw tight.

The cop studied her driver's license, his gaze flicking between the card and Lisa. "Lisa Turner. You're an out-of-towner?"

"Well, I'm actually from here, sir," she replied with careful politeness. "I just haven't been home in about seven years."

"Is that right? What about your friend? She looks very familiar."

Josey, matching his serious tone, answered firmly. "Actually, I'm not from here. I was born, raised, and currently reside in Georgia. I'm just accompanying my friend on her visit."

The cop's expression remained unreadable. "You look like a suspect we've been searching for in the area. I'm gonna have to ask you to step out of the car, please."

Josey's mouth dropped open as she turned to Lisa with a look of disbelief. Her eyes flashed back to the officer. "Sir, I just told you I've never been here before!"

Lisa gave a subtle shake of her head. "Please just do what he asks so we can get outta here," she whispered urgently.

Before Josey could respond, the officer's firm voice cut through the tension. "Ma'am, please step out of the vehicle."

"I can't believe this bullshit," Josey muttered as she unbuckled her seatbelt and reluctantly climbed out.

The officer's sharp gaze followed her. "Stay in the car, ma'am," he instructed Lisa, who nodded stiffly.

Circling around the vehicle, the cop stood before Josey. "Turn around towards the car, put your hands on the roof, and spread your legs apart."

Josey complied with a frustrated scoff, her hands splayed across the sun-warmed roof. The tension crackled in the air as the officer leaned closer, his voice low. "How long have you had eye contacts?"

Caught off guard by the unexpected question and his sudden proximity, Josey hesitated. His cologne — a warm blend of lavender, sandalwood, and something else subtly intoxicating — momentarily distracted her. By the time she registered what he'd asked, he was already patting down her shoulders.

"I don't wear contacts," she hissed, her voice dripping with irritation. "This is my real eye color."

The officer's hands continued down her back, then slowly along her legs. When his hand brushed her inner thigh, Josey jerked in outrage. "Hey!"

"Sorry, ma'am," he said coolly, unbothered by her reaction. "It's police procedure to search there. Women have been known to conceal weapons in that area. You're clear. You can turn around now."

Josey spun to face him, her eyes blazing.

"What's your name?" he asked.

"Josephine Duncan," she shot back, practically daring him to make another comment.

"I need to see your license."

Her glare hardened. "Don't you think you should've asked for that *before* you felt me up?"

The officer stood unwavering, waiting as Josey stormed to the car, yanked her wallet from her bag, and thrust her license toward him.

He examined it with a slow nod, then without another word, shifted his attention. "Ms. Turner, step out of the car and come over here."

Lisa obeyed, her heart pounding. Josey's eyes darted between them, the tension in the air thick enough to cut.

"What did you stop us for anyway?" Josey demanded.

The cop's stern expression abruptly softened. "Because I needed to do this."

Before either woman could react, he stepped forward and wrapped Lisa in a tight, affectionate hug. His voice shifted to a warm, joyful tone. "Hey there, little sis. I've missed you!"

"I've missed you too!" Lisa returned the embrace, her arms tightening around him. It had been about two years since they had last seen each other. The familiarity of her brother's embrace tugged at her heart. She blinked away the tears welling in her eyes. For the first time in a while, she felt the comfort of being a little sister.

Josey's jaw dropped. She stared in shock, trying to reconcile the no-nonsense cop with the man hugging Lisa. "You're... You're *Devan*!" she exclaimed, her voice a mixture of disbelief and astonishment.

Devan's warm, charming smile widened as he turned to Josey. "You're right, Lisa, her eyes are very pretty. You can really see 'em now since her eyes are stretched wide open. She's really intelligent too. She knows who I am," he added sarcastically, chuckling.

Lisa giggled, her laughter light and teasing. "Now you know how it feels to be felt up!"

Josey, still reeling from the bizarre turn of events, shifted her gaze between the siblings. Shock and disbelief were etched across her face. Finally, she found her voice. "I'll admit, you guys got me. But don't think y'all are gonna just get away with it!"

Devan's grin only grew. "Here are your documents." He handed back their licenses and registration with an amused flick of his wrist.

Lisa turned towards Devan, a playful twinkle in her eye. "Now that you two have been properly introduced, Josey and I can head to your place."

"There was nothing *proper* about that introduction!" Josey huffed, still fuming.

Devan, intentionally ignoring her complaint, pulled a key from his pocket and handed it to Lisa. "Here's my spare key. I get off at 3. Where are you guys gonna be?"

"We're going to the hospital after we unpack."

"Okay. When I get off, I'll go home, change, and meet y'all there." He shifted his attention back to Josey, flashing another one of his signature smiles. "Nice meeting you, Josey."

Josey, unimpressed, folded her arms tightly. "You can call me Josephine," she snapped, her glare as sharp as daggers.

Devan let out a low chuckle, waved, and got back into his car.

As Lisa pulled away, Josey's frustration bubbled over. "I can't believe you set me up!" she yelled, her hands flailing in exasperation.

"You were asking for it," Lisa giggled, completely unapologetic.

"You're lucky your brother's fine. I started to kick him in his privates."

Lisa burst into laughter, her amusement echoing through the car. "You weren't gonna do shit!"

Josey shook her head, a reluctant smile tugging at the corners of her lips. Lisa's laughter was contagious, and despite herself, she couldn't help but join in as they sped down the road, the city of Donaldsonville sign welcoming them home.

Chapter Four

THE WELCOME IN-BETWEEN

Lisa and Josey stepped into Devan's apartment, immediately enveloped by a captivating blend of jasmine, sandalwood, and a subtle hint of musk. The fragrance wrapped around them like an invisible embrace, warm yet fresh, mingling with the faint, earthy scent of the lush greenery scattered throughout the space. Towering tropical plants and cascading pothos vines softened the sleek modern look of the apartment, their deep green leaves catching the light from the recessed ceiling fixtures.

To their right, a silver leather sofa shimmered under the ambient glow, its surface smooth and cool to the touch. Silver accent pillows, each adorned with large, intersecting dark and light blue circles, were arranged with meticulous care. A silver and royal blue striped throw was draped across the back with effortless elegance, the fabric's subtle sheen giving it a graceful, almost liquid quality.

The living room held a curated mix of global treasures. Exotic figurines, some no taller than a coffee mug and others nearly reaching their waists, stood proudly on sleek glass-topped tables. Their intricate carvings and metallic finishes gave the space a museum-like allure, each piece whispering stories of distant lands and rich cultures. The tables themselves featured etched silver X designs, their sleek silver legs reflecting the soft glow of circular lampshades perched atop sculptural stands composed of varying sizes of silver circles. Shadows danced across the walls, adding depth to the already striking décor.

One wall boasted two rows of six black and white inspirational quotes, the bold print commanding attention without overwhelming the space. Another wall held larger-than-life black and white portraits of Biggie Smalls and Michael Jordan, their intense gazes seeming to follow Lisa and Josey as they moved further inside. The contrast of their iconic images against the modern elegance of the room made a statement—one of ambition, legacy, and style.

Beyond the living area, a small kitchen table with a smooth gray marble top and two royal blue chairs marked the transition to the kitchenette. The chairs' upholstery was plush yet firm, inviting yet undeniably stylish. The kitchen's sleek counter featured an array of royal blue appliances, their glossy surfaces gleaming under the under-cabinet lighting. Near the sink, royal blue and silver kitchen towels were carefully hung, the colors tying together seamlessly with the rest of the apartment's aesthetic. Two matching royal blue barstools were neatly tucked beneath a bar, their polished chrome legs gleaming against the pristine floor.

Lisa trailed her fingers along the cool marble surface of the table as Josey stepped toward the bar, curiosity flickering in her eyes. Everything in Devan's apartment felt purposeful—no clutter, no excess, just a seamless blend of urban sophistication and natural beauty. Even the plants, arranged in corners and along window ledges, brought in texture and warmth, as if they belonged exactly where they were.

Lisa took another slow glance around, appreciating the space as a whole. The thoughtful coordination of colors, the balanced mix of modern and organic touches—nothing about it felt accidental. *He always had a sense of style*, she thought, admiring how effortlessly the space reflected Devan's personality.

Josey let out an appreciative whistle. "Your brother is really tidy. Was he like this growing up?" She ran a hand over the smooth leather armrest of the sofa, her fingers gliding across its cool surface.

Lisa smirked. "Pretty much, yeah. He always took pride in his neatness. I can guarantee that even the kitchen utensils and bath towels are royal blue and silver."

Josey chuckled, nodding toward the hallway. "I like the way he decorated the place. I'm gonna go check out his bedroom!" A mischievous glint flickered in her eyes as she started toward the door.

Lisa laughed, shaking her head. "Ok. You go do that. I'm going to grab my things and put them in our bedroom."

Josey gently pushed open the door to Devan's room, her fingers tingling with curiosity. As she stepped inside, the cool air carried a faint trace of his cologne—a mix of warm spice and something clean, like fresh linen. The bedroom was a flawless continuation of the apartment's aesthetic, every detail intentional.

A towering silver headboard framed the bed, its sleek surface reflecting the dim lighting. The royal blue comforter was neatly spread, the fabric looking plush and inviting. An array of silver and blue accent pillows were arranged with military precision, giving the bed a showroom-like perfection. Above it, three striking African art pieces in black, silver, and royal blue drew her gaze. Their bold colors and intricate designs added depth to the space, complementing the modern elegance of the room. The remaining furniture—sleek silver nightstands, a minimalist dresser—continued the theme of refined sophistication.

Josey's eyes wandered back to the bed. Her lips parted slightly as a slow smile crept onto her face. She could almost see him there, stretched out beneath the sheets. The covers would be pulled down to his waist, exposing his taut, brown abs. Her gaze drifted higher, imagining the smooth rise and fall of his chest, the rhythmic movement almost hypnotic. The thought sent a shiver down her spine, and before she realized it, she was biting her lower lip.

"Hey! Are you ready to go to the hospital?"

Josey jolted, her heart leaping into her throat. "Oh!" she yelped, spinning around so fast she nearly stumbled.

Lisa stood beside her, one brow arched, amusement flickering across her face.

Josey cleared her throat, desperately trying to compose herself. "Ugh, sure! Just let me throw my things in our room," she blurted, her voice pitched an octave higher than usual.

Without waiting for a response, she turned on her heel and practically sprinted into the living room, her cheeks burning as she tried to shake the vivid image from her mind.

Victoria Rose

The drive to the hospital was uneventful, but the silence between Lisa and Josey felt thick, stretching longer than it should have. Lisa's hands gripped the steering wheel, her posture stiff, her gaze locked on the road as if she were trying to outrun her thoughts.

Josey considered asking if she was okay but decided against it. From their conversation during the flight, Josey could tell there was more to the story. But Lisa made it clear she wasn't ready to unpack it just yet. *It's best to stay quiet*, she told herself. Pushing now might just make her shut down even more.

Instead, she let the quiet settle, filling the car with nothing but the hum of the engine and the occasional tap of Lisa's fingers against the steering wheel.

When they pulled up to the hospital, Lisa exhaled sharply, as if shaking off whatever had been weighing on her. Without a word, she put the car in park, unbuckled her seatbelt, and stepped out.

Josey followed her lead, adjusting her bag as they made their way through the automatic doors. The cool, sterile air of the hospital replaced the thick humidity outside.

Then—

"Hey!"

Lisa's head snapped up just as Miriam approached.

A genuine smile tugged at Lisa's lips, pushing past the tension that had been perched on her shoulders. She closed the distance, wrapping Miriam in a tight hug.

When they pulled back, they took a moment to study each other.

"You look good Miriam." Lisa said, a teasing lilt in her voice. "I see you've put on a few pounds in all the right places!"

Miriam smirked, one hand settling on her hip. "You look wonderful yourself!"

Lisa still had that same effortless beauty that exuded confidence and poise. Her smooth brown skin had the same radiant glow, accentuated by her high cheekbones. Her sleek bob framed her face perfectly, as polished and confident as ever.

For a moment, it felt like no time had passed at all.

Lisa cleared her throat. "How is Ma doing?"

"She is doing well since she has no choice but to take her insulin. She's been in a very good mood since she found out you were coming. That's all she's been talking about."

Lisa chuckled, shaking her head. "Sounds like her."

The shift was subtle but noticeable. The tension that had weighed down their reunion started to lift, replaced by something easier—something that felt like home.

Miriam turned her attention to Josey.

Lisa gestured between them. "Speaking of my visit, I want you to meet Josey."

Josey stepped forward, her smile warm. "Hello Miriam."

"Hi. It's nice to meet you. Lisa mentioned you'd be coming along." Miriam said with a smile.

They shook hands.

For a moment, Lisa simply watched them—two parts of her life meeting for the first time. It wasn't quite the past, and it wasn't fully the future, but something in-between. And for the first time in a long while, it felt like a welcome place to be.

Miriam turned to Lisa. "I told her doctor you were coming. He'd like to speak with you. In fact, there he is now."

Lisa's eyes followed Miriam's outstretched hand, expecting to see a balding, middle-aged man in a white coat. Instead, her gaze landed on a young, undeniably handsome man. She quickly checked herself, making sure her mouth hadn't fallen open. *Damn*, she thought, *there should be a rule that doctors aren't supposed to look like that.*

Dr. Crane walked up to Miriam, his posture relaxed but professional. "Hello there, Ms. Butler."

"Hello, Dr. Crane. I want to introduce my friends Lisa and Josey."

He shook Josey's hand with a polite nod before turning to Lisa. The moment their eyes met, his heart stumbled. *She's beautiful*, he thought, momentarily caught off guard.

Lisa felt it too — that magnetic pull. She couldn't quite put it into words, but there was something undeniably attractive about him. He gave off a Steve Urkel/Stefan Urkel vibe - a smart, somewhat smooth, sexy, yet nerdy vibe.

"Hello, I'm Lisa," she said, her voice steady despite the flutter in her chest.

"Nice to meet you. I'm Dr. Crane, Sean Crane." As the words left his mouth, Sean inwardly cringed. *That sounded like a line straight out of a movie, dummy!*

"I'd like to talk to you about Mrs. Butler, if you don't mind."

"Of course not. Go ahead."

"I'm sure Miriam has already explained that she refuses to take her medicine when she's released."

Lisa nodded.

The doctor continued, his tone gentle but concerned. "Nathaniel and Miriam have both tried talking to her without success." He offered a small, hopeful smile. "She talks about you like you're her own daughter. I was hoping you might succeed where we couldn't — convince her to take her medicine."

Lisa's face lit up with a reassuring smile. "I'm pretty sure I can do that for you."

"Great. I knew I could count on you." *Okay, that definitely sounded like I know her way more than I actually do*, Sean scolded himself. The intensity of her gaze — those dark brown eyes — had a way of derailing his ability to think straight.

Suddenly, a loud crackling noise pierced through the air and a female voice blared, "Dr. Crane, please report to the nurses station."

Saved by the intercom! Sean thought, almost relieved. "Looks like I'm needed elsewhere," he said, quickly pulling a business card from his pocket. He scribbled his cell number on the back and handed it to Lisa. "Please don't hesitate to call me if you need anything."

"Thanks. I'll make sure I keep this handy, just in case."

He gave a small wave, then turned and strode down the hallway.

As soon as he disappeared, Josey mimicked in a husky low voice, "I'm Dr. Crane, Sean Crane."

"He didn't give *me* a card!" Miriam protested dramatically.

"Stop joking around, you two. He's cute." Lisa shook her head, her smile lingering. "Miriam, why didn't you tell me her doctor was so young and handsome?"

"Sorry, it didn't cross my mind — you know, with my mom being in the hospital!" Miriam shot back with mock sarcasm.

Lisa smirked. "You know I meant after she was okay. Don't hate, congratulate."

They quickly looked around at each other then burst into laughter.

"Where's Nathaniel?" Lisa asked, her tone low and serious.

"He's at Mom's house," Miriam replied, her expression tightening.

"Does he know I'm here?"

"NO!" The word shot out of Miriam's mouth, her voice sharp and unwavering.

Lisa held her gaze for a moment before nodding. "We'll deal with him when the time comes. For now, I'm going to have that talk with Mom. Why don't you two get acquainted while I do that?"

"Okay," Miriam said, her tone softening. She slipped an arm around Josey's shoulder, steering her gently down the hall. "I'll take you to the cafeteria."

Lisa watched them go, a small smile tugging at the corners of her lips. She could tell they'd become fast friends.

Taking a steadying breath, Lisa made her way to Mary's room. With one last exhale, she reached for the door handle and stepped inside.

When Mary saw Lisa, her face lit up. She opened her arms wide, her voice bursting with joy.

"Lisa!"

Lisa rushed over, wrapping her arms tightly around her. The warmth of the hug brought back memories, but so did the familiar ache of guilt. She had stayed away too long, and the weight of that choice pressed down on her. Pulling back slightly, she kissed Mary's cheek, forcing a smile.

"How are you?" she asked, her voice soft and tentative.

"I'm good, Bae. Look at ya. You so beautiful! Time sho' do fly by. It's been seven long years since ya left. I guess I'm gonna have to get hospitalized every time I wanna visit from ya," Mary teased, a playful sparkle in her eye.

Lisa tried to laugh, but the lump in her throat made it difficult. "Ma, please don't start the guilt trip. Believe me, I don't need it. I feel guilty enough without it. I know I stayed away too long. I'm sorry for that."

Mary smiled. "I guess I can let ya off the hook dis time."

Lisa nodded, then turned to gaze out the window, as though the sprawling sky could help her gather her thoughts. The moment of silence stretched, but she knew there was no easy way to start. She shifted her focus back to Mary, determination in her voice.

"I'm going to get straight to the point. I know you're not taking your medicine. I want to know what's going on with you, and I want the truth. You can't fool me like you've been fooling Nathaniel and Miriam."

Lisa locked eyes with her, but kept her gaze steady. Mary held her stare, but the weight of Lisa's words lingered in the air. After a moment, her shoulders sagged, the fight draining from her.

"Aight," Mary mumbled, her voice low. "I'll tell ya, but ya have to keep dis to yoself."

"Agreed. Now go on."

Mary's hands twisted the blanket in her lap as she spoke, her words fragile and strained. "I been thinkin' bout what happened in da past lately. I feel like I let Nathaniel and Miriam down. When I think 'bout ya, I feel like I let ya down da mos' of all."

Her voice cracked as she shifted in the bed, turning fully toward Lisa. The raw pain etched on her face was impossible to miss.

"No chil' should have to do what ya did, and no woman should let a chil' go tru dat. I think dat's why ya stayed away for so long. It's all my fault. I feel like I should be punished for lettin' dat happen to ya!" The last words escaped in a choked cry, and then Mary fell silent, her breaths uneven.

Lisa's chest tightened, but she forced herself to stay composed.

"So you think by purposely not taking your medicine, you'll get the punishment you *think* you deserve?" Lisa's voice shook, frustration and sorrow intertwining. "Ma, I chose to do what I did because I love you. We all needed you — we still do! I also chose to leave. And it sure wasn't because of you or what people were saying. I couldn't care less about what they think."

She leaned in closer, her voice softening but steady. "You're one of the biggest reasons I came back. If you do this, all you're going to accomplish is throwing away my reason for everything I did. Do you know how devastated I'd be if you died? Did you ever think about Nathaniel and Miriam? As far as I'm concerned, the person who was supposed to be punished got theirs a long time ago. You have no reason to feel guilty or think you need to be punished."

Mary wiped at her damp cheeks, her fingers trembling. Her gaze dropped to her lap, as if the shame she carried was too heavy to look past. "I didn't think 'bout it like dat," she murmured, her voice barely above a whisper. "I guess it is selfish a me to act like dis. But I can't help feelin' guilty."

Her eyes flicked back to Lisa's, glassy and uncertain, searching for forgiveness.

Lisa reached out and gently took Mary's hand, her grip firm but tender. "I'll tell you what we'll do," she said, her voice warm and light. "You take your medicine like you're supposed to and I'll come visit more often, and we'll both work on making peace with the past. Deal?"

"Deal," Mary whispered, her voice cracking just a little. Her mouth quivered, caught between tears and a smile.

Chapter Five

THE THINGS WE DON'T KNOW

Miriam and Josey entered the hospital's small cafeteria. The air held a faint scent of reheated food, and the hum of a vending machine blended with the occasional chatter of staff on their breaks. It reminded Josey of the size of a Subway restaurant, cramped yet functional. The selection was limited to pre-packaged sandwiches, bags of chips, and bottled drinks lined neatly in a refrigerated case. After a quick scan, they each grabbed their meals and headed toward a quiet table in the corner.

Sliding into the plastic chair, Miriam gave Josey a small smile.

"How are you liking the trip so far?" she asked, unwrapping her sandwich.

"It's going great. Except for Lisa and Devan pranking me!" Josey exclaimed, her eyes narrowing playfully.

"What!" Miriam gasped, a chuckle escaping her lips.

"Other than that, it's going great. I really like everyone I've met so far. Except for Devan. The jury is still out on him," Josey added with a grin. "I think the only ones I haven't met are your mom and brother. I'm getting the sense that Lisa and him don't get along."

Miriam's smile faltered, her fingers picking idly at the crust of her sandwich.

"He doesn't get along with her. It wasn't always like that, though," she murmured. "When we were young, he loved her like a big sister. He always wanted to be around us. I used to have to beg Mom to make him play with his friends around the corner."

"So what happened?" Josey asked, curiosity lacing her voice.

"Lisa didn't tell you?" Miriam's brows knitted together.

"Tell me what?"

"I guess that's a no. Did she say anything about my dad?"

"Well, yeah. She said he was very abusive and that he passed away. But what does that have to do with Lisa and your brother?" Josey's voice rose slightly, her interest piqued.

Miriam exhaled slowly, as if bracing herself. "I'll tell you while we eat." She tore a small bite from her sandwich, though her appetite seemed diminished.

"My mom said my dad was a really gentle, smart, caring, and funny person. They would talk for hours about anything and everything. That's what made her fall in love with him," Miriam said, her voice soft with the echo of a distant memory. "He was also patriotic and cared a lot about others. He felt it was his duty to join the army to help out in Vietnam."

Josey nodded, pulling a chip from her bag and crunching down on it, though the sound felt almost intrusive against the weight of Miriam's words.

"Unfortunately, I never had a chance to know that version of him," Miriam continued, her eyes fixed on a distant spot as if the past played out before her. "My mom said when he came back, he was different. He started drinking and taking drugs. He gradually started abusing her. Then, when we were born, he got even worse. All I've ever known was the mean, violent, hatred-filled version."

She paused, the tension in her jaw visible as she gripped her bottle of water tightly.

"By the time Lisa and I got to the seventh grade, he was threatening to kill us. I remember waking up every morning wondering if that would be my last day on Earth."

Josey's eyes welled with tears. She pictured twelve-year-old Miriam, lying rigid beneath thin blankets as the warm morning sun slipped through the curtains. What should have been the promise of a new day turned into a nightmare on a daily basis.

Miriam was surprisingly calm, considering this was the first time she'd spoken about what happened. The memories hovered over her like an ever-present shadow, but the words flowed freely. She hadn't planned on talking about it—not really.

PEACE AMID THE CHAOS

Growing up, she and her mom had tried to reach out to adults, hoping someone would step in. But time and time again, no one did. The dismissive looks and hollow reassurances taught her that it was easier to keep quiet.

But now, across the table, Josey listened with unwavering attention. Her eyes brimmed with empathy, her body leaned slightly forward as though willing to absorb the weight of Miriam's words. Even though Josey hadn't said much, the concern etched on her face spoke volumes. For the first time in years, Miriam felt a strange sense of relief. *Having someone show they care makes all the difference*, she thought. It gave her the confidence to continue.

"About a month after school ended that year, that's when it happened," she began, her voice steady despite the ache that came with the memories. "Lisa was supposed to come over to play after I finished helping Mom with the chores. Nathaniel was around the corner playing with his friends. Mom and I were in the kitchen cooking lunch. We always ate at twelve thirty. That day, my dad decided we ate at twelve, and since we weren't ready, we were being lazy."

Miriam paused, her fingers absentmindedly tracing the edge of her water bottle.

"The buildup of my dad's anger was like a tea kettle on the stove. Slowly, quietly at first, his temper would simmer and heat. As the pressure mounted, like water nearing its boiling point, his rage got worse. Eventually, unable to contain itself, it would erupt. It was like a scalding burst of steam accompanied by a piercing whistle that left everyone scarred and trembling in its wake."

Josey swallowed, the mental image pressing down on her.

"It got to the point that when it started, we knew we had about ten minutes before it became a full onslaught," Miriam continued, her gaze fixed on some distant point. "He would always start out with a small mumble as he walked past. A few minutes later, he'd be back. His mumbles turned into mean whispers of whatever paranoia had captured his mind. Then the whispers would escalate to full-out screams."

Miriam's voice grew quieter, as though each word chipped away at a barrier she'd built long ago.

"Mom tried to reason with him that day, but as usual, it was no use. He started hitting and choking her. Screaming how he was going to kill her. I couldn't take another minute of it. I grabbed a skillet and hit him with it." She winced, remembering the moment as if it had just happened.

"He turned on me." Her voice trembled. "His eyes were so cold, so filled with hatred. As if I wasn't even his flesh and blood. He knocked me out." She ran her hand through her hair, as though trying to shake away the lingering echoes.

"By the time I came to, the cops and ambulance were there... and he was dead. Lisa had taken his gun and shot him."

Josey's hand, mid-reach for a chip, froze. Her eyes grew wide as she leaned back in her chair, exhaling a heavy, "Whoa."

Miriam nodded slowly, her lips twisting into a sad, knowing smile.

"No wonder she didn't tell me. You guys were only twelve!" Josey shook her head in disbelief. "Your brother was being abused too, right?"

"Yeah, but not as often as Mom and me. I think Dad had a big grudge against the female gender." Miriam's tone was laced with bitterness.

"So why is he upset with Lisa?" Josey pressed.

Miriam sighed deeply. "My brother hardly remembers any of the beatings. Although he's never been properly diagnosed, I believe he's suffering from either repression or dissociative amnesia. His brain tried to protect him, so he's either unconsciously blocked the bad memories and associated feelings or his brain hit what I call a permanent delete. If it's the latter, he may never recover those memories."

Josey nodded slowly, processing the weight of it.

"This is where I think another psychological mechanism, called projection, comes into play. I believe that deep down, he feels responsible for what happened. Perhaps he thinks he did something wrong because he can't remember. He also paints our dad as a misunderstood army vet, taking the few good times he can recall and using them as proof to justify his version of our father. He wants his view of Dad to be true so desperately that someone has to replace him as the bad guy. I guess in his eyes, the only option is Lisa."

"Wow. How do you know all of this? And how do you feel about your dad?" Josey asked softly.

"After Dad died, Nathaniel became angry and withdrawn. He stopped playing with his friends and started getting into fights. I thought becoming a psychologist would help him — and Mom. But no matter how hard I've tried, it feels like I haven't helped them at all. If anything, I think I've made things worse," Miriam whispered, her voice heavy with defeat.

Josey reached out and squeezed Miriam's hand. "You do realize you were just a child yourself, right? I hope you don't mind me saying this, but it sounds like you've heaped a whole lot of responsibility onto that little twelve-year-old's shoulders. Try not to be so hard on yourself, okay?"

Miriam looked away, nodding softly.

"Don't forget, psychologists are people too!" Josey sang in an uplifting tone.

Miriam chuckled through her tears, dabbing her eyes with her sleeve.

"To answer your other question," she said, "I have to give two answers. From my professional point of view, my father was suffering tremendously from the trauma he endured. He obviously turned to drinking and drugs to deal with his pain. The military didn't really offer soldiers psychological support like they do now. And on top of that, Black folks tend to shy away from seeking that sort of help. The community has this idea that if you seek emotional help, something is wrong with you—you ain't right in the head."

Josey nodded knowingly.

"He probably felt alone and helpless in what he was going through, but the child in me can't quite bring myself to forgive him. Fathers and husbands are supposed to protect their family, not become the enemy within."

"It's only natural that you have mixed emotions," Josey reassured her. "What about your mom? How does she feel about what happened?"

"I don't really know. She avoids it. She pretty much does anything she can to *not* talk about it. But she loves Lisa like she's her own." Miriam's shoulders relaxed slightly.

"What does she say when your brother starts in on Lisa?" Josey probed.

"She tells me it's just a phase... and not to worry. That he'll eventually grow out of it."

That's one hell of a long phase, Josey thought, but kept the comment to herself.

Miriam's voice dropped. "But to be honest, he's gotten worse. We usually end up arguing until I storm out."

Miriam could see the concern in Josey's eyes. She realized up until this point, their entire conversation was about her. *This is not how I want our first time getting to know each other to be*, she thought. She shook her head slightly from side to side as if shaking off the tension. Taking a deep breath, she smiled mischievously—a genuine smile because she truly did want to get to know Josey more.

"Enough about me. Tell me more about you. What do you like to do for fun when you're not getting pranked by Lisa and Devan?"

"Oh, I see everyone around here got jokes!" Josey chuckled, tapping her fingers on the table thoughtfully. "Mmm, let's see. Well, I'm obsessed with shopping—especially for shoes. High heels, boots, sandals, sneakers, even crocs—I love them all. I'm also a people-watcher at heart. There's something fascinating about seeing unlikely pairs spending time together and observing what people choose to wear." She leaned forward, eyes widening. "It drives me absolutely crazy when I see folks running around in socks and sandals. Wearing socks defeats the whole purpose of sandals!"

Miriam laughed. "You know what? I never thought about that, but you're absolutely right."

"Oh, I know I am," Josey shot back playfully, then her expression softened. "But the most important thing I do in my spare time is volunteer." Her eyes sparkled with genuine passion. "I work with the Myles Singleton Foundation hosting Thanksgiving events for battered women's shelters across metro Atlanta. We cook for the ladies and children, serve them, provide entertainment—the whole experience. It's up to all of us to make this world better, you know? No matter if it's something small or something big, it all matters. It all adds up in the end."

"Wow, that's so awesome!" Miriam's voice filled with admiration. "That is so true! That's why I'm part of a mentor group!" She hesitated, wanting to talk more about her mentoring experience but not wanting to shift focus back to herself. Instead, she asked, "How many siblings do you have?"

"I have two sisters," Josey said.

"Really?" Miriam's eyes widened, a wistful expression crossing her face. Growing up with only Nathaniel, she'd missed that special bond she imagined sisters shared. The secret exchanges, the late-night conversations, finishing each other's sentences. Her fingers absently traced patterns on the table as her mind drifted to Lisa. In the beginning, they were just like that, but the way their relationship stood now, it was far from a sisterly bond. Wanting to know more, she asked, "What was it like growing up with sisters?"

"It was okay until we hit puberty," Josey said, pursing her lips and shaking her head as the memories played through her mind. "Then it was like all hell broke loose."

"What do you mean?" Miriam leaned forward, intrigued.

"We're all just one year apart. Imagine sharing everything with two other people—clothes, hair products, accessories, shoes—and all living in one small, cramped room! Every day it felt like someone was arguing with someone about something."

Miriam gasped as her hand flew to her mouth, her eyebrows shooting upward. The chaotic image Josey painted clashed with her romanticized vision of sisterhood.

Josey's voice grew animated, her hands punctuating her story. "I remember one time I had this favorite shirt. Usually I just wore my sisters' hand-me-downs. But there was this one time when we were out shopping, and I begged my mom for this purple shirt with sparkly butterflies on it. My mom usually told us no, but I guess she saw how much I wanted it, so she bought it for me. It was my prized possession! I wore it at least two or three times a week!" She chuckled. "Then one day, I went to wear it, but couldn't find it anywhere. I looked in the drawers, in the closet, under the bed, in the dirty clothes basket—but it's nowhere to be found. I walked into the kitchen and there sat my sister with my favorite shirt on!"

"What!" Miriam exclaimed.

"I was so mad. She knew that was my favorite shirt but thought she could get away with wearing it. Well, she thought wrong. I walked right up to her and punched her."

Miriam's jaw dropped, her water bottle frozen halfway to her lips.

"Don't worry. We only went at it for a couple of minutes before my mom pulled us apart," Josey said with a wave of her hand. "After hearing what happened, she made my sister give me my shirt back, but then we both got whippins—her for stealing my shirt and me for starting the fight." She finished with a chuckle.

Miriam, still stunned, asked, "How do you all get along now?"

"Oh, we're as thick as thieves now." Josey winked. "I couldn't ask for more supportive and caring sisters."

A shadow crossed Miriam's face, her lips pressing into a thin line. The thought of Nathaniel surfaced. Their heated conversations that escalated into arguments within minutes. Their fundamentally opposing views on almost everything that mattered. The distrust that had grown between them over the years. Nothing like the warm, resilient bond Josey described with her sisters. Her eyes darted to the wall clock, and her stomach tightened. He would arrive soon—his punctuality, at least, was reliable. She smoothed her expression, breathing deeply to calm her suddenly racing pulse, not wanting her anxiety to betray her to Josey.

She touched Josey's arm lightly and forced brightness into her voice. "Look at the time, we should head over to my mom's room."

As they stood, Josey glanced at Miriam—something about her smile didn't quite reach her eyes. It passed quickly, just a flicker, but Josey caught it. She didn't press. Everyone had things they carried, pieces of themselves they wanted to keep hidden.

The things we don't know, she thought, *but somehow still feel.*

Chapter Six

Cold Hard Facts

With a twinkle in her eye, Mary grinned. "When ya gon' tell me 'bout da city life in..." She paused, tapping her chin playfully. "How do da youngins say it? ATL?"

Lisa laughed, shaking her head. "What do you know about the ATL?"

"That's what I'm tryna get ya to tell me!" Mary shot back, her laughter ringing through the room.

Suddenly, the hospital room door swung open. Nathaniel walked in, "Hey momma, how you..." His voice trailed off as he stopped short at the sight of Lisa. He stood in the doorway for a moment, then took a step into the room, letting the door close behind him. His jaw clenched and his eyes narrowed as he stared at Lisa.

Lisa tilted her head to meet his gaze, her thoughts racing. He had grown much taller since she'd last seen him; he had to be about six feet now. The last time she saw him, he was 15—just before she left mid-summer when he revealed how he really felt about her.

Looking at them now, no one would guess they were once so close. When he was little, he'd run up to her eyes gleaming whenever she'd arrive. When he got a little older, he would trail behind her and Miriam, begging to be part of their adventures. Miriam found him annoying, but Lisa thought it was sweet having a little brother figure. Especially since she only had a 'most of the time' annoying older brother. Sometimes, she and Miriam scraped together enough money to buy candy. Lisa would secretly save some to give to Nathaniel when Miriam wasn't looking. Occasionally, he'd muster up enough courage to ask them to play with him. Miriam always refused, aggravated by his persistence. But Lisa had a soft spot for him. She'd agree, giving him 30 minutes, while Miriam stood impatiently on the sidelines, arms crossed, foot tapping, her face twisted in frustration.

After the incident, Nathaniel changed. He spoke to Lisa less and less until the conversations stopped altogether. Sometimes, she'd catch glimpses of him lingering in doorways before disappearing. But most of the time, he was nowhere to be found. When he did appear, he'd simply stare at her with an unreadable expression before slipping away. He used to wear his emotions openly, but now she couldn't tell what he was thinking.

Finally the time came for her to leave for college and that's when it happened. Miriam had already said she most likely wouldn't be home. At this point, their relationship had become what it was today-distant. So they decided to say their goodbyes over the phone. Mary was sitting on the porch in her favorite rocking chair when Lisa walked up. They went inside to get some cold drinks. After talking back and forth for a while, they hugged each other tightly and Lisa promised to write to her as soon as she settled in. Mary remembered there was some laundry she wanted to finish up so she headed to the back of the house while Lisa let herself out.

But as she stepped onto the porch to leave, Nathaniel stood in the middle of the driveway. His face was expressionless as usual, but this time, there was something lurking in his eyes. As she bounded down the steps and closed the gap between them, it dawned on her then that his eyes looked just like his father's did that day-full of rage.

She chose to play it cool. She didn't want to misread the situation. Deciding to plan for the worst, but hope for the best, she smiled and said, "Hey, just the person I wanted to see. I'm heading out tomorrow and wanted to make sure I said goodbye."

For a moment, silence hung between them. Then, a slow, sinister smile twisted his face. "It must be nice," he said, his voice low and dripping with malice. "To be able to enjoy life, go off on adventures and make new memories. You know... to actually be alive. Too bad my father couldn't say the same."

Lisa took in a deep breath and slowly let it out. She had hoped it wouldn't come to this, but a part of her knew it was inevitable.

Mary believed Nathaniel just needed time, but all the time in the world wouldn't be enough to help him realize what happened was for the best. The loss would have been far greater if it hadn't gone down the way it did. But Nathaniel would never see it that way. She understood now that he was a "grass is always greener" on the other side kind. There was only one way to deal with that type—with cold hard facts.

"You're right. It is nice to be alive," her voice steady. "And it is too bad that your father couldn't have been a better husband and father. If he were, I'm sure he'd still be alive too."

Nathaniel's eyes widened as his nostrils flared. "That's all you got, isn't it? Blaming the victim to justify what you did. It's the same shit you've been spewin' for years." He spat, his voice rising. "I'm so sick of this shit. You're too much of a coward to admit you planned the whole thing. You murdered my dad in cold blood." His last sentence exploded into the air.

"That's enough!" A hushed familiar voice rang out.

They both turned as Miriam's footsteps pounded the pavement. "Don't you think you put mom through enough as it is?" She asked as she jabbed her finger at Nathaniel.

Before he could respond, the creak of the screen door stole their attention. Mary stood in the doorway, concern etched on her face.

"Is everything ok? I thought I heard yelling."

Lisa forced a smile. "Everything's all good. Just stirring up some trouble for the neighbors to gossip about while I'm gone."

She waved as she turned to leave, the heat of his stare burning into her back. She didn't have to look back to know the hatred in his eyes mirrored his father's. And now, seven years later, those same eyes were staring at her once again. Only this time, they were framed by a pair of glasses.

His jaw unclenched just enough to let the words escape. "What in the hell are you doing here? You're trying to finish my mom off too?"

"I'm here because she asked me to be." Lisa shot back.

Rolling his eyes, he turned toward Mary. "Mama, did Miriam talk you into seeing her?"

Mary gave Nathaniel a don't play with me look. "She's here cause I told Miriam to call her and ask her to come. Now, you gon' behave while she here."

"I can't believe you Ma!" Nathaniel launched into two quick, small jumps, stomping forcefully as he landed each time, his voice rising to a childish pitch. "How could you stand to be around a murderer? She killed your own husband and yet you sit here with her smiling in your face!" He threw his hands up, fingers splayed dramatically. "Stop letting her brainwash you."

Before Mary could answer, Lisa walked swiftly up to Nathaniel and said between clinched teeth, "Your father beat the crap out of you, Ma and Miriam on a daily fucking basis. He broke Ma's jaw and knocked Miriam out! Do you really think that was going to be the end of it that day?"

"He didn't deserve what you did to him!" Nathaniel's face contorted, spit flying from his lips as he leaned forward.

"And Ma deserved to get her jaw broken and Miriam deserved to get a concussion that day?" her eyebrows raised in mock question. "Did y'all deserve all the other things he gave you: the bruises, black eyes, broken and fractured bones? The fear, the sadness, the hate? Did you?" Lisa's voice escalated with each question, her fingernails digging half-moons into her palms.

Nathaniel's mind scrambled for an answer, but nothing came. Some questions simply had no answers — or maybe his mind refused to find them. Every time he tried to recall an abusive incident, a thick fog seemed to settle over his thoughts. The memories stayed just out of reach, and maybe that was for the best.

He didn't want to think about that part of his childhood. As far as he was concerned, it didn't happen. Mama never talked about it, and if it had really been that bad, surely she would have said something.

Before he could dwell on it any further, the sound of footsteps pulled him from his thoughts. Miriam and Josey walked in, Devan trailing closely behind.

Nathaniel's eyes gleamed, a smirk tugging at the corner of his mouth, "While we're asking questions here, why don't you tell us how you knew where daddy's gun was?"

Miriam's voice vibrated with anger. "Don't start your accusations again. If it were up to you, we'd be dead and your precious father would still be alive!"

Devan gently pulled Lisa back maneuvering himself between her and Nathaniel. "Everyone, calm down." His voice low and steady, he eyed Miriam and Nathaniel. "You don't want to upset your mom, right?"

Staring at Lisa, Nathaniel's voice dripped with fake curiosity, "You know what, I have an even better question. Aren't cops supposed to investigate and arrest the guilty?"

Devan's voice lowered to a growl, "I became a cop because of your father, and it sure wasn't to investigate his death. If you want an investigation, do it your damn self."

Nathaniel turned his focus to Devan. "Anybody could tell that it was a setup. All she needed was some key info from an ungrateful child and a reason to provoke his anger. You better believe I'll do my own investigation," his eyes turned to Lisa, the heat just as intense as ever, "Even if I have to interrogate the suspect myself."

The sudden creak of the door drew everyone's attention. "What's going on?" Dr. Crane asked, his voice quiet yet authoritative. "I could hear you from down the hall."

Nathaniel's eyes narrowed as they swept across the room, lingering on each face. His jaw clenched, and his fists tightened at his sides. Without a word, he spun on his heel and strode out, the door slamming shut behind him with a resounding thud that seemed to echo the tension he left in his wake.

Miriam walked over to her mother's bed, her voice tight with frustration. "How come you never tell him anything when he does that? He thinks dad was so great when we know he wasn't.

Why don't you just tell him the truth and make him face reality? Maybe if he knew the truth, he'd finally decide to get counseling."

Mary's shoulders sagged, the weight of Miriam's words seeming to pull her down. Her fingers traced the worn edge of her blanket, tugging at a loose thread. She kept her gaze fixed there, as though the fabric held answers she couldn't find. A soft sigh escaped her, barely louder than the rustle of the blanket

"Oh, I know." Miriam rolled her eyes dramatically. "He's just going through a phase."

Dr. Crane stepped forward, "That's enough Miriam." his voice calm, but firm. He placed a reassuring hand on Mary's shoulder. His voice softened as he continued. "Your mother doesn't need to be upset anymore than what she already is."

"Yeah, I am a lil pooped." Mary said tiredly.

Josey added, "Me too!"

"I'm sorry about all this Josey. I know you came to have some fun." Lisa apologized.

"Let me introduce you to Mrs. Mary. Ma, this is my friend Josey."

Mary forced a tired smile. "Hello sweetie. I'm sorry 'bout my son's behavior."

Josey grinned as she energetically tip toed over to the bed. "Don't worry about it." She waved her hand back and forth as she leaned in to give Mary a hug.

Mary opened her arms wide and squeezed tight. After a few moments, Josey started to pull away, but Mary held on—wanting to enjoy the warmth and comfort for a little while longer. After a few more moments, she released Josey and sat back in the bed.

Lisa went over and gave Mary a kiss. "We'll let you get some rest. We'll come back tomorrow and have a better visit." Lisa's voice lowered, her eyes lingering on Mary's weary face.

Dr. Crane pulled her aside as everyone left. "Don't worry, I'll take care of her."

"Thanks. I'm truly sorry for what went on."

"Don't worry about it."

"Ok, I'll try." Lisa exhaled slowly, the tension visibly draining from her shoulders. "I'll call you later to see how she's doing."

Victoria Rose

As Lisa rejoined the group, Devan asked, "Is everyone alright?"

They all solemnly nodded yes.

"What are we going to do now?" Josey asked.

"I'll leave that up to you ladies." Devan answered.

"You haven't been to my place yet. Let's go there." Miriam offered.

Everyone agreed, and they had just started heading for the door when a sharp beeping noise broke through the air.

"It's my pager," Miriam said, unclipping it from her waist and glancing at the screen. The code flashing back at her was a 1013 — a tough one. It meant someone had been involuntarily committed due to an emergency mental health crisis.

"I'm being paged for work. We usually rotate on-call shifts, but I volunteer almost every week."

Lisa raised a brow. "When was the last time you had a date?"

Miriam shot her a pointed look. "For your information, I take my work very seriously. I volunteer to show the patients I care and that they can count on me."

Before Lisa could respond, the pager beeped again. Miriam sighed. "Sorry, guys. I really have to go."

Victoria Rose

Miriam rested her head against the steering wheel as she gripped it tightly. She shouldn't have snapped at her mother. She knew that. But when Nathaniel's voice rose, when his fists clenched just so, and her mother fell silent—just like she used to—Miriam's stomach twisted with something hot and unbearable. It was like watching a ghost rise from the past.

She would never understand it. Never understand how her mother stayed. How she let their father's fists and words break her down, let him turn their home into a battleground. How she let him hurt them too.

As a child, Miriam had raged silently inside, blaming her as much as him. But she learned, over time, to swallow the anger, to pack it away like an old, unwanted keepsake and shove it into the farthest corners of her mind. She became the perfect daughter—the one who smiled, who said all the right things, who never let the resentment slip past her lips.

And yet, it was still there. A quiet, simmering thing that sometimes escaped, like it had today.

She, of all people, should understand. As a counselor, she was trained to untangle trauma, to help people heal. She told herself she empathized with her mother—that she saw the fear, the learned helplessness, the cycle of abuse. And she did.

But the daughter in her—the wounded, angry girl still trapped in the past—wasn't ready to forgive.

And beneath all of it, something colder lurked. Fear. The kind that gripped her chest late at night, whispering a truth she could never quite shake.

What if she ended up loving a man just like him?

Miriam always started with the best intentions. She wanted to connect, to open herself up, to believe that love—real love—was possible. And for a while, it was. A few months of effortless conversations, warm touches, and hopeful what-ifs.

But then, the shift.

A certain tone in his voice. A fleeting look in his eyes. A moment of frustration that lingered just a second too long. It didn't matter if it was real or imagined—her mind twisted it into something familiar, something dangerous. She would see her father in the way he moved, in the way he spoke, in the way his presence filled a room.

And that was enough.

Before it could go any further, before she could risk being trapped, she would end it. The men never understood. They searched her face for answers, asked what they had done wrong, and when she told them it was her, not them, she meant it. But that never made them believe it.

She had unraveled so much of her past, learned to stitch the broken pieces of herself back together. But this—this lingering fear—was the wound that refused to close.

She should confront it. She knew that. But the thought alone made her skin crawl. Facing it meant peeling back old scars, inviting the memories to breathe again. Instead, she buried herself in work, in other people's pain, in problems she could actually solve. It was easier that way.

She exhaled sharply and loosened her grip on the wheel. Another day, another client, another excuse to ignore the things clawing at the back of her mind.

Maybe someday she'd deal with it.

But not today.

Chapter Seven

FANTASY OF POSSIBILITIES

With a sharp exhale, Nathaniel slid his glasses from his face, the world around him immediately transforming into a collage of undefined colors. Between deep, frustrated breaths, he closed his eyes and massaged the bridge of his nose between his thumb and index finger. The beating of his heart pounded against his temples like a prisoner trying to escape. He roughly grabbed the bottom of his shirt, as if it were the cause of his stress, and used it to clean his glasses. Guiding them back into place, he watched as visitors streamed in and out, their faces blurred together as he remained fixed in place. His spine stiffened as his gaze sharpened, narrowed eyes fixed on the hospital doors.

The glass doors slid open and instantly he recognized the familiar profile of his sister. Miriam moved swiftly towards the parking lot, eyes fixed forward, unaware of her surroundings.

"She's so deep in her thoughts, she doesn't even see me," he scoffed, shaking his head.

Shortly after, two women and a man emerged. His breath escaped in a low, loathsome sigh, fingers simultaneously clenched into a fist as he recognized the siblings.

"There goes the Murderer and the supposed cop," he mumbles.

Grabbing the steering wheel with both hands, he pulled himself forward, zeroing in on the other woman. He didn't get a chance to really look at her before, but figured she most likely came with the Murderer. The one thing he did notice was those fake green eyes. "Of course she would surround herself with fake people, just like her," he spat.

She hadn't wasted any time back then spewing her fake lies either. Making everyone believe his dad tried to attack her, leaving her no choice but to defend herself. He leaned back into his seat, jaw clenched. And to add insult to injury, Miriam seemed to be in on it too. He just needed to find proof. It was going to be hard though. Those sneaky little bitches covered their tracks very well. On top of that, the damn cops hadn't done much of an investigation. The only thing they did was take down his mother's, Miriam's, and the Murderer's statements, as if it were an open-and-shut case!

More than once, he had confronted Miriam. The very first time he asked, he swore he saw a tinge of guilt wash over her.

"Just admit it," he'd growled, his eyes wild with anger. "You and the Murderer planned it all out didn't you?"

But in an instant, Miriam's expression was replaced with a cold-like resolve. "You don't want the truth. You only believe in your little fantasies and daydreams," she snapped back.

No longer able to contain his anger, his voice boomed, "You helped her murder your *own* father?"

And then just like every time afterward, she turned on her heels without another word, slamming the door behind her, leaving him alone with his anger and unanswered questions.

As a last resort, he even turned to his mom, hoping she might remember something—some detail that hadn't made it into the report. But every time he asked, she gave the same response: *What's in da report is all I remember.*

He didn't believe that. Not entirely. A nagging suspicion told him she knew more but was too kind to turn the Murderer in. Maybe she thought staying silent would keep the peace.

He could have pushed harder, pressed her for the truth. But with her health declining, he couldn't bring himself to do it. She had already endured so much.

She never talked about his dad, though he knew she loved and missed him just as much as he did. Maybe even more. The pain of losing him—losing everything—and then raising two kids alone must have been unbearable. He winced, thinking about all the trouble he had caused, the extra weight he had added to her already heavy burden. And yet, she never got angry, never lashed out.

Most parents would have given up on a kid like him. But not her. Hell, she was practically a saint.

He never once wished she had died instead of his father, but he couldn't shake the feeling that if his dad had been there—if they had both been there—his life would have turned out differently.

Even though he has trouble remembering most of his childhood, Nathaniel remembered the beginning of that fateful day with startling clarity. He had been crouched around the corner with his friends, Bobby and Russ, locked in a heated game of jacks. With five jacks already claimed, he was in the lead, but Russ was close behind with four. The stakes felt high—at least, as high as a game of jacks could feel to a kid.

They had heard the sirens in the distance, but the game had held their focus. For most kids, they don't hold the same urgency as they do for adults. Not until they have an up close and personal experience with them.

As they continued to play, a murmur rippled through the street as people stepped outside, whispering in hushed tones. Then, a sudden shift—an awkward silence. A strange sensation crawled over Nathaniel's skin—as an unseen force penetrated through his awareness. He swallowed a gulp of air as he slowly turned around. He glanced up from his crouched position, his fingers still curled around the tiny metal jacks. A sea of pitying adult eyes were staring at *him*. All at once, a big heavy metal ball seemed to drop from his throat to his stomach. Sweat erupted from every pore, releasing water like a dam giving way under pressure.

And then, before his mind could catch up, his body took over.

The jacks, his prized possessions only moments ago, clattered to the pavement. His legs propelled him forward as he ran, blinded with fear, his heart hammered against his chest. The familiar path home blurred past him. But as he rounded the final corner, the flashing blue and white lights stopped him in his tracks—sapping his energy. His blood pounded in his ears, drowning out the world. His vision wavered—sharp one second, hazy the next—as if his body was rejecting reality itself.

A deep, sinking dread gripped him. His mom was dead. He felt it. Knew it.

He forced himself forward, toward the porch, but a firm hand stopped him before he could reach the first step.

"Lil Nate," a voice said gently. "Come on over to my squad car so I can talk to you."

Nathaniel turned toward the cop. He could barely process the words over the noise in his head. He wanted to ask, *Is it my mom?* But he couldn't make his mouth form the words.

The cop guided Nathaniel over to his squad car and crouched down, meeting him at eye level. "Now son, what I have to tell you is not easy. I want you to be brave, okay?"

Nathaniel gave a stiff nod, his gaze was drawn back toward the house. The front door opened. Paramedics emerged, two of them maneuvering a stretcher down the steps. His breath caught when he saw Miriam lying on it with Lisa trailing close behind. Then a second stretcher appeared.

His eyes narrowed and his head tilted to one side. His eye brows furrowed in confusion.

His mother was on the stretcher—moving. If she was moving, how could she be dead?

He turned back to the cop, shock and uncertainty etched across his face.

The officer exhaled, his face lined with sorrow. "Son, your father is dead."

Nathaniel's eyes became distant as the cop's words faded away and the world went silent.

That was the last thing he remembered from that day. It wasn't until later that he found out the truth.

Lisa had pulled the trigger.

From that day forward, nothing was ever the same for Nathaniel. He would sit in class, staring blankly at the chalkboard, lost in thoughts that stretched far beyond the four walls around him. Time slipped away without him noticing until—

"Nathaniel."

His name, sharp and sudden, pulled him back. Blinking, he found himself under the weight of his teacher's glare, the amused whispers of his classmates rippling around him. The same way the adults had whispered that day. He could feel their eyes on him, dissecting, judging, mocking.

At first, he withdrew. Words felt useless. There was no one he could talk to, no one he could trust. But the quiet only seemed to make him an easier target. The stares and whispers hardened into cruel laughter, and the taunts came soon after.

"Your dad was nothing but a drunk coward."

"He beat up on women and little girls."

Nathaniel's blood would boil. He'd yell that they were wrong, that they didn't know anything. But they wouldn't stop. And so, his silence turned into rage. That's when the fights started.

His grades plummeted. His mother gave up on punishments—she couldn't keep up anymore. Between the suspensions and the days he skipped altogether, school became a place he barely existed in.

But in his mind, he lived somewhere else entirely.

There, his father was still alive.

He would picture himself outside, tossing a football in the air, waiting. Then, the rumble of an engine. His father's car would roll into the driveway, and Nathaniel would sprint over, flinging the door open before his dad could even unbuckle.

"Dad, come throw the football with me!"

His father would smile, patting him on the head. "I'm tired, son. Maybe tomorrow."

"Please, Dad! Just for a little bit?"

A pause, then a sigh—then a grin. "Alright, alright. Just for a little bit."

But "a little bit" would turn into hours.

Sometimes, his mind would take him fishing with his father, or to a football game where he stood on the sidelines, cheering him on.

Occasionally, Nathaniel's daydreams included his mother. In his mind, she was the perfect wife—warm, loving, and devoted. He imagined her gliding through the house, humming softly as she vacuumed the living room rug, folded fresh laundry, and prepared his father's favorite dinner—red beans and rice, collard greens, and cornbread.

As the day wound down and the clock inched closer to his father's arrival, she would pause for a final check, smoothing out the couch cushions, adjusting a picture frame, ensuring everything was just right. Then, with a bright, contented smile, she'd turn to Nathaniel and say, "It's almost time for your father to come home!"

The warmth in her voice lingered in his mind, wrapping around him like a soft embrace. Even now, the memory of that imagined love filled him with comfort.

But it wasn't all fantasy. Somewhere in the depths of his childhood memories, he could still recall moments when his mother fussed over the house before his father walked through the door—straightening things, adjusting details, making sure everything was perfect. It made him smile to think that she had loved his father so much, she had gone to great lengths to make sure he was well taken care of.

But his favorite daydreams were the ones where his father showed up at school. Maybe for a father-son event, maybe just because. And in those dreams, the other kids weren't laughing at him. They were staring in awe, whispering about how cool his dad was. How lucky he was.

The daydreams always felt real—until reality came crashing in.

"Nathaniel!"

The voices would shift, morphing from admiration to irritation, and suddenly, he was back in class, looking up at his teacher's disapproving face. The laughter came next—sharp, relentless, clawing at the edges of his patience.

Something inside him would snap.

Books smacked the floor. His chair toppled over. The laughter cut off, replaced by startled gasps. He saw the fear in their eyes, and for a moment, it filled him with a twisted sense of power. But the teachers weren't so easily shaken. They shut it down fast, sending him straight to the principal's office. Again.

In-school suspension became his second home. A whole week in a silent room, away from the others. He was still expected to do schoolwork, but it gave him more time to escape into his mind. To live in the world he preferred.

Expulsions came next. Those were harder. His mother would have to leave work, her face tight with disappointment as she signed the paperwork to take him home.

"Why can't ya jus' behave like ya used to?" she would ask, her voice heavy with something deeper than frustration.

At first, he told her the truth—the kids wouldn't leave him alone. But eventually, that stopped being the reason. Now, he was the one starting the fights.

Because it didn't seem like anyone cared about his pain.

And if no one else felt it, he would make them.

The one person he thought he could turn to was Miriam. He was certain she was having the same problems at school that he was, but he soon realized their experiences were like night and day. Suddenly, it seemed like she was one of the most popular girls at school. She started making the honor roll and joined the cheerleading team. She always had something to do—always off somewhere doing some extracurricular activity or another. And Mom, well, she was always working or cleaning up around the house. It seemed like everyone had something to do but him. He increasingly found himself wishing his dad was still alive, knowing he would understand what he was going through.

Over time, the truth settled in—everything had started the day his father died. The anger, the resentment, the aching void inside him. At first, he had lashed out at the kids at school, making them feel a fraction of his pain. But they weren't the ones who deserved it.

Only one person did.

Lisa.

If she hadn't murdered his father, his life would have been completely different. She had stolen everything from him—his childhood, his innocence, the memories he should have made with his dad. Every ounce of his suffering could be traced back to her. And for that, she would pay.

He had promised himself that.

One day, he would uncover the proof—that it was all premeditated. He wouldn't settle for an easy way out like the death penalty. No, that would be too merciful. She needed to suffer. Slowly.

He wanted her to know what it felt like to be utterly alone just like he had growing up. To wake up one day to laughs and sneers and realize her reality is just a fantasy of possibilities that will never happen.

And most of all, he wanted to see the fear in her eyes—the moment of realization that there was no escape, no way to undo what she had done.

The thought sent a thrill through him, a dark excitement curling in his chest.

He just had to figure out how to prove it.

The deep rumble of an engine snapped him back to the present, shaking him out of his thoughts. He blinked, glancing down at his watch. Over an hour had passed since he stormed out of his mom's hospital room.

His belly growled in agreement that he had sat there far too long, lost in his thoughts. But despite the hunger gnawing at him, he felt confident—more focused than he had in years. A sense of purpose coursed through him, fueling his determination.

"First order of business—grab some grub," he muttered, gripping the wheel. "Second—come up with a plan to take down the Murderer."

He started the car and drove off. A slow smirk creeping across his face.

Chapter Eight

It's Me

Lisa, Josey and Devan left the hospital, the weight of the night settling over them as they made their way home. The car ride was quiet, each lost in their own thoughts. By the time they reached Devan's apartment, the somber mood clung to them like a heavy blanket.

Devan stepped ahead, unlocking the door and pushing it open. With a small, welcoming smile, he gestured for the ladies to enter. "Ladies first," he announced, holding the door wide. Lisa and Josey stepped inside, the lingering chill from the hospital fading as the apartment's warmth wrapped around them.

Lisa let out a long sigh before flopping onto the sofa, sinking into the cushions. "I need a nap," she mumbled. already making herself comfortable.

Josey stretched her arms out on each side then rolled her shoulders. "After all the excitement, I'm wide awake," she said, shaking her head.

"I'm hungry." Devan declared, rubbing his stomach as he marched towards the kitchen with purpose.

Lisa groaned, forcing herself back up with exaggerated effort. "I'm going to take a nap." she decided, trudging toward the bedroom without another word.

She shuffled into the guest room, took off her shoes, and closed the door. She sighed deeply as she padded herself down, taking everything out of her pockets and placing all of it on the nightstand. She laid on her back with her hands on her stomach and closed her eyes. Her mind wandered back to that day. She even remembered what she had on. Light blue jean shorts with a yellow short sleeve shirt, her favorite colors.

She remembered passing Mrs. Blanchard's white picket fence on her way to Miriam's house, the familiar sight barely registering in her rush. Gripping the handlebars tighter, she pushed the bike to its limit, pedaling as fast as her legs would allow. As she rounded the corner, a chilling sound stopped her cold—screaming.

Oh no, this isn't happening! she thought.

The bike performed a slight bounce as it hit the ground, wheels spinning as feet bounded up the porch steps. Even though she couldn't see clearly beyond the mesh of the screen door, she knew something terrible—frightening was on the other side. Her fingers grasping the handle, she pulled.

Every muscle tightened. Her jaw clenched almost causing her to bite her tongue as her teeth grinded together. Invisible ropes squeezed around her chest, legs and arms keeping her feet frozen in place. Each breath came in small, ragged gasps against her throat.

"What have you done to my child!"

The agonizing scream pierced through the air, sending a chill down her spine. "Miriam, please be okay," she silently prayed. Her heart pounded against her chest as she battled to slow her breathing and clear her mind. She needed to think quickly.

She started to calm down until she heard him say coldly, "This is what I did you fucking dumb bitch!"

"No, don't!" Mom's voice tore through the air, followed by a sickening crack—loud, sharp, final. The sound reminded Lisa of a baseball bat connecting with a perfect home run, only this wasn't a game.

The shock shattered her paralysis. Her legs finally obeyed, propelling her forward. She veered left, flying through the living room and into the master bedroom, dropping to her knees beside the bed. Her hands fumbled frantically beneath it until her fingers struck cold metal.

The black, heavy box scraped against the floor as she yanked it into the light. With sweaty fingers, she flipped it open. Relief and dread tangled in her chest—it was exactly where Miriam said it would be.

Her hands trembled, but her resolve didn't. She grabbed the gun, bolted back through the living room, and charged toward the kitchen.

The double-hinged door swung wildly as she burst through. The massive island stood at the room's center, flanked by

L-shaped counters. To her right, sunlight streamed through the breakfast nook's windows, golden and indifferent.

Her gaze darted right, then dropped. A gasp strangled in her throat.

Miriam lay motionless on the floor, small and still.

Lisa's eyes traveled from her friend's limp form to a pair of scuffed boots. She realized...

"Stop torturing yourself with this shit!" Lisa scolded herself. She would never get to sleep at this rate.

She looked over at the nightstand. Her cell phone lay beside the doctor's card. She picked both of them up. She flipped the card over and hesitated. *It won't hurt just to check up on mom.* she thought. She quickly dialed the number before she could change her mind.

Sean blew out a breath of air as he slowly shook himself out of his white coat. He grimaced a bit as he placed his hands on his hips leaning backwards then forwards, stretching his back. He smiled to himself, thankful there were no major issues with any of his patients today. He learned early on to appreciate these types of days. The phone in his pants pocket buzzed him out of his thoughts. "Hello."

"Hi, it's me." Lisa's voice came through the receiver barely above a whisper.

His eyes widened in recognition, his tiredness evaporating instantly. His heart hammered against his chest, but his voice answered with a light hearted ring. "Hey, me."

"Do you know who this is?"

"Of course I do!" His shoulders squared, chin lifting as if she could see him through the phone.

A pause stretched between them. Lisa bit her lower lip, eyes narrowing. "Who am I?"

"You are me." His lips twitched into a smile.

"Stop stalling. You have no idea who this is!" Her knuckles tightened around the phone.

"I know exactly who you are. You're the person who called me for the very first time and said, "It's me." He chuckled.

"So you do know who I am. Unless you give your number out to all the new girls." Her eyebrows arched, a reluctant smile beginning to form.

"Darn, I'm busted!" he joked. "Are you calling to check on Mrs. Butler, Lisa?" He said in a more serious, but still laid back tone.

Lisa felt her stomach flutter. Her name sounded sexy coming from him. She wondered how it would sound if he said it while they... *Focus girl!* She shouted at herself mentally. *Hold your horses. You don't even know him yet!*

"Yes. That's exactly why I called Dr. Crane. I hope I'm not interrupting you." She wasn't lying, but she also wasn't being totally truthful.

"Please, call me Sean. Of course you're not. Actually, I just got off so I have some time to spare. She's doing well. She just needed to calm down after what happened."

Lisa's shoulders dropped, a long breath escaping her as the tension eased from her body. "That's such a relief!" Her voice softened, a weight lifting from her. "I was afraid all of that might have stressed her out even more so. I want to apologize again for the fuss we all made. I'm really sorry about that."

Her tone grew quieter, a touch of regret in it. "It was childish of us. You see, Nathaniel and I don't get along anymore."

On the other end of the line, Sean waved his hand as though dismissing her words, even though she couldn't see the gesture. "It's ok," he said with an easy tone. "I know all about it. This is a small town and you know how people gossip. I was told about what happened a long time ago."

The doctor usually rushed through conversations, but this one felt different. He found himself pausing, wishing the conversation wouldn't end just yet.

"So you knew who I was when you met me?" Her eyebrows arched, head tilting slightly as she listened intently.

"I sure did," his tone turning serious. "There was one thing they hadn't told me though."

Lisa's curiosity piqued, her brow furrowing slightly. "What's that?"

"They didn't tell me how beautiful you are."

The words left his mouth before he could stop them. He swallowed hard, feeling suddenly exposed. It was like she was his truth serum.

Oh, my God! Lisa's mind screamed, but her voice betrayed her. "Wow, I'm flattered... Thanks." She fumbled with the words, trying to hide the flutter in her chest.

Sean felt his pulse race. He couldn't tell if that was a nervous 'cause I like him too' or a nervous 'cause he's a stalker' response. With a slight cough, he shifted, deciding to try a different route.

"Well, there was something else they didn't mention," he said, the tension hanging between them.

"What's that?" Lisa asked, intrigued.

"They didn't say anything about your friend, Josey."

Lisa chuckled softly, the sound light in the quiet of the conversation. "She's a relatively new friend. She's from Georgia. This is her first visit down here."

"She seems nice." He hesitated, a brief pause before gathering his courage. "How come your boyfriend didn't come?"

Lisa response was cool, measured. "I don't have one."

Sean's voice faltered slightly in disbelief. "Really! That's hard for me to believe," he said, his voice rising a pitch. His eyes flickered upward in silent gratitude, his thoughts a quick prayer: *Thank you God!*

"I've found most men don't like confident women." Lisa added, a touch of bitterness slipping in.

"That's because they don't have confidence in themselves." Sean shot back with ease.

Lisa's tone softened, curiosity mixing with a hint of playfulness. "You seem like a confident man. Where's your girlfriend?"

Sean's chuckle vibrated through the line. "I am confident, but unfortunately, I'm not a good conversationalist."

"You're not having any problems talking now." Lisa observed, leaning forward slightly as she sat on the bed, a smile tugging at the corners of her mouth. Her eyes sparkled, impressed by how open he was about his weaknesses without being embarrassed.

"Usually I'm nervous and all I can think of is nerdy things to say." Sean admitted, his voice a little more sheepish now.

Lisa tilted her head, her smile widening. "Why aren't you nervous now?"

Sean paused for a moment, his gaze shifting as he considered her words. "That's because you put me at ease. I don't feel foolish telling you the truth." His voice took on a deeper sincerity. "You're not like women from here or from where I'm from."

Lisa's heart soared at his honesty, though he had no idea how much he had just brightened her day. "That's really sweet," she said softly, her smile lingering.

Wanting to keep the conversation light, she decided to shift the focus. She didn't want to rush anything even though the curiosity was bubbling up in her "Where are you from?"

"Chi-town," he replied with a grin, pride slipping into his voice.

"I've never been there before," she said, her eyes sparkling. "I'll have to make a special trip out there."

"I'll go with you and show you all the sights," he offered quickly, his voice playful. "You'll have your own personal guide.
"

Lisa laughed, the sound carefree. "Good, you can take me to the Oprah show!" she said dreamily.

Sean grinned to himself. He loved the way she was happy just thinking about going. He loved even more that she didn't mind him in her thoughts. "I'll take you there and any other places you want to visit. It will be great. I haven't been home in a while."

"What made you move down here from such a big city?"

"I did my internship here. I liked the closeness of the community. Everyone knows everyone else and their business. It wasn't like that where I grew up. Big isn't always better."

"What did your parents say about you moving?"

"My mom died giving birth to me. I'm the only child they had. My dad raised me alone. He always said he spoiled me. He thought it was great that I moved out here. He said I stayed under him too much instead of getting out and discovering the world."

"I'm sorry about your mom. Your dad sounds like he's really nice."

"He is. I couldn't imagine him not being my dad. I'm sorry about your parents passing too."

"How did you know...Oh, I forgot. The gossip."

"Yes, that and I know your brother."

"You know Devan. How?"

"Occasionally cops have to bring in prisoners to get treated. During my first week as an intern, he brought in one that I had to treat. I was pretty nervous since that was my first time treating a prisoner. I think your brother picked up on that because he talked to me the entire time. It wasn't about anything in particular, but for some reason it helped calm my nerves. We've been friends ever since."

"I had no idea you knew each other. I'll have to ask him about you two. Maybe he can give me some gossip about you!"

A slight smile played at the corners of Sean's mouth. "I have an even better idea."

"Oh, really, what is it?"

"Why settle for second hand gossip when you can get a first hand account. How about we take a trip to New Orleans on Saturday. I have to check on some of my patients early in the morning and then I'm free the rest of the day. I've always wanted to do the tourist thing and see some of the awesome sites." Sean's heart skipped a beat as he held his breath.

Lisa closed her eyes and silently performed a happy tap dance jiggle with her feet. She quickly regained her composure as she calmly answered, "Only on one condition."

Sean's shoulders relaxed, the tension melting away as he exhaled, his eyebrows lifting. "What's that?"

"I drive. I heard some thangs about how people drive from Chicago!"

Sean's head tipped back, a little snort followed by a deep belly laugh escaped before he could stop it. He had no idea what the condition was going to be, but he never expected this. In the most dignified and royal British voice he could muster through his laughter he responded, "I do not know anything about these unfounded rumors, but I'll have you know I am an excellent driver. Nevertheless, I shall accept your terms."

The air hung still for a heartbeat before they both doubled over, their laughter echoing through the phone line. Tears rolled down their cheeks as they gasped for breath, each fresh wave of giggles setting the other off again until their sides ached.

As they both worked to draw steady breaths, she remembered his long day at the hospital. She softened her voice. "As much as I'm enjoying this, the long day is finally catching up with me. I should probably try to get some sleep."

"Yeah, you don't want to overdo yourself," he said, his tone matching hers.

"Sean?"

"Yes?"

"I'll see you tomorrow," she said, her voice honey-sweet.

Sean drew in an audible breath, words failing him.

"Bye." Her giggle floated through the phone.

"Bye!" He smiled as he hung up.

Sean stared at his phone for a moment, then exhaled sharply, shaking his head with a grin. He paced to the window, gazing out at the hospital parking lot, but all he saw was her.

"Of all people," he whispered, half laughing to himself.

"She calls, says 'It's me'—and just like that..."

He trailed off, an unexpected warmth settling in his chest.

"I think I'm in love," he murmured, rubbing the back of his neck.

Chapter Nine

Almost Beautiful

From the loveseat, Josey watched as Devan moved around the kitchen. He pulled open the fridge, grabbed a pack of salami, some cheese, and a loaf of bread. "You want a sandwich?" he asked over his shoulder.

"Nah, I'm good. Thanks for asking."

Devan poured himself a cup of orange soda before joining her on the sofa. As he ate, Josey studied him, curiosity tugging at her. She wondered what he thought about what happened today. Did he think they planned it?

She hesitated for a moment, then decided to ask.

"What do you think about what Miriam's brother said?"

Devan tipped his cup back, draining the last of his drink. "Which part?"

"The part where he accused Lisa and Miriam of murdering his father."

"I'm not sure. If they did, I couldn't blame them. The day it happened was horrible. My dad was working offshore on an oil rig. Mom and I were home.

I was sixteen that year. Like any other teenager in the summer, I stayed up late and slept in. That day, I rolled out of bed around noon. Lisa was already gone. I was in the kitchen eating a bowl of cereal when the phone rang.

It was Mrs. Miller. All the kids called her Big Red behind her back. She was big and red as fire."

Josey smiled slightly, picturing a fiery, no-nonsense woman standing outside, wagging her finger at a teenage Devan.

"She was screaming into the phone," Devan continued, "I had to tell her to calm down and talk slowly. That's when she said the cops and ambulance were at the Butler's place. Someone told her Lisa was there too, but they didn't know if she was okay."

He paused, staring down at the empty plate in front of him.

"I was one of those big brothers who tormented their younger siblings, always acting like I didn't care," he admitted. "Lisa was there for me to pick on when I was bored. But in that moment—" he closed his eyes briefly, his voice softening—"it hit me that I might never see her again. Never talk to her, never hear her laugh, never see her smile." He exhaled, shaking his head. "That was the first time I can truly say I felt real fear."

A gentle warmth settled over his hand. He looked up to find Josey's emerald eyes fixed on him, full of quiet understanding. Her fingers wrapped around his, grounding him.

"When I hung up with Mrs. Miller, I prayed with all my might. I begged God to please let Lisa be safe. I promised if He did, I would never be mean to her again."

His voice grew distant as he lost himself in the memory.

"I took off running to the laundry room, shouting what happened before I even got there. My mom's eyes were wild with panic. She grabbed me by the shoulders, demanding I repeat myself. I forced myself to slow down, to explain it right. As the words sank in, she leaned against me, trembling, struggling to breathe. I had never seen my mother that shaken before. Somehow, we made it to the car and over to the Butler's house.

The street was packed with a sea of people, whispering, craning their necks. My mom clutched my arm so tight it hurt as we pushed through the crowd toward the police barrier. I scanned the scene, desperate—until I finally spotted Lisa standing by an ambulance. Relief flooded through me, it was like a thousand-pound weight lifting from my shoulders in an instant.

I pointed her out, and my mom gasped, 'Thank God!'

The cops let us through once we explained who we were. And then Lisa saw us and ran straight into Mom's arms. She had a black eye. Bruises." His jaw clenched. "Mom wrapped her up, holding her like she'd never let go, kissing her face between sobs. I pulled them both in, my own tears falling before I even realized I was crying. The paramedic who had been with her came over, his expression serious as he told us what happened."

Devan's fingers curled into a fist. His voice, raw with emotion, dropped to a low growl.

"I can only imagine how afraid Lisa must have been." He swallowed hard. "I was angry. I wished he was still alive so I could kill him again. They were just children!" His hand curled into a fist.

"I don't know how he called himself a man. I could never beat on my wife let alone my children or someone else's!"

Josey listened quietly, her hand moving in slow, soothing circles along his arm.

"When my dad heard the news, he rushed home and ended up staying for two weeks. I think he felt guilty about not being there when it happened. Every time he would leave after that, he would pull me aside and say, 'Take real good care of your sister, ya hear?'

Mom got into the habit of inviting Lisa's friends over - filling the house with chatter and laughter. Lisa never seemed to mind. I think she enjoyed the constant company and distraction.

I tried over and over again to make sense out of what happened, but I couldn't. I felt powerless and that made me angry. Eventually I realized there was one thing I could do. Keep my promise to my dad and take care of Lisa. That's why I became a cop. In a lot of ways Lisa seemed like her old self, but we could all tell she was different."

"Different how?" Josey asked.

"Before it happened, she used to be so annoyingly loud." Devan laughed lightly. "But after, she was quieter and seemed to be in her thoughts a lot. She still smiled and laughed, but in her eyes, I saw worry and fear. We were all worried about her, but she insisted she was fine."

I see I'm not the only one she keeps a certain amount of distance from, Josey thought.

Devan continued. "She and Miriam became even closer after that, practically inseparable until our parents died. I'm not sure what caused the shift, but suddenly, an awkward distance settled between the two. No matter how many times I asked her what was going on, she would just say everything was fine. Right before they graduated, Lisa announced she was going to college in Georgia. That really was a shock for me. I had always envisioned us living out our lives here. I also knew not to try to change her mind though. Once she has her mind made up, you might as well give up. So I had to be the bigger big brother and support her decision."

Josey leaned forward, her brow furrowed in concentration. The weight of his words hung in the air between them as she continued to gently caress his arm, processing what he'd shared. When she finally spoke, her voice was gentle, barely above a whisper.

"What happened to your parents?" she asked.

Devan swallowed hard, his gaze drifting toward the window. "My dad died in an oil rig explosion. My mom died of a stroke five months after that. My mom and dad were really close. I think it was too much for my mom to be here without him."

She squeezed his arm softly. "I'm sorry you guys had to go through that."

"Thanks. I think it was worse for Lisa. That was her senior year. Instead of thinking about what color she would wear to prom, she was helping make funeral arrangements. I think that's why she moved to Georgia. This is her very first time visiting since she left."

"Did you visit her in Georgia?"

"Of course I did. We also took vacations together. We would plan everything over the phone and then meet each other at the vacation spot."

"That was very sweet of you. You'll make a good husband."

Devan's voice rose a notch. "Why you say that?"

"I always judge a man by the way he treats the women in his family. You treat your sister with respect and love. I don't see that very much."

Wow, I can't believe I said all that, Devan thought. He had never shared so much details about what happened before. And she picked up on everything. He shifted in his seat, suddenly self-conscious. *I don't want to come across as self-centered. Besides, I definitely want to know more about her.*

Clearing his throat, he changed the subject. "Thank you. So, enough about me. I want to know more about you. Do you have any siblings?"

"Yes. I have two sisters. I'm in the middle. One is a year older than me and the other a year younger."

"What about your parents?" Devan asked.

"My mom raised us alone. Her and my father never got married. After my mom had my youngest sister, he split. He visited us a couple of times while we were growing up. We didn't have a real relationship with him. My mom is great. I look up to her. I don't think I could raise three children on my own."

"I don't think you'll have to. A man would be a fool to leave a beautiful, caring woman like you."

He found himself drawn to her, wanting to know her thoughts, her dreams, her fears. Yet at the same time, his body yearned for hers. In the past, women had appealed to either his mind or his physical desires—never both with such equal intensity. Until now.

Bathed in a gentle glow from the overhead light, Josey looked radiant. The rich tones of her dark brown skin made her green eyes all the more vivid, making her look almost too perfect for this world. Her wavy, black hair flowed past her shoulders like a silk curtain, framing her face. Her full, soft lips were parted just slightly, as if suspended between a thought and a breath, as she looked back at him.

Devan's body moved instinctively toward Josey—like a magnet pulled to a rare and precious metal. His gaze locked with hers, the air between them thick with unspoken desire.

"I know when I look into those pretty eyes, I couldn't imagine hurting you."

As if she was suddenly standing by a blazing fire, heat spread across Josey's skin from head to toe. The room seemed to fade away, her pulse thundering in her ears. *It feels so good to be close to him*, she thought.

He slowly moved his lips close to her ear and whispered, "You are so beautiful."

That sent ripples of pleasure through her body. Usually she was the one making men want her, not the other way around. He had her stumped. All she could do was look him in the eyes and let him lead.

He grazed his lips back and forth against hers. He gave Josey a long and slow kiss as he slid his hand up her thigh. She caressed his chest through his shirt. His hand traveled from her thigh to her breast.

Devan took a deep breath. Desire coursed through him, urging him to whisk her away to his bedroom. Yet it was like her essence was calling out to him - connecting them on more than just the physical level.

He realized she hadn't said one word the entire time. He pulled away slowly until her entire face was in view. She gazed back at him, eyelids low, lips slightly parted in anticipation. As he leaned in to taste her lips once more, the guest room door creaked open. Startled, they sprang apart, backs rigid, eyes fixed straight ahead while their hearts threw jabs at their chests.

Lisa walked into the living room.

"What are you guys up to?" Her last words faded on her lips as she looked at how they sat.

"Oh, nothing." Josey mumbled.

"I'm, uh, going to bed. Goodnight." Devan tripped over his words, nearly knocking over his empty plate as he bolted from the loveseat. His footsteps echoed down the hallway, followed by the resounding click of his bedroom door—leaving their unspoken "goodnights" hanging in the air behind him.

Before Lisa could ask any questions, Josey said, "I thought you were sleeping. You don't look like you even closed your eyes."

"I didn't go to sleep."

"What were you doing?"

"I was upset about what happened at the hospital and I couldn't go to sleep. So I called Sean."

"Sean? You mean Dr. Crane?"

"Yup. He made me feel better, but then I couldn't stop thinking about him. So, I thought I'd get me something to eat." Lisa said gleefully as she carried Devan's plate back into the kitchen.

"You sound like you guys made a love connection!"

"Let's just say our visit has turned out a hundred percent better than I thought it would."

"I second that." Josey murmured.

"I heard that!" Lisa shot back. "I knew what you guys were doing as soon as I saw your faces."

"Ok. I admit it. I like your brother a lot."

"I'm glad. You two are perfect for each other. I realized that when we played the joke on you earlier today. You guys had instant chemistry."

A long sigh escaped Josey as her shoulders relaxed. "I've never met anyone quite like him," she confessed, all smiles. "The way he thinks, how deeply he feels things..." She traced her finger absently along the couch cushion. "And those soft lips of his..." She shook her head, amazed. "I keep wondering how someone so incredible could still be single."

Lisa shivered "Eew! For future reference, I don't want to hear any of the personal details. Keep that to yourself. Unfortunately, most women want a "Bad Boy". Devan doesn't fit that criteria. He's the complete opposite."

"He definitely fits in mine. I could see myself in a long term relationship with him."

"Sean is the same way. He makes me feel like he would be happy just spending time getting to know me." Lisa came out of the kitchen with her food. "I can't wait to see him tomorrow."

"Look at you. All happy and shit!" Josey beamed at her friend.

Lisa sank into the couch beside her with a grin. For a moment, the room felt full—of warmth, laughter, the kind of quiet comfort that didn't need explanation.

It was almost beautiful.

The kind of night that made you forget the hard ones.

"Well, now that all the festivities have wound down, I'm going to take a bath and go to bed."

"Okay, don't take up the whole bed. It's only a full size. I don't want you all over me calling out you know who's name either." Lisa joked.

"Same goes for you, missy!" Josey replied.

Victoria Rose

Lisa opened her eyes, confused by what she saw. It can't be, she moaned to herself. She was back in Miriam's house, standing in the doorway of the kitchen. It looked just like it did the day *it* happened. She looked down and saw Miriam and Mary's legs. Her heart quickened as she realized they weren't moving. She called out in a shaky voice, "Ma... Miriam?" No answer. She clutched her chest; her breathing became ragged and choppy as she continued to stare at their legs.

She reached her hand out towards them as she finally willed her eyes to move from their legs to their midsections. Her whole body started to shake as her eyes reached their blood-stained, lifeless faces. In the blink of an eye, she was twelve again. Her face contorted into a heaping sob of tears as she started to scream in agony, "Aghhhhhhhhhhh!" The sound reverberated from every crevice and corner of the house. She screamed and screamed until there was no more breath in her lungs.

She looked up and took a breath only to find the person who had caused all of this pain looking back at her. Their face was solemn and confused, as if they had done nothing wrong. All of a sudden, in her outstretched hand was Miriam's dad's gun. Her tears were quickly replaced with pure hatred and anger. Her screams finally found their way into words, "WHAT HAVE YOU DONE? WHAT HAVE YOU DONE?" she screamed out one last time as she pointed the gun and fired. The sound of the gunshot drowning out her screams.

Chapter Ten

BENEATH THE SURFACE

BANG!

Lisa's heart hammered against her ribs as the gunshot morphed into a familiar echo of a slamming door. Sweat dampened her hairline as she turned her head sideways on the pillow. Next to her, Josey's chest rose and fell in a peaceful rhythm.

She released a hollow sigh as recognition settled in—her old nemesis, the nightmare, was back. After the incident, it had stalked her nights like a faithful shadow. Strangely, after Josey hosted their first poetry reading night, the nightmares had stopped. But here it was again, trying to swallow up her new found happiness. The familiar feeling of disgust crept over her. An invisible film of grime clinging to her skin, making her want to scrub herself clean. Her mind went back to yesterday

- Nathaniel's hateful glare as he hurled his accusations at her. That's what resurrected the beast from its shallow grave.

She forced her lungs to follow a steady count. In-two-three. Out-two-three. The muscles in her neck and shoulders relaxed little by little.

She eased herself from the bed, careful not to disturb the sheets where Josey slept. She padded quietly down the hallway, each step carrying her farther from the nightmare. Morning light poured through the living room window, catching the brass of Devan's badge as he straightened his uniform. The sight of her brother washed away the nightmare's lingering shadow.

"You look good." Lisa flashed a knowing smile. "I'm sure Josey would agree."

Devan chuckled, running a hand over his freshly pressed shirt. "you think so, huh?"

"I know so." Lisa sang in a sing song voice.

Devan shook his head, amused. "What are you doing up so early?"

Lisa stretched her arms over her head and leaned against the counter. "I wanted to see you off to work and say thanks."

He tilted his head. "Thanks for what?"

"For sticking up for me at the hospital yesterday."

Devan scoffed, waving a hand. "That was definitely my pleasure. Besides, that's what big brothers do. It's in the big brother contract I signed."

Lisa's face lit up as she laughed. "Well, I just want you to know that I appreciate all the things you do for me."

Devan's face softened. "I have to tell you thanks, too."

She blinked. "What for?"

"For bringing Josephine of course!"

Lisa grinned, "She likes you too, but I guess you know that already."

Devan nodded, a slow smile spreading across his face. "She's different from any woman I've ever met. I want to spend as much time with her as I can."

Lisa studied her brother, noticing the way his eyes softened at the mention of Josey. It was a rare look—one she'd never seen him wear. Love looked good on him.

"You really care about her, don't you? It's nice seeing you both so happy together."

She paused, fidgeting with her sleeve. "And since we're on the subject of romance... I might have someone special in my life too."

Devan's eyebrows shot up. "Who?"

Lisa looked past Devan dreamily. "He's cute, smart, polite, and you know him."

Devan narrowed his eyes playfully. "Okay, that narrows it down to about two guys."

Lisa rolled her eyes before sighing dramatically. "Sean Crane."

"*What?*" Devan's eyes widened with recognition, making Lisa grin. "I should have known it was him." He broke into a slow smile as he nodded his head up and down. "He's really cool, down to Earth and actually cares about his patients." He touched her shoulder, his expression warming. I was worried for a second, but..." He squeezed her arm gently. "Looks like my little sister knows what she's doing after all."

Lisa couldn't contain her excitement. "Of course I do! We're going on a date to New Orleans Saturday."

"Y'all not wasting any time, are y'all." *Actually, I need to take a cue from them. I'm off Saturday too so that would work out perfectly*, he thought. Devan snuck a peek at his watch. "What are you and Josephine going to do today?"

"First stop's Nottoway Plantation, then we'll head over to the hospital." Lisa's lips curved into a mischievous smile. "You should try to stop by there around three so you can continue what y'all started on the loveseat last night."

Devan's face froze mid-smile. He spun on his heel like a soldier at inspection and marched toward the front door. "And I'm out."

"Bye." Lisa giggled as the door slammed behind him.

Lisa eased the bedroom door open, wincing at the smallest creak. She gathered her clothes and toothbrush in a bundle against her chest, tiptoeing back out towards the bathroom. While brushing her teeth, her mind wandered to last night's phone call - imagining how Sean must have looked as he smiled and laughed.

Her socks slid across the kitchen tile as she made her way to the fridge to make breakfast. She tossed two slices of bread in the toaster. As she waited, her mind gradually rewound back to the hospital and her argument with Nathaniel. But before the thought could intrude any further, the toaster's sharp pop snapped her back to the kitchen.

She turned on the TV hoping it would keep her centered. The morning anchor's voice faded in and out as her mind drifted. One moment, she was reliving Nathaniel's hateful expression, his insistent questioning echoing in her ears. The next, she found herself smiling at the memory of Sean's British accent impression. She shook her head, trying to find focus. Yesterday felt like a movie reel spliced from two different films - one a dark drama, the other a sweet romance.

Josey shuffled into the living room, her socks whispering against the carpet. The morning news buzzed softly from the TV. She spied Lisa curled up on the sofa, before her eyes wandered over to the loveseat.

Without looking away from the TV, Lisa said, "He already left for work."

The couch cushions sank as Josey dropped onto them, her shoulders slumping. "That means I have to wait all the way until he gets off from work to see him." Her lower lip jutted out, head tilting back against the couch like a deflated balloon.

Lisa smirked. "Yup. I talked to him before he left though."

Josey perked up instantly, sitting up straighter. "What did he say?"

Lisa shrugged. "We talked about a couple of things."

Josey's eyebrows raised. "Did he say anything about me?"

Lisa tapped her chin, gazing upward as if deep in thought. "Hmm...I think he did mention your name."

PEACE AMID THE CHAOS

Josey leaned in, gripping a couch pillow. "What did he say?"

Lisa pursed her lips, drawing out the suspense. "Hmm...I can't really remember."

Josey's eyes narrowed as her lips curled. "Lisa if you don't tell me, I swear I'll—"

"Ok, ok." Lisa threw up her hands, fingers spread wide like a traffic cop stopping oncoming traffic. "I'll tell you. You sure you want to know?"

"Yeah."

"Fine, don't say I didn't warn you."

Josey hesitated, her fingers twisting anxiously in her lap. "It's... that bad?" Her voice came out small, uncertainty flickering in her eyes.

"I guess I should let you be the judge." Lisa clamped down on the smile threatening to break through her serious facade.

Josey swallowed hard, giving a quick nod. She wasn't sure if she wanted to, but it was too late to back down now.

"He said he won't be able to hang out with me because he wants to spend time with his special someone."

"He told me he wasn't dating." Josey murmured, her voice tinged with both surprise and disappointment.

Lisa was having fun, but she knew Josey was going to kill her when she told her the truth.

"Apparently he wasn't until he met you!" Lisa jumped up and ran into the bathroom locking the door quickly behind her.

Josey's hand flew to her chest, her breath escaping in a rush as tears welled in her eyes. "Oh my God. Thank you Jesus!" she shouted.

She ran over to the bathroom door where her fingers wrapped around the handle, tugging uselessly against the locked door. "I ought to wring your neck Lisa!" Her fist pummeled the door.

"He also said..."

The pounding ceased mid-strike, Josey's furrowed brows softened. "He also said what?"

"I'll tell you if you meet my demands!"

"What do you want?"

"I want you to guarantee my safety once I open this door and you have to promise to take care of my brother."

A smile tugged at Josey's lips as Devan's face flashed through her mind. With a light air to her voice she responded, "The latter request is no problem." Her tone dipped low, sweet as syrup laced with poison. "I don't know if I can fulfill the first."

"No deal then."

"Ok. I promise I won't hurt you."

"If you don't hold up your end of the bargain, I promise you I'll never tell you anything else he says." Lisa matched Josey's sugary threat with her own sing-song warning.

"I won't do anything to you. Now come out scaredy cat."

Lisa slowly opened the bathroom door and peeped out. Standing off to the right, she could see Josey standing with her arms folded with a pout on her lips. They stared at each other for a few seconds.

"Ok, out with it!" Josey exclaimed.

"He also said he never met anyone like you. He is very serious about starting a relationship with you."

Joy spread across Josey's face, her smile stretching wide enough to make her cheeks ache. "I never thought I'd find the perfect man for me. I'm so glad God is proving me wrong!"

"I think you need some alone time." Lisa trotted off towards their room. "I'm going to see if Miriam can meet us at the hospital."

Lisa used Devan's home telephone to call Miriam on her cell.

"Hello." Miriam's professional voice rang.

"Hey, it's me. Where are you?"

"On my break in between sessions. What's up?"

"Guess who I had a long conversation with last night?"

Miriam was silent as she thought then said, "Ahh, it must have been Dr. Crane."

"Yup! We're on a first name basis now."

"You two must be about to hook up."

"We're actually going on a date Saturday." Lisa beamed.

"Nice!"

Guess who else is hooking up."

Miriam was stumped this time. "Who?"

"Josey and Devan."

"What! I didn't see that one coming."

"I did. You should have seen them when they first met."

"I'm happy for you and them." Miriam smiled into the phone, genuine warmth in her voice. She meant every word, but she also knew where this conversation was headed. As she sank deeper into her office chair, she could picture Lisa's expression - that knowing look she always gave when she knew something wasn't quite right. She really didn't want Lisa lecturing her about her non-existent dating life. Miriam sat up straighter, phone pressed to her ear. "Speaking of being happy, I joined a foundation called Magnolia's Light about nine months ago. The organization pairs mental health professionals with children in foster care and orphanages as mentors. My mentee's name is Angellica Lewis. Though it's been a slow process, it's been wonderful seeing her emerge from her shell little by little. I was hoping you could meet her."

"Oh, wow," Lisa said, surprised, masking the flicker of something sharper beneath her voice. Even though Miriam's job now revolved around helping others, she hadn't expected it to spill over into her personal life.

In high school, Miriam had been the social butterfly, always flitting from one activity to another, but never focused on helping others. Lisa felt a jolt hearing this newfound compassion in Miriam—a side completely absent during their senior year.

Lisa swallowed the bitterness that wanted to rise up in her throat. "Sure," she said evenly. "I wouldn't mind meeting Angellica."

"Great! How does tomorrow afternoon look for you? We can take her to the fair uptown."

"Uhm, that should work."

"Awesome!"

"Sounds good." Lisa steered the conversation in a new direction. "How's your afternoon looking today? I'm taking Josey to Nottoway Plantation, and then we'll head to the hospital around three. I wanted to see if you could meet us there."

Miriam's shoulders slumped as she ran her fingers through her hair. "Unfortunately, my day is packed with appointments. I missed a couple of days when Mom first went into the hospital, so I had to reschedule everyone to catch up. I'm going to miss you guys today, but tell Josey I hope she has fun!"

Victoria Rose

Josey wandered the grounds of Nottoway Plantation with conflicting emotions churning inside her. Her fingers traced the rough bark of the massive oak trees dedicated to the owner's children, each trunk and sprawling branch holding nearly 150 years of stories.

Following Lisa through the grand entrance, Josey stepped from the humid Louisiana afternoon into the cool dimness of the main house. The tour guide's voice faded to background noise as she moved from room to room, trailing her fingertips along ornate wallpaper and polished banisters. A small laugh escaped her lips as she peered at the low-set beds in the bedrooms—people back then must have been tiny. The dual staircases made her roll her eyes; all that architectural extravagance just to prevent men from glimpsing women's ankles.

But her amusement faded as she walked through what used to be the slave quarter's area where countless enslaved people had lived. Her chest tightened thinking of the lives destroyed here: human beings stripped of their rights, subjected to physical and sexual abuse, children torn from their mothers' arms—all for profit. Her throat constricted as she tried to comprehend how anyone could reduce another person to property, valuing wealth over human dignity. The hypocrisy struck her hardest—slave owners who would fight desperately for their own freedom while denying it to others.

"Ready to go?" Lisa's voice broke through her thoughts. Josey nodded silently, unable to articulate the heaviness in her chest.

The late afternoon sun cast long shadows as they made their way back to the parking lot. Josey slid into the passenger seat of Lisa's rental car, her mind still lingering among the ghosts of Nottoway. As Lisa navigated the winding road toward town, Josey leaned her forehead against the cool window glass, watching the plantation recede in the side mirror until it disappeared around a bend. The weight of history traveled with her, questions without answers spinning through her mind as miles of sugarcane fields blurred past the window.

The gentle jolt of the rental car settling into a parking space at the hospital yanked Josey from her thoughts.

The hospital's automatic doors came into view, and with them, a figure that made Josey's heart skip. Devan stood at the entrance, his hands tucked into his pockets, rocking slightly on his heels.

"Hi. How was the visit to Nottoway?" His warm smile, welcoming.

Josey clasped her left elbow with her right hand. "It was... educational."

Lisa stepped forward to give Devan a quick hug. "I'm going to head to Mom's room. Y'all can catch up with me there." The doors whooshed open with a blast of air-conditioned breeze, then sealed shut behind her retreating form.

"I'm sorry I slipped out without saying good morning earlier." Devan shuffled closer, his voice dropping to a softer tone. "And I've been thinking about how I could get into your good graces to have the privilege to call you Josey like everyone else."

Josey had all but forgotten that she had demanded that he call her 'Josephine'. She leaned forward slightly, one eyebrow arched, her smile inviting him to continue.

"Would you be interested in a home cooked meal as a peace offering?"

Her heart raced at the thought of spending time with him, but she kept her voice deliberately casual. "I think that will work."

Devan's face lit up, his grin transforming his entire expression into pure joy. "Saturday it is then."

He hesitated briefly, rubbing the back of his neck. "I was thinking of making my grandmother's famous gumbo. Any chance you're free tomorrow? We could pick up the ingredients together. I know a little market where they have the freshest okra and andouille."

"Friday works for me," Josey replied without hesitation.

As they walked through the entrance, Josey turned her face slightly away, unable to hide the smile spreading across her face. She found herself looking forward to tomorrow—and the Saturday that would follow. Two dates in two days. Not that she was counting.

Chapter Eleven

Lunch Date

Miriam's small frame slumped over her neatly organized desk, her chin propped up by one hand, eyes glazed as she stared at the soft glow of her computer screen. The fingers of her other hand drummed a restless rhythm against the keyboard. It was 11:45 — just fifteen minutes to go.

A long sigh escaped as she leaned back in her chair, eyelids fluttering shut. After a beat, she inhaled sharply, her brows tightening as her eyes flicked open with a burst of energy. She snatched up her pen and scribbled something across her notepad—then paused, frowned, and drew a firm line through it.

Her gaze flicked to the wall clock again, then toward the door. Still no buzz. Still no knock. With a quiet huff, she tapped her fingers faster, trying to outrun the growing anticipation. Just a little longer.

A wave of relief loosened the tension in her neck and shoulders, and a radiant grin spread across her face as she registered the time. She jumped to her feet as she threw her hands in the air and shouted, "Only five more minutes!"

She glided over to the side of her desk and eyed the bags of goodies she bought for today. Her smile dimmed as memories from the past few weeks crept in—hospital visits, arguments and suffocating anxiety. Her shoulders tensed for a moment, then relaxed. The thought of her special lunch date pulled her back, rekindling her smile.

Miriam tapped a finger against her chin, her gaze shifting between the bags of groceries and the too-small space on her desk. "Is this enough room?"

The question swirled in her mind as she reached for the framed photos, sliding them aside to make room. Her fingertips lingered on the edge of one frame—younger versions of her and Lisa frozen in time. A quiet ache tightened in her chest as her emotions clashed. She hadn't realized how much she had missed her until now—Lisa's laugh echoing in her mind. But then there's Nathaniel. His name alone cast a shadow over the reunion. The tension between him and Lisa lingered like an unspoken threat, pressing against the edges of her excitement. And beneath it all, something deeper stirred—memories she had long buried, now rising, uninvited, to the surface.

A sharp vibration sent tremors through the surface of her desk, snatching Miriam from her thoughts. Her eyes widened as she drew in a sharp, audible breath. Her hand fell away from the photo as reality yanked her back into the present.

Miriam cleared her throat as she pressed the intercom button. "Yes?"

The secretary, Mrs. Foster replied, "Your visitor has arrived. Would you like me to escort them to you?

"Yes, please."

A few minutes later, Miriam's office door opened. Mrs. Foster peeped her head in as she smiled and announced "Your special guest has arrived."

Before Miriam could respond, a small figure darted past Mrs. Foster and flung themselves into her arms, wrapping her in a tight embrace. A surprised laugh bubbled up in Miriam's throat as she steadied herself, warmth spreading through her chest. She shot Mrs. Foster a grateful smile.

With a knowing nod, Mrs. Foster quietly closed the door behind her.

Miriam glanced down, meeting a pair of wide, dark brown eyes that shimmered with excitement. The little girl's honey-brown skin glowed under the office lights, her long lashes blinking up at Miriam before she finally released her grip. A pair of deep dimples appeared as she smiled, then took a step back, turning her attention to the room. Her gaze moved swiftly over every detail.

Miriam watched, amused, as the girl's micro braids, neatly gathered into two playful pigtails, bounced with every turn of her head. Curiosity danced across her face as she soaked in her surroundings, her wonder almost tangible. Miriam spread her arms out wide from her sides. "So, what do you think of the place, Angellica?"

"It looks very grown up and serious." Angellica replied thoughtfully.

Miriam chuckled. It had been too long since she'd last seen Angellica—life had pulled her in too many directions, between caring for her mom, juggling work, and Lisa's unexpected visit. She'd asked Angellica's foster mom to drop her off today, hoping to steal a little time together. At least something good had come from the chaos. It gave Angellica the unique opportunity to visit her office since she'd never been before. "I'm going to take that as a compliment! How have you been?"

"I don't think I could have waited another minute, Miriam. I missed you so much. I felt like I was..."

She stopped when she spotted the bags of groceries near Miriam's desk. She squealed with delight as she jumped up and down. "You remembered!"

Miriam smiled, "Of course I did. I couldn't wait to see you too. You want to help me put everything on my desk?

"Yeah, what are we having?"

As Miriam pulled items from the bags, she handed them to Angellica one by one, letting her arrange them on the desk. "Let's see," she said with a playful tone, "we've got ham and cheese sandwiches, apples, grapes, chips, and some nice cold drinks." She paused, her smile widening as she revealed the final treat. "And to top it off—your favorite—pecan pie." She set it down with a flourish. "Go ahead, take your pick."

"Yay!" Angellica giggled as she grabbed a sandwich, a handful of grapes, a bag of chips, and a grape soda. As she tore open the bag, the crisp crunch of the first chip filled the air. Miriam, meanwhile, picked up an apple, taking a slow, thoughtful bite.

"So, what have you been up to?" Miriam asked with a smile.

"Well, I got a progress report from school and all my grades are back up!" Angellica chimed through her crunches, "Here it is. I saved it so I could show it to you."

She dug in her jeans pocket and produced a yellow paper. She handed it over to Miriam.

Miriam beamed as she reviewed the report. "From C's and D's to all A's and B's, huh. Wow! I'm so proud of you!"

She raised her hand in the air. Angellica instantly smacked it with a triumphant high five.

"You worked so hard to bounce back and earn these grades," Miriam continued, her eyes shining. "We have to celebrate! How about a summer trip? There are so many places we could go—hiking in the mountains, a day at the water park, or even the beach."

Angellica's eyes widened, her voice rising with excitement. "I've never been to the beach!" Then, as if catching herself, she softened. "I knew you'd be proud of me. But you don't have to take me on a big, expensive trip. I'd rather just spend time with you here."

"Nonsense. I was thinking about taking you on a vacation before this anyway. Besides, I haven't been on a trip in so long."

Miriam planted one hand on her hip, waving the other in the air with flair. Her tone turned playful, a teasing sass creeping into her voice as she snapped her neck dramatically from side to side. "I think I deserve it too! Don't I?"

Angellica giggled, "Of course you do."

"I'm glad we're on the same page!" Miriam quipped before shifting gears. With a gentle smile, she asked, "So, how have you been feeling?"

Angellica's smile faded to a thoughtful look. She opened her mouth then closed it. Miriam knew that she was deciding on whether or not to tell her something.

Miriam said softly, "Whatever you want to say, you can take your time to tell me."

Angellica gave a nervous smile and said hesitantly, "Ok, but I'm scared you're going to be mad at me."

Miriam's smile remained bright, unwavering. She had no idea what Angellica was about to say, but she wasn't about to let it show. "Whatever it is you have to tell me, I'm sure it won't make me upset. Go ahead and tell me what's on your mind."

Angellica took a couple of moments to collect herself. She closed her eyes and took in several deep breaths. She opened her eyes and looked into Miriam's. "I've been feeling sad, mad and lonely since the last time we saw each other. I've been sad and lonely because we weren't able to spend time together."

She stopped to see what Miriam's reaction would be. Miriam smiled at her and said, "I've been sad and lonely without you too. Why were you mad?"

Angellica looked down at her hand in her lap. "Because... because." Her voice became low and shaky.

Miriam knew she was about to cry. She stood up, walked around the desk and knelt down in front of Angellica. She lifted her face up by her chin. Angellica's eyes were filled with tears. Miriam had to fight back her own tears.

"Don't cry sweetie. You know you can tell me anything. Have you ever regretted telling me anything before?"

Angellica shook her head from side to side as tears streamed down her face. "Well, you should know that you won't regret telling me this." Miriam said as she hugged her.

Miriam rocked her back and forth as she cried. Through her sobs she whispered, "I was mad because your mom got sick. She took away our time together. Ever since I had to move into my foster home and you became my mentor, you've been here for me. I know I'm being selfish for being mad at your mom. I've tried to make it go away, but I can't. I just wish she would go away so it could be you and me again. After all you've done for me, this is the way I act. I'm sorry. Please forgive me. I know I can behave better if you give me another chance. Please don't be mad and leave me. I'm sorry, I'm sorry..." Angellica began to cry uncontrollably.

Miriam felt overwhelmed with love for Angellica. She couldn't believe she thought her being upset would make her leave.

"It's ok. I'm not mad with you and I'm definitely not leaving you. It's ok for you to be upset. You're human just like everyone else."

Angellica swiped at her tear-streaked cheeks, drawing in a deep breath as she tried to steady herself. She looked up and asked with a hopeful expression. "You're really not mad with me?"

Miriam reached towards the box of tissues on her desk and handed it to her.

"I'm not mad with you at all," Miriam said gently. "If I were you, I'd be mad too if someone took away time I enjoyed with someone else. Don't worry, I could never be mad at you." She hesitated for a long moment before adding, "I do have a question."

Angellica sniffed and nodded. "What is it?"

"Why would you think I'd leave you? I know it's not because you were mad. Something else had to have happened."

Angellica clutched the tissue, twisting it between her fingers. "There's this girl at the foster home named Permilla ," she mumbled, her gaze dropping to her lap. "She always stares at you from the kitchen when you come to pick me up."

Miriam's expression darkened slightly. "I know exactly who you're talking about."

Angellica let out a shaky breath. "She is always picking on me about you."

Miriam's brow raised. "Oh, how so?"

Angellica's words tumbled out before she could stop them. "She tells me I think I'm special because you take me places and buy me things. She says I'm no better than the rest of them. She said you'll lose interest in me after a while and then I'd see for myself that I'm nothing." Her voice wavered with frustration, her hands balling into fists in her lap. "I always tell her she is just jealous."

But then her tone dropped, her eyes darting away twisting the tissue harder. "That was until your mom got sick," she murmured. "She started teasing me constantly. Telling me this was the beginning. You would start by not bringing me places and only call me. After a while, you wouldn't call me at all."

Her throat tightened, and she swallowed hard. "I started thinking maybe it was true when you called me and said you couldn't come and get me." She glanced up at Miriam, searching her face, then looked away again. "I thought what she said was true."

Angellica's fingers trembled as she wiped away fresh tears. "She kept asking me when were you coming to get me. I didn't have an answer so I stayed silent." Her voice wavered, fragile and strained. "She would say, 'You finally found out you're worthless like the rest of us!' and then start laughing." A sharp inhale shuddered through her. "I just knew you didn't want to see me again."

Miriam's voice was calm but firm as she met Angellica's gaze with a reassuring smile. "She's upset because no one visits her. Don't be mad at her for it—if the shoe were on the other foot, you'd probably feel the same way." She paused, choosing her words carefully. "If she asks whether I'm coming to get you, stay silent like you've been doing. She'll figure it out sooner or later."

Angellica let out a slow breath, her shoulders loosened as she met Miriam's steady gaze. A quiet nod followed, the tension in her eyes softening under the warmth of Miriam's reassurance.

She reached over, wrapping Angellica's hand in a gentle squeeze. "Listen," she said softly, "life is full of tough moments—stress, sadness, even chaos. It can make you feel lonely, like there's no hope."

Silence settled between them as Miriam's gaze drifted, her thoughts pulling her back – back to the chaos of her own past. The weight of old memories flickered across her face, but when she spoke again, her voice was steady, calm, almost rhythmic.

"But finding peace amid the chaos is what keeps you going. It's about having something—or someone—you can count on, something that reminds you things will get better."

As if the truth of her own words anchored her, Miriam blinked, her focus returning to Angellica. She gave Angellica's hand another squeeze, this time lingering just a little longer, as if sealing a promise between them. "Next time you feel sad, mad, scared, or lonely, talk to me about it. I'll always be here for you."

Angellica's eyebrows bunched together as her voice grew quiet, almost thoughtful. "I kept saying Permilla's teasing didn't bother me until after your mom got sick... but now I'm starting to think maybe it always did. I just didn't realize how much until everything started falling apart." She smoothed the crumpled tissue in her hands, her fingers working gently over the creases as if trying to make sense of her thoughts. Then she looked up at Miriam, regret flickering in her eyes. "I'm sorry I didn't talk to you sooner. I feel stupid now that I think about it."

"You just remember that I would never do that to you. You are very important to me." Her voice softened, deliberately shifting the mood. A playful glint sparked in her eyes. "In fact, you get to meet my best friend tomorrow. She's in town and I've already told her all about you. We're going to take you to the fair."

Angellica's eyes went wide, and in an instant, the weight on her shoulders seemed to lift. A grin stretched across her face as she bounced excitedly in her seat. "I get to meet your best friend and go to the fair?" she squealed. "I hope she likes me!"

Miriam chuckled. "She already does."

Chapter Twelve

ONE SIMPLE QUESTION

Lisa paused at the entrance of the fairgrounds, the familiar bustle washing over her like a gentle breeze. Laughter rang out from children darting between booths, their voices weaving through the blaring music from distant speakers. Vendors called to passersby, enticing them to test their luck at games lined with colorful prizes. The air was thick with the scent of cotton candy, the sweetness clinging to the warm breeze.

Stepping further inside, the aroma shifted into the savory scent of buttered popcorn and corndogs crisped to golden perfection. The familiar scents stirred memories of all the favorite foods she had been missing since she left. A sudden craving for pecan candy made her mouth water. Not pralines—though people often confused the two—but that soft, melt-in-your-mouth confection that yielded at the first bite, unlike the brittle texture of pralines.

A slow smile tugged at her lips as she began compiling a mental feast of all her favorite foods she would savor before the trip ended - because if there was one thing she didn't want to leave without, was the taste of home.

As Lisa added to her mental list, a familiar voice cut through the hum of the crowd, calling her name. She turned, scanning the sea of faces until she spotted Miriam, grinning and waving with an energy Lisa hadn't seen in a while. Relief washed over her—Miriam actually looked happy for a change. Ever since Lisa had been back, she couldn't shake the feeling that something was off with her. But now, with the sun catching the gleam in her eyes, she looked like the Miriam she remembered.

Miriam rocked a pair of dark, form-fitting jeans and a Mary J. Blige t-shirt—classic Miriam. No surprise there. Lisa had lost count of the nights they'd spent belting out Mary's songs at their sleepovers, their voices hoarse by morning. Beside Miriam bounced a small figure in black tights and a bubblegum-pink shirt, her grin a mirror of Miriam's. Lisa couldn't help but smile at the little cutie pie as she waved back. *This must be Angellica*, Lisa thought, as she began weaving through the crowd toward them.

Lisa crouched slightly to meet the little girl's gaze and held out her hand with a warm smile. "Hey there! You must be Angellica. I'm Lisa—it's so nice to finally meet you."

Angellica's eyes widened with excitement as she grabbed Lisa's hand, shaking it up and down with an enthusiasm that made Lisa chuckle. "Hi! I can't believe I'm really meeting you!"

Lisa laughed. "Same here! It's great to finally put such a cute face to your name."

"Thank you!" Angellica gushed as she swung from side to side.

"Did we keep you waiting long?" Miriam asked, as she snuck a peek at her watch.

Lisa shook her head. "Nah, I just got here a few minutes ago."

"Oh, good," Miriam said with a nod. "Well, what should we do first?"

Lisa turned to Angellica, her eyes playful. "I say we let the little boss lady decide."

Angellica's entire face lit up. "I made a list!" she announced, bouncing on her toes.

Lisa laughed, "You're a list girl too. I knew the moment I met you, I'd like you! What's up first?"

Angellica's mouth opened in a half drool, "Cotton candy! I just love the way it melts in my mouth!"

"Sounds good to me," Miriam chimed.

The trio followed the sugary aroma wafting through the air, weaving through the crowd as laughter and carnival music played in the background. The vibrant swirls of pink and blue spun on the vendor's stand like clouds plucked from a cartoon sky. Angellica's eyes sparkled as Lisa handed her a puff of cotton candy, the sweetness dissolving on her tongue in a burst of sugary delight.

After savoring the treat, they made their way to Angellica's next request—the bumper cars. The line stretched long, a clear testament to the ride's popularity. Excitement buzzed in the air as the sounds of clashing metal and laughter echoed from the arena.

When it was finally their turn, they each hopped into a car. Lisa and Miriam exchanged competitive grins, an old rivalry stirring to life. Without the need for words, their challenge was clear. Angellica clutched the steering wheel, determination flickering in her eyes. But before she could figure out the controls, the other two sped off with mischievous glee.

Lisa, still grinning ear to ear, glanced back to check Miriam's position, expertly weaving through the tangle of traffic. Her laughter rang out, mingling with the hum of engines. But after a few daring twists, turns and near misses, she found herself boxed into a corner.

With a satisfied look of victory, Miriam rammed into Lisa. "Gotcha!"

Lisa's face crumpled into mock defeat. "Oh, no!"

Angellica pulled up just shy of them, eyes wide with fascination. Her head swiveled back and forth, watching the exchange like an eager spectator.

Miriam, seizing the moment, reversed and bumped Lisa again, a mischievous grin spreading across her face. "You like it? You like that? You like it, huh?"

Lisa replied in a comical pleading whining voice, "I don't like it, I don't like it!"

A loud, bubbly laugh startled them both. They turned to see Angellica clutching her stomach, tears of laughter forming at the corners of her eyes. Her giggles came in gasps, the contagious kind that quickly swept up those around them. As they realized who the laugh belonged to, they exchanged glances of mocked outrage. But Angellica's laughter was quickly stopped short by a sudden jolt pitching her forward. Another car had blindsided her. The force whipped her around, leaving her wide-eyed.

There was a roar of laughter as Angellica turned to see Lisa and Miriam pointing at her.

"Hey, no fair!" Angellica huffed, crossing her arms in an exaggerated sulk.

Miriam's attention slipped for a second—just enough for Lisa to seize her chance. She sped out of the corner with a triumphant cheer.

"Oh, no you don't!" Miriam bellowed, jerking her wheel to give chase.

Determined not to be left behind, Angellica slammed her foot on the pedal, her laughter echoing as she joined the pursuit.

All too soon, the attendant's voice crackled over the speaker, announcing the end of the ride. Groans of disappointment filled the air.

"That was fast," Angellica pouted.

"I know, right?" Lisa said, still breathless.

Miriam turned to Angellica, her smile warm. "You want to go again?"

Angellica paused, the temptation lingering. The bumper cars had been a blast, but the day was still young, and curiosity bubbled inside her.

"Nah. Let's do something else. Ooh, I know. What's your favorite ride?" She bounced on her toes, her excitement contagious.

Lisa and Miriam shared a knowing look, their eyes gleaming. Without hesitation, they declared in unison, "Tilt-a-Whirl!"

As they made their way through the bustling fairground, the lively chatter and colorful stalls passed in a blur. Every few steps, someone called out an enthusiastic "hey" or "what's up," their faces lighting up as they spotted Lisa and Miriam.

Angellica couldn't believe how many people knew them. She could see it plainly in everyone's reactions – those genuine smiles lighting up their faces, the warm, welcoming tones as they called out greetings – they were popular and respected here. But what touched Angellica's heart the most was the way people greeted her the same way. As if she already belonged. The joy of it wrapped around her like a warm embrace, leaving her with a feeling she couldn't quite describe.

Halfway to the Tilt-a-Whirl, a distinct joyful Creole voice cut through the carnival's clamor, "Lord, look at you two! I haven't see y'all in so long."

Miriam and Lisa whirled around. Their 9th-grade typing teacher, Mrs. Baptiste, stood before them, her trademark gold tooth catching the sunlight with a brilliant wink. She looked exactly the same – timeless, vibrant, her smile spreading wide across her face.

"Well, fancy meeting you here Mrs. Baptiste. How are you?" Lisa's voice bubbled with surprise and warmth.

"I've been good, Bae. Whatta 'bout y'all two?"

"We've been good." They exchanged a quick glance, the unspoken words lingering between them—a silent acknowledgment of, "It's not like it isn't true."

Mrs. Baptiste's knowing chuckle filled the air. "I see y'all still two peas in a pod, huh. When you saw one, you saw the other. Y'all was always in the centa' of somethin' or notha.'"

Lisa and Miriam gave slightly nervous laughs as they looked away. Mrs. Baptiste's words hung in the air, a sudden reminder of how things had changed. The laughter faded as they exchanged a glance, the unspoken truth settling between them.

Oblivious to the shift, Angellica's eyes lit up with curiosity. Her brows arched, and a playful grin tugged at her lips. "Do you mean they were in trouble a lot?"

Privately, Lisa and Miriam were relieved by Angellica's innocent curiosity, grateful for the lighthearted shift.

Mrs. Baptiste waved a hand through the air, her laughter rumbling softly. "Oh, goodness no, bae. They were good, smart girls, but sometimes a little mischievous."

"What do you mean?" Angellica's eyes widened, clearly eager for a juicy story.

Mrs. Baptiste's grin turned sly. "Well, there was this one gal in class—now, I won't say her name. That wouldn't be right for a teacher to go tellin' all the details about a former student. But let me just say, this gal had some mighty big—"

Lisa quickly cut in, her playful grin matching the mischief in her eyes. "Whoa there, Mrs. Baptiste! You can't spill all of *our* details either! Don't we pay you enough hush money to keep quiet?"

Mrs. Baptiste's laughter bubbled up, her shoulders shaking. "Chil', you know y'all ain't paid me no money. If you had, I wouldn't still be working, now would I?"

Miriam seized the moment, placing her hands gently on Angellica's shoulders and steering her away with exaggerated urgency. "It was so nice listening to you tell all our secrets—ahem, I mean talk about the past. See you later!"

"Bye y'all!" Mrs. Baptiste called after them, her laughter lingering in the air.

Angellica twisted back, her face scrunched in exaggerated disappointment. "Ahh, I wanted to hear the story!"

"That's not happening," Miriam shot back, her response swift and final. The trio's laughter trailed behind them, the fairground bustling with the sounds of joy and anticipation.

After the Tilt-a-Whirl's dizzying spin, Angellica's legs wobbled as she stumbled off the platform, giggling through the rush of dizziness. She blinked a few times, steadying herself before her eyes landed on the balloon pop game. Determination sparked within her.

The sharp pop of each balloon brought a surge of satisfaction, the sound like tiny bursts of triumph. Every time the thin, taut rubber gave way beneath her dart, she felt a thrill. When the final balloon burst and the attendant declared her a winner, her excitement reached its peak.

Scanning the prize rack, Angellica's gaze locked onto a ButterCup plushie from the PowerPuff Girls. Strong, vibrant, unapologetic—just like she wanted to be. But not mean, she reminded herself. More like Miriam and Lisa: kind, supportive, genuine.

The sno ball stand beckoned next, the colorful syrup bottles lined up like a rainbow. Angellica's mouth watered at the thought. She adored the way the crushed ice transformed into a canvas of flavors, each bite a refreshing burst of sweetness. Her favorite had gummy bears hidden at the bottom, the chewy candy adding a delightful texture. On a day like this, with the sun blazing overhead, the icy treat was pure magic.

But the grand finale was still ahead. Angellica tilted her head back, taking in the towering Ferris Wheel. Its massive frame loomed against the sky, each glowing carriage rising and falling in a slow, mesmerizing rhythm. A flicker of anticipation lit her eyes.

"That's next," she declared, her heart drumming with excitement. "I've never ridden one before," she added, her voice dipping to a whisper.

Concern flashed across Miriam's face. "You sure you want to ride it? You've never been up that high before."

"Of course, I'll be fine! That's not that far up at all. I'm not a kid anymore, I'm practically grown," Angellica blurted, her tone filled with mock confidence.

Miriam hesitated, uncertainty flickering in her eyes before she sighed. "Okay, but only two people can ride in one cart."

Angellica's grin widened as she spun toward Lisa. "Will you do me the honor of accompanying me?"

Lisa laughed, giving an exaggerated bow. "Anything for you, little boss lady!"

After what felt like an eternity of waiting, it was finally their turn. They were the last group to board. The operator guided them to their cart, securing the safety bar with a firm click.

"I'm really glad I have some time to talk with you alone," Angellica said softly, her voice carrying a rare note of vulnerability.

A small smile played on Lisa's lips. "Oh, really? Why's that?"

Angellica fidgeted, her fingers tracing the edge of her seat. "I wanted to ask you something important."

Lisa's brow lifted in curiosity. "Okay."

But before Angellica could speak, the Ferris Wheel jolted into motion. As their cart began to rise, Angellica's stomach twisted. She clamped down on Lisa's arm, her eyes wide. "Oh, my God!"

Lisa patted Angellica's hand reassuringly. "There's nothing to be afraid of. This is how it usually feels."

Angellica's grip loosened slightly, but her face remained tense. Then, as the wheel made its second loop, another surge of fear swept over her. She squealed and tightened her hold once more.

Lisa chuckled, though a hint of concern lingered. Hoping to distract her, she asked lightly, "So, what did you want to ask me?"

Their cart slowed near the top, offering a breathtaking view of the fairground below. Angellica took a few shaky breaths.

"I... I wanted to know what makes a great friend. I want to stay friends with Miriam forever, just like you two. I figured you'd know because you're the expert."

As soon as the last word left her lips, the cart jolted to a stop. Angellica let out a loud squeal, her eyes wide as she clutched the safety bar. She didn't get a chance to see the struggle in Lisa's face.

Lisa barely flinched, but her gaze instinctively dropped to the ground below. Her stomach twisted, though it had nothing to do with the height.

Angellica's words echoed in her mind soft but heavy: *What makes a great friend?* It was such a simple question—so innocent so earnest—yet it landed like a stone in her chest.

Lisa hated that she didn't have an answer, at least not one she could say out loud. She felt like the last person qualified to define great friendship.

The truth gnawed at her: there was nothing great about her relationship with Miriam now. They'd barely spoken over the last seven years. Most of their interactions were laced with tension, their connection a threadbare version of what it used to be. Hell, today was the first time in ages that they'd even laughed like they used to.

When her parents died, Lisa's world collapsed. In the span of months, the warmth and laughter that had filled her childhood home disappeared. It's like the world didn't make sense anymore. Her father's quiet, dependable presence, her mother's voice belting out her favorite gospel songs in the kitchen—gone.

She could still feel the ache of her eyes as they cried oceans every night. The world was all wrong. She desperately needed something to feel normal, to feel right. She thought she could find that in Miriam. But she was wrong.

The memory rushed in uninvited. Lisa could still hear the tremor in her own voice as she made the call, desperate but hopeful.

"Hey. I was wondering if you weren't busy, if you could come over."

Silence. For a moment, Lisa thought the line had gone dead. Then came the faint sound of rustling.

"Uhm... well, I was planning on studying for this big history test I have tomorrow... So I wasn't really planning on going anywhere tonight."

Lisa's heart sank. The words had stung, but it was the emptiness that followed that twisted the knife. She wanted to scream, "I need you!" but the weight of rejection clamped her throat shut. She had swallowed it all down, forcing her voice into something that resembled indifference.

"Oh, don't worry about it. We can catch up another time."

But 'another time' never came.

Her chest tightened as tears threatened. The pain, hurt and the rejection she felt back then suddenly erupted its way back up to the surface.

A sudden thud of Angellica's shoe against the cart jolted Lisa from her thoughts. She blinked, forcing the tears back before they could betray her. By the time Angellica turned toward her, Lisa's face wore a carefully crafted smile.

"To answer your question..." She waited until Angellica's eyes locked onto hers. "It takes two people to make a great friendship. Both have to put in the effort to support each other. If one doesn't hold up their end, the relationship becomes unbalanced, broken."

Angellica's eyes shone with admiration. "That makes a lot of sense. I knew you'd have the answer!"

Lisa's smile never faltered, though it felt like a hollow mask. The Ferris wheel lurched forward again, and Angellica squealed, clutching Lisa's arm. This time, Lisa found herself laughing. The sound was genuine—Angellica had that effect on people.

As soon as the operator lifted the safety bar, Angellica bolted toward Miriam, her words tumbling over each other in excitement. Miriam laughed, hugging her tightly.

"I can't understand a word you're saying," she teased. "Slow down and try again."

Angellica beamed, taking a deep breath before launching into the story again.

Lisa lingered behind. Her steps dragged, and she could feel the distance growing between her and the others. By the time they reached the fairground's exit, Miriam finally turned, her brows furrowing slightly.

"So, did you enjoy the ride, Lisa?"

Lisa's smile reappeared, practiced and smooth. "The ride was good."

For a moment, Miriam's eyes lingered, as if searching for something deeper. Lisa held her ground. Then, with a playful grin, she added, "But I think I enjoyed Angellica's reaction more. You know, with her being almost grown and all."

Angellica's eyes widened as she blinked. She opened her mouth, but no words came out.

They erupted in laughter.

"I'll see y'all later," Lisa said, pointing at Angellica. "You be good, little boss lady."

"Don't worry, I will!" Angellica beamed.

Victoria Rose

On the drive home, Lisa's thoughts drifted back to her and Miriam. The more she replayed their strained moments, the tighter the anxious knot in her chest grew. The questions, the regrets—they swirled like a storm she couldn't outrun.

When she reached Devan's apartment, a wave of relief washed over her. The empty space greeted her, silent and still. No need to pretend, no need to push the feelings away. Not this time. She couldn't lock them up, even if she wanted to.

Devan and Josey must still be out shopping for their date tomorrow, she thought. *Good.* She had no energy to force a smile or fake small talk.

Her restless feet carried her across the living room, back and forth. She could feel the emotions clawing at her chest, demanding release. Lisa knew herself well enough to recognize this sensation. When her mind twisted itself into knots, there was only one way to find clarity—she would drag it into the light, kicking and screaming if necessary.

She turned abruptly, striding toward her bedroom. The moment her eyes landed on the familiar notebook resting on the nightstand, her shoulders eased slightly. The cover was worn, the corners bent from years of use. Her ink pen lay beside it, always ready. Lisa never knew when inspiration might strike—or, in this case, desperation.

With determined fingers, she lifted the notebook and settled onto the edge of her bed. She closed her eyes, inhaling deeply. The air filled her lungs, and she held it for a moment, then released it slowly—a quiet surrender.

Clearing her mind, she opened her eyes. The first blank line stared back at her. Without hesitation, she touched the pen to paper. There was no planning, no second-guessing. Just the raw flow of her emotions, spilling out in every stroke of ink. Her pain, her longing, her unanswered questions—they all took shape on the page. Word by word, she let them go.

Chapter Thirteen

SUPPORTING CAST

Lisa let out a yawn as she made her way down the hallway to room ninety-eight. Sleep had been elusive—tugged away by frustration over her relationship with Miriam and excitement about her date with Sean. Her thoughts had bounced back and forth like a ping-pong ball: one moment, she was agonizing over the rift between her and Miriam; the next, she was wondering what she should wear.

Somewhere in the quiet, early hours of the morning, she finally found a bit of clarity. No, the situation with Miriam wasn't magically fixed, but at least she knew what her next step would be. That small sense of direction was enough to let her drift off to sleep.

She opened the door to room ninety-eight, her shoulders sagged slightly at the sight of Miriam, seated on the far side of Mary's bed. Lisa had expected they'd cross paths eventually—just not this soon. Still, she kept her facial expression and voice light for Mary's sake.

"Hey, Ma. How are you?" she said with an easy smile.

"I'm fine, babae. How you?"

"I'm good." Lisa turned her attention to Miriam. "Hi."

Miriam shifted in her seat. Her eyebrows raised, eyes questioning. "Hi," she replied, her tone hesitant and cautious.

Mary looked between them, a faint trace of confusion etched across her face.

Just then, the door opened, and Dr. Crane stepped inside, his cheerful presence slicing through the tension.

"Hello, ladies," he said, beaming.

"Hello," they chimed in unison.

He walked to Mary's bedside, unwinding the stethoscope from around his neck. "Let's see how you're doing today."

As he began his exam, Lisa caught Miriam's eye and motioned her over to the other side of the room. With a quiet breath, she leaned in slightly, her voice just above a whisper.

"I wanted to talk to you about something," she said. "Are you available tomorrow?"

Miriam held her gaze, brows knitting slightly. "Sure."

"I can come to your place. Does around eleven in the morning work?"

"Yes, but…" Miriam's voice rose a little, "can you tell me what this is about?"

Lisa hesitated. She didn't want to go there—not now, not here. She knew that if she did, it would cause a scene, and Mary didn't need that. Not again.

They locked eyes, the silence between them tight and loaded.

Dr. Crane broke through the silence. "Well, good news!" he announced. "Mary's insulin levels are back to normal, and all her vitals look great. If this keeps up through the weekend, she'll be ready to go home Monday."

The tension melted like a sandcastle under an incoming tide.

"Yes!" Miriam grinned.

"Awesome!" Lisa echoed.

"'Bout time!" Mary whooped.

Her sass drew a round of laughter from them all.

Dr. Crane gave Mary's hand a gentle pat. "You'll be my first visit on Monday."

"I'll hold you to it!" she replied, beaming.

As the conversation shifted, Lisa maneuvered her way toward Dr. Crane, ensuring she had a clean path out of the room—and away from any more questions from Miriam. She felt a subtle wave of satisfaction flow through her. She'd taken the first step toward something she'd been avoiding for years. Late? Maybe. But it was still a step.

She tucked the weight of tomorrow behind her and focused on today. Today was for her and Sean.

With a smile and a wave, she said goodbye to Mary—and to everything waiting for her at eleven the next morning.

Victoria Rose

After leaving Mary's room, Sean wrapped up his rounds with a quick briefing with the hospital staff. Once that was out of the way, he and Lisa made their way to the parking lot to begin their adventure.

Sean slid into the passenger seat, his knees bumping awkwardly against the dashboard. It took him a few moments to locate the seat controls and adjust it to something more comfortable.

Lisa smiled, watching him with quiet amusement before starting the car. "Danger" by Mystikal exploded through the speakers at full blast. She chuckled, reaching to turn it down. New Orleans' Q93.3 had been her favorite station growing up—always spinning the latest hits, especially from local artists. It was clearly still holding it down, playing her all-time favorite home-state rapper.

She nodded her head to the beat as she remembered spending hours by the radio, finger poised over the record button, waiting for her favorite tracks to come back around. Then came the marathon sessions of memorizing lyrics just so she could join in with the girls at school during lunch.

She turned the volume down to elevator-music level, then glanced at Sean, ready to bring him into her sentimental memory—but paused. Something caught her off guard.

Sean noticed her puzzled expression and followed her gaze. "Oh," he said casually, lifting a light jacket into the air. "I always like to be prepared. You never know when you'll need one."

Lisa nodded, thoughtfully. "True."

She pulled out of the parking lot and headed toward Highway 70, her mind racing. Now what? They were finally together—alone, in the same car, with nothing but time—but the words wouldn't come. Or rather, too many came at once. She wasn't sure which to say first.

They filled the space with easy banter as the car sped past the chemical plants that lined the highway. As they rounded a bend, the Sunshine Bridge came into view. Lisa held her breath for a moment, then let it out when she realized what she was doing.

The Mississippi River always commanded her attention—equal parts awe and fear. As a child, she used to hear the adults say the levee might break when the water got too high. During those times, families were called to help lay sandbags. It scared her, but her parents would always reassure her and Devan that everything would be okay.

There was one memory in particular that was sharp and vivid. She, her mom, and Devan had planned to eat lunch at the Pavilion overlooking the river, a tradition she loved. But this time, her mother must have forgotten to check the water level. As they reached the top of the levee, ready to descend, all they could see through the windshield was water. Lisa glanced out the side window, heart hammering, and saw the river lapping hungrily at the car's wheels.

No one moved. No one spoke. They sat still, like tightrope performers mid-walk, afraid a single shift might tip the balance. Then, quietly, her mother put the car in reverse and inched them back to safety. Since then, Lisa always looked down when crossing the Sunshine Bridge, just to check the water level.

The bridge disappeared behind them, giving way once more to highway. A Kris Kross song played softly in the background, pulling her back into the moment.

Suddenly aware of the silence, Lisa glanced over at Sean—only to find him staring at her playfully, his jacket now on... backwards.

Right on cue, Sean started swaying side to side, jumping in with the song.

"The Mac Dad will make ya (jump, jump)
The Daddy Mac will make ya (jump, jump)
Kris Kross will make ya (jump, jump)"

"Oh no, not the backward clothes!" Lisa half-screamed, half-laughed, doubling over with laughter. Tears welled in her eyes as gut-wrenching giggles took over. She tried to catch her breath, gripping the steering wheel as she wiped at her face.

When she finally managed to compose herself, she dared another glance at Sean.

Grinning like the sun had parked itself on his face, he asked, "What? You don't like my moves? Back in the day, I swore I was gonna be the third Kris. Wearing my clothes backwards felt like the coolest thing ever."

That set Lisa off again. "They always reminded me of that part in Mary Poppins when Bert pulls his pants down to dance like the penguins. It just looked like he threw on some oversized pants backward!"

Without missing a beat, Sean burst into song.

"*When Mary holds your hand, you feel so grand!*"

Lisa's mouth dropped open in amused surprise. "Nah! What you know 'bout dem old school movies?"

Sean did a double take, enchanted by the unexpected slip into her Creole accent. She sounded adorable. He cleared his throat dramatically, puffed out his chest, and responded in a crisp, dignified British tone.

"I'll have you know," he began, "that I am well versed in the classics. My repertoire includes such cinematic masterpieces as *Little House on the Prairie*, *Bonanza*, and *Anne of Green Gables*."

He gave her a once-over, eyebrow raised for effect. "Furthermore, my expertise extends to vintage sci-fi royalty such as *Lost in Space*, *Doctor Who*, and the original *Star Trek*—featuring none other than Sir William Shatner himself."

Then, for good measure, he gave her a slow, disbelieving glare, turned his head with a dramatic *hmph*, and looked out the window like a man wounded by doubt.

Lisa erupted into another fit of uncontrollable laughter.

The laughter and playful banter lingered between them as they eased through the lively streets of Jackson Square, the rhythm of the city rising to meet them. Lisa navigated the turn onto Toulouse Street Wharf, the Mississippi glittering just beyond the edges of the Quarter.

As they pulled up behind Jax Brewery, the Natchez Steamboat came into view, its iconic paddlewheel glistening proudly in the afternoon sunlight.

Sean let out a low whistle. "Now that's a boat," he said, his eyes wide with admiration.

He ran a hand along the gleaming rails as they boarded, drawn in by the vintage charm. They climbed to the top deck, alone for now, the hush of the river offering a quiet kind of welcome.

Lisa found a perfect spot near the rear, a cushioned bench tucked beneath a modest overhang. A warm spring breeze teased the edge of her hair as she settled in beside him. The sun wrapped around them like an easy promise.

As they sat in silence for a moment, the sound of the overhead speaker crackled to life.

"Ladies and gentlemen, welcome aboard the Steamboat Natchez," the captain's voice boomed with practiced ease. "We'll be embarking shortly for a scenic cruise along the mighty Mississippi River. Sit back, relax, and enjoy the ride."

Their eyes met in the quiet of the moment. Lisa could hear her heart pounding in her ears as Sean leaned in close.

"I'd really like some booty," he said, his voice soft and sincere.

Lisa blinked, stunned, her mind scrambling. *Is he really asking for some—you know what—already?*

But then she caught the look in his eyes—calm, wide, and completely innocent. She opened her mouth to respond, then closed it again. She wasn't sure how to ask if he meant what she thought he meant. And if he did... well, she had no idea how to answer.

Sensing her hesitation, Sean added, "You know, booty. That sausage with the rice and pork in it. It's delicious."

"Oh my God!" Lisa burst out laughing, the tension snapping in an instant.

Sean tilted his head, clearly confused. "What's so funny?"

"It's pronounced *boo-dah*, not *booty*," she managed through her laughter. "It's spelled B-O-U-D-I-N."

Sean's eyes widened as the realization hit. His mouth dropped open in horror and he immediately covered his face with both hands, like he could shield himself from the embarrassment.

"What made you even think about that?" she asked, still grinning.

"Well," he muttered, lowering his hands, "I was just thinking about how unique Louisiana is compared to the rest of the states. Especially when it comes to food—it's so flavorful. That reminded me of the time I had some boo..." He stopped short, catching himself. No point in butchering it again. He sighed. "Now's one of those times I *really* wish I had a time machine."

Lisa tried—and failed—to hold back another giggle.

"There are different *levels* of English Black folks use down here," she said, teasing. "You're gonna have to learn the lingo if you want to survive."

He gave her a mock-serious nod.

"They are: Creole, Black, and proper English. For example—'Hey dey bae. How ya mom'n'nem?' translates to 'Hey, how yo' people?' which then translates to 'Hello. How is your family?' in proper English. You following me?"

Sean nodded again, like a student desperate to pass the final exam.

"Okay, let's work on your pronunciation. Try saying *boudin*."

"Boodang?" Sean released the word slowly, almost like a question.

Lisa doubled over with laughter.

Sean hung his head. "This is too embarrassing to keep up," he said. "So I'm gonna use my imaginary *change-the-subject card.*" With a shy grin, he made a motion like he was pulling something out of his front pocket.

"How has your visit been so far?" he asked, smoothly switching gears.

Lisa looked away at first, but then forced herself to meet his eyes.

"Well... in some ways it's been great. And in other ways... not so much."

Sean gave a small, encouraging nod, smiling gently. "Okay. What's been great?"

"Meeting you," she said, her voice soft and shy.

Sean let out a dramatic breath and brought a hand to his chest. "Whew! For a second there, I thought I didn't make the cut!"

Lisa laughed lightly, shaking her head, but her smile faded as his next question came.

"So... what's in the 'not so much' section?"

She drew in a deep breath, hesitating. "For a long time, I was haunted by the same nightmare. Over and over, I'd find Ma and Miriam lying dead on the kitchen floor. Nothing I did could make it stop."

A chill raced down her spine just thinking about it. She stood, turning her back to him, trying to shake off the memory—trying to hide the fear she didn't want him to see.

Behind her, the soft hum of the steamboat's engines shifted into motion, followed by a sharp whistle. The boat gave a gentle lurch, and the sensation of movement rolled beneath her feet as they pulled away from the dock.

This was the first time she had ever told anyone about it. She had always been too afraid people would think she was weak.

"After I moved to Georgia and met Josey, the dreams finally stopped. I thought they were gone for good... but now they're back."

Her final words came out as a whisper.

Sean stood too, watching her closely. He noticed the way her fists were clenched and her shoulders slumped beneath an invisible weight. He stepped forward and gently took her hand, turning her to face him. When she didn't look up, he lifted her chin with a soft touch, guiding her gaze to his.

"Nightmares are usually your body's way of working through emotions you haven't fully faced," he said, calm and reassuring. "Eventually, what it's trying to tell you will rise to the surface. Just give it time."

Lisa exhaled, releasing a breath she hadn't realized she was holding. Tears threatened to fall, but she blinked them back.

"Well, I wish I'd hurry up and figure out what I'm trying to say to myself, then," she muttered, half-laughing, half-choked.

Sean chuckled gently, rubbing her shoulders with comforting hands.

"Is there anything else in the 'not so much' section?"

She hesitated. Opening up about the nightmare had lifted something heavy, but part of her still worried about sharing too much—worried she might overwhelm him.

But Sean, sensing her reluctance, leaned in just a little closer. "I'm here. I'm listening. And I'm not going anywhere."

There was no doubt in his voice. Just quiet sincerity that melted the wall she hadn't realized was still standing.

"Miriam and I used to be best friends," Lisa began. "Close, like sisters. But when my parents died our senior year, she wasn't there for me. Not in the way I needed." Her voice wavered. "So, for the past seven years... we've barely spoken. And now that I'm back, all those feelings are back too. It's been hard. On top of Ma's condition. On top of Nathaniel."

She paused, collecting herself. Sean continued to rub her shoulders, grounding her with his presence.

"Last night, I just couldn't take it anymore. It felt like there was a civil war going on inside of me. So, I did what I always do when I get overwhelmed."

Sean raised an eyebrow, his voice soft. "What's that?"

"I put it all in a poem."

"You write poetry?" He asked, astonished.

The shock in his voice brought a little smile to her face. "A poem is categorized as poetry, so that would be a yes."

He laughed, relieved that she could still dish out some good old fashioned humor, especially after everything she'd just shared.

"Can you recite it for me?"

She took a small step back, surprised by the request. "You mean right here, right now?"

"Yes," he said, his smile warm and full of encouragement. "I'd love to hear it. Please."

Once again, his sincerity chipped away at her nerves.

"Okay... but only if I get to recite it with my eyes closed," she said with a nervous laugh.

Sean nodded quickly before she could change her mind.

"The name of the poem is *Supporting Cast*," she said softly, taking a breath and steadying herself before beginning.

"Even when I'm 1st to show up
I end up being last

I'm never given the leading role
Invariably assigned to supporting cast

Even so, I show up every day
My focus only on you
I diligently learn my lines
No need to tell me what to do

I know exactly how you need me to perform
I come into the scenes right on cue
Nail every detail flawlessly
I give a strong performance for you

As the credits roll, it's announced
The next movie is mine
I'm the main character
Our roles reversed this time

When we start to film,
I look around
But you're nowhere
To be found

I search and when
I finally do find you
You don't know your lines
You don't know what to do

Disappointed, I've finally realized
The importance of your role
You haven't grasped
Leaving me to be my own...

Supporting Cast"

Lisa waited for a response—but there was only silence.
She cracked one eye open and peeked up at him.
Sean's expression was a blend of awe and quiet disbelief.
She is so cool... and smart, he thought.
"Wow," he finally said, his voice soft. "That was beautiful. So full of emotion."

Lisa opened her other eye, still unsure. "You think so?"

"I know so." He nodded, his gaze steady. "And I also know that you two weren't best friends just for the sake of being best friends. You've been through a lot together. That kind of history—it leaves scars. It can take a toll on any relationship. But I really believe you two can overcome this."

He reached out and pulled her into a hug—warm, strong, safe. "I think you should tell Miriam how you feel."

As he said it, his arms tightened around her.

The tears she'd held back for so long finally declared victory. They slid down her cheeks as she leaned into his embrace. She hadn't realized just how much she needed this—the hug, the understanding, the encouragement.

What Sean didn't know was that talking to Miriam was exactly what she planned to do tomorrow.

He had this way of making her open up, bare all her wounds—which was scary and new. But just when the vulnerability felt too raw... he somehow knew how to hold her together too.

In that moment, it hit her.

Maybe she had spent all those years mourning the loss of one kind of "supporting cast," never realizing someone else *could* quietly step in to take the role—if only she let them.

Chapter Fourteen

FLASHBACK

Miriam's arms folded tightly across her chest, hands gripping the insides of her elbows like she was trying to hold herself together. Her body trembled with a quiet urgency she couldn't suppress, even as she stood motionless, rooted to the linoleum floor.

She'd meant every word of her excitement when Dr. Crane said her mother might be discharged by Monday—but joy had been quickly replaced by something else. Something heavier. Lisa's icy words echoed louder than the doctor's good news.

The image she saw of herself in Lisa's eyes wasn't a friend—but a stranger. A foreigner in once-familiar territory. Someone viewed with suspicion, kept at arm's length. An outsider, granted only the occasional glimpse inside.

Just yesterday, they'd been laughing and joking like the girls they used to be. For a moment, it had felt like the past was still within reach. But in the blink of an eye, the distance between them had returned, stretching like a canyon—and this time, Miriam wasn't sure there was a bridge back.

She remembered the strange look on Lisa's face as they were leaving the fair, the slight shift in her tone—one she'd dismissed too easily. Now, it felt like a warning she should've paid attention to.

Her mother had turned her attention to saying goodbye, seemingly oblivious to the tension that lingered in the room. Lisa never acknowledged Miriam. No nod. No glance. No goodbye.

As Lisa walked out with Dr. Crane, Miriam didn't move. Didn't speak. Shockwaves of confusion and disbelief rippled through her mind. Lisa's silence had spoken volumes.

That, more than anything, had left her stunned.

A lump rose in her throat, but she forced it down. Falling apart now wasn't an option—not with her mother still glowing from the good news.

She wanted nothing more than to slip away, retreat to the quiet of her apartment, and wallow in the confusion and hurt that clung to her like smoke. But she knew better. For now, she'd share in the excitement—and find her exit the moment the timing felt right.

Plastering on a smile, Miriam took a few carefully measured strides toward the bedside, doing her best to look casual.

"I bet you can't wait for Monday, can you?"

Mary looked up, her eyes bright as she grinned.

"Babae, you don't kno' the half of it! Monday gon' feel like my birthday, Christmas, New Year's, and Valentine's Day all rolled into one!"

Despite the ache in her chest, Miriam let out a small laugh.

"Well, now that we know you're getting sprung from prison— I mean the hospital— I should probably start getting everything ready. We already made a list of the foods you want from Dr. Crane's approved list."

To her relief, an escape route began to form.

"I can knock out the grocery shopping today and go through the fridge and cabinets to toss anything you aren't supposed to eat."

Mary's smile dipped as she poked out her lip, clearly unimpressed by that part.

"Okay," she replied with a hint of playful reluctance.

"If I get too busy tomorrow with all the prep, I'll just give you a call instead," Miriam added, laying the groundwork for tomorrow's alibi.

"Okay, bae. Thanks for takin' care of yo' ol' momma," Mary said, her voice warm and content.

"No problem, Momma. I'll talk to you tomorrow."

As Miriam stepped out of the hospital room, a pang of guilt stabbed her square in the gut.

Victoria Rose

Nathaniel pulled into a spot in the hospital parking lot and threw the car into park. Resting his arm on the door, he scanned the lot, his fingers absently rubbing the back of his head.

Despite the pep talk he'd given himself the other day, he still hadn't come up with a solid plan to catch the Murderer. Time was slipping through his fingers, and he knew she wouldn't stay in town for long. She was too smart for that—too slippery. He had to act while he still had a chance.

But how?

With a frustrated grunt, he raked his hand over his head a few more times before flinging it away, as if disgusted with himself. Just sitting here wouldn't solve anything.

He blew out a sharp breath and yanked the door handle. The door snapped open with more force than necessary, creaking on its hinges as it rebounded halfway back. He started to step out—left foot on the ground, hand reaching for the door—

Then froze.

Just across the next aisle, a familiar figure made his hand stall in mid-air.

His eyes narrowed in stunned disbelief. Lisa.

With Dr. Crane.

Nathaniel slowly pulled his leg back into the car and eased the door shut. His jaw clenched.

"You've got to be fucking kidding me," he muttered, voice laced with venom.

He craned his neck to keep them in view as they strolled past, walking close together, smiling like they didn't have a care in the world.

They looked... comfortable. Familiar. Like a real couple.

The sight made his blood boil.

In tight-lipped silence, Nathaniel curled his hands into fists. His teeth ground together. He knew Lisa was capable of some horrible things, but this? Cozying up to his mother's doctor?

Was she trying to finish the job? Take his mother out too—just like she did with his father—and no one would ever suspect a thing?

It wasn't enough that she'd already destroyed one part of his life. Now she was circling the rest, ready to strike again.

She wanted to take everything he loved. Everything that still mattered.

His instincts screamed at him to follow them. But then another thought pushed its way forward—

What if this was part of her plan? A diversion? What if she'd already set something in motion, and the moment he drove off, his mom would be left vulnerable?

No. He had to check on her first.

Nathaniel stayed in the car, eyes locked on Lisa and Dr. Crane as they pulled out of the lot. Only after their taillights vanished did he finally open the door and step out, heart pounding with suspicion—and something darker.

He'd barely made it a few steps past the car parked beside him when another familiar figure caught his eye.

Miriam.

She was moving fast, head down, completely oblivious to her surroundings—as usual. Lost in her own thoughts.

As Nathaniel drew closer, he could see it on her face—she was upset. His stomach dropped. His gut must've been right. Panic surged through him, pumping his body with adrenaline. He quickened his pace.

The moment she was within earshot, he called out in a high-pitched panic, "What's going on? What happened to Mom?"

Startled, Miriam halted and snapped her head up. Her eyes flicked to him in recognition, but confusion still clouded her features.

"What are you talking about?" she asked, her voice sharp with irritation.

"What did that Murderer do to Mom?" he demanded.

"I just left her room. She's fine."

"Are you sure?"

"Yes, I'm positive. Why are you even asking me this?"

"I just saw the Murderer leaving with Momma's doctor," he said, breath short. "She's trying to cozy up to him so she can take Momma out too!"

Miriam's expression shifted—confusion and irritation melting into something harsher. Anger. Disgust.

She was already hanging on by a thread. Trying to stay calm. Trying to keep it together. And now here he was, again, with his wild accusations. His *bullshit*.

Yes, she and Lisa weren't on the best terms right now. Yes, maybe they'd never be the kind of friends they used to be. And yes, what had just happened between them cut her deep.

But Lisa would never hurt their mother. Not in a million years.

She didn't understand how she and Nathaniel were even related—how two people who grew up in the same house could see the world so differently. She was exhausted from his constant paranoia, his endless conspiracy theories. Everyone was always out to get him.

A sudden jittery energy fired through her limbs. The anger was in her muscles now, in her bloodstream—buzzing and bouncing like electricity. She felt like she could run all the way home and still have energy left to burn.

She stormed past him, taking a few tight, furious steps before spinning around to face him.

"Mom is absolutely *fine*," she snapped.

She threw her hands in the air. "In fact, she'll probably be getting out Monday!" Her voice cracked at the end, frustration spilling over the edge. Her arms dropped to her sides with a sharp slap as her hands struck her hips.

She leaned toward him, her face twisted in a sarcastic, disbelieving glare. "Imagine that."

Nathaniel staggered back a step, stunned. The disgust and disbelief radiating from Miriam practically rolled off her in waves.

But then... why was he surprised?

This was how it had *always* been between them. She never truly listened. Never tried to understand his point of view. To her, his feelings didn't matter. His thoughts didn't matter. And no matter what happened, she always—*always*—sided with the Murderer.

"Look," he shot back, voice edged with defiance, "I know what I saw. She's trying to worm her way into his good graces so she can hurt Momma."

Miriam let out a sharp, humorless laugh.

"Well, you got one thing right," she said, bitter. "She *is* cozying up to the doctor. But it's got nothing to do with Momma. They like each other. Plain and simple."

Her eyes blazed with fury now.

"I know your paranoid little mind can't handle that most folks are just out here trying to *live*. Nobody's plotting against you. Nobody's checking for your 'everybody's out to get me' ass! But I guess that's the real problem, isn't it? Deep down, you're miserable because nobody seems to care—"

"Once upon a time, I thought out of anyone, *you* would," Nathaniel cut in, his voice trembling, raw.

There it was.

The truth he'd carried in silence for years.

"I don't know why I thought this time would be any different," he said, resentment creeping in. "You've never been there for me."

His voice rose with the weight of long-buried pain.

"After Dad was killed... the kids used to tease me. Say all kinds of cruel shit about him. And at first, I'd run to you. I'd tell you. I needed you to back me up."

He paused, his breathing ragged. "But you just stood there. Silent. Letting them say whatever they wanted. You didn't defend him. You didn't defend *me*. You left me out there. Alone."

"Do you know how that made me feel?" he yelled, pounding his fist into his chest with each word, each strike driving the pain deeper.

Miriam flinched.

She hadn't meant for him to feel abandoned. Not ever.

In the beginning, she had tried—gently, carefully—to explain what their father had done. But Nathaniel had refused to hear it. It's as if his heart had hardened against the truth.

And that... that had enraged her.

To believe *his* version of events was to erase her truth. It felt like betrayal. Like he thought what their father had done to them was somehow *justified*.

So how dare he stand there, screaming about being left behind, when *he* was the one who turned his back on *them* first?

And over the years, she watched it happen—slowly, unbearably—as that one lie festered like a body-snatching alien virus. The kind you'd see in horror movies. It crept through him like poison, until he started to look, sound, and act more and more like their father.

Her fury ignited, all the heat inside her funneling straight into her voice.

"Yeah?" she snapped. "Well, instead of facing the truth, you chose to believe a lie. You *chose* misery."

She shook her head, her voice beginning to shake too.

"I don't get it. I really don't. God forbid anyone else is happy or finding a little peace—because you can't have that, now can you?"

Her arms flung wide, eyes flashing.

"Nah, you gotta drag them right back down into your paranoid little pit of misery. Every damn time!"

"I chose? I didn't get to choose *shit*! The Murderer chose for me!" Nathaniel exploded, closing the distance between them in a blink.

He grabbed Miriam by the shoulders and yanked her toward him until their faces were only inches apart. His grip was so tight, she let out a startled gasp.

Spit flew from his lips as he growled through clenched teeth, "But you're fucking right. If I don't get to be happy, neither does she. I'll drag both of our asses to hell before I let that happen."

His voice trailed into silence.

In that instant, Miriam didn't see Nathaniel anymore. She saw *him*—their father.

Her eyes went wide, lips trembling as terror swept over her like a tidal wave. A roar filled her ears, like rushing water. Her heart pounded against her ribs, desperate to escape what she knew all too well came next. What *always* came next when he got like this.

She smelled the sharp linen scent of their father's cologne. Saw the harsh cut of his jaw just inches from her face. His eyes blazed with that same wild rage—untamed and dangerous. Her arms ached as phantom pain pulsed through them, remembering how his hands would dig into her skin. Trap her. Break her.

In the blink of an eye, Nathaniel saw a ten year old version of Miriam. Her face small and fragile—fear etched across it. She whimpered helplessly as tears started to form in her eyes as she stared up in horror.

At him!

In that moment, the depths of his mind flashed back to a long buried memory—Miriam, cornered, her tiny body bracing for the worst as their father loomed over her. Nathaniel's chest tightened. He looked down at his hands, still clenched around her arms, and recoiled.

He let go immediately, stumbling back a step, the breath escaping his lungs in a startled gasp. *What have I done?*

Her face—the fear on it—was undeniable. And he was the reason it was there.

Panic swirled in his mind, scrambling for answers, for a way to undo it.

Before he could say anything, a deep voice called out, "Everything okay over there?"

Nathaniel turned. A middle-aged man and woman stood on the next aisle over, watching closely. The man's eyes were locked onto him—unflinching, suspicious. The question, though, was clearly meant for Miriam.

Nathaniel looked back at her, unsure what she'd say.

The terror in her face had vanished. In its place was something even harder to read: a blank, expressionless mask.

"Everything's fine," she said quietly, her head bowed. "Thanks for asking."

"You're welcome," the man replied, still sounding concerned.

Without another word, Miriam turned and walked away.

Nathaniel started to reach out after her but stopped himself. From the corner of his eye, he could see the couple hadn't moved—still watching him like sentinels guarding something sacred.

Mind racing, he turned and made a beeline for the hospital entrance. He moved deliberately, staying in plain sight so they'd know he wasn't circling back. Just a harmless man walking away.

But even as he moved, one thought stayed crystal clear:

This was all the Murderer's fault.

Victoria Rose

Miriam fought the urge to break into a full sprint—but even if she tried, she wasn't sure her legs would carry her far. They felt like rubber, weak and unsteady, barely keeping her upright. She gripped her car keys tightly, like a lifeline, each step forward requiring more willpower than the last.

Her ears stayed alert, straining to catch any hint that Nathaniel might be behind her. But she didn't dare look back. She was too afraid of what she might see.

It felt like forever before her car came into view. Relief washed over her in a weak wave as she approached it. But just as she reached the front bumper, that fragile sense of safety shattered.

A presence—dark and suffocating—crept up behind her.

Her eyes widened. Sweat dripped down her face. She turned her head slightly, peering out of the corner of her eye—

Then gasped and spun around.

Her brother's—no, her father's—outstretched hand loomed before her, monstrous and massive, ready to drag her back into the hell she thought she'd escaped.

Terror surged through her like a tidal wave. Her chest tightened, crushed beneath the weight of memory and fear. It felt like a star collapsing inside her heart.

She shrieked and threw her hands over her face.

Something struck her foot.

Another scream tore from her throat as she jumped back, kicking wildly, blindly, as if fending off an invisible attack. Her foot connected with something hard—a clink of metal against pavement followed.

Her keys.

Somehow, she'd dropped them when she covered her face.

Panic swelled again, sharper now. If she couldn't find her keys, she couldn't escape. Her breath came in fast, shallow gasps as hot tears finally broke free.

The dam had burst.

She dropped to her hands and knees, frantically sweeping her hands across the pavement, searching, desperate. Her vision blurred from tears, her lungs burned from sobbing, and the pounding in her chest grew unbearable. The terror of being caught—*again*—sank its claws into her, pushing her toward the edge.

Her field of vision narrowed to a tunnel. Her hands trembled, brushing under her car.

And then—cold, hard metal.

She clutched the keys to her chest like a sacred artifact. Then turning around to sit, she collapsed, curling into herself against the side of the car. Her body shook violently, wracked with sobs, but her mind screamed: *Get out. Now.*

She forced herself upright, legs quaking beneath her. Somehow, she made it into the car, slamming the door shut and locking it in one frantic motion.

Her fingers trembled as she jammed the key into the ignition.

She shifted into drive and peeled away, whispering a prayer as her tears kept falling.

"Please, God. Just let me make it home."

Chapter Fifteen
VICTORIA ROSE ORIGINAL

Josey lifted the lid off the pot and peeked inside. It looked like some kind of stew—but she knew better than to say that out loud. A Native Creole might skin her alive for calling gumbo "stew." Steam curled upward, carrying with it a rich, spicy aroma that made her stomach flutter in anticipation.

She'd watched Devan move around the kitchen with practiced ease, slicing ingredients with care, sautéing some, layering in others—all at just the right time, just like his grandmother's recipe instructed. It always amazed her how a handful of raw ingredients could transform into something completely different, something tasty and wonderful.

I Wanna Know by Joe played softly in the background. She smiled to herself as she watched Devan wipe down the counter, then start putting away the dishes he'd already washed. She had offered to do them, but he refused—with a grin that rivaled the sun—saying it was part of his peace offering.

He'd thought of everything.

A miniature flower arrangement added a burst of color to the small kitchen table. A bottle of wine chilled in a bucket of ice. Even the playlist—a dreamy mix of R&B hits—set the mood just right. And then there was his apartment itself. She still couldn't get over how stylish and sophisticated it was.

You know what, Joe? she thought to herself. *I want to know, too.*

She crossed the room, eyeing Devan sweetly until he noticed her presence.

He turned, that same easy grin spreading across his face. "What?"

"I don't know if I said this already," she began, "but your apartment looks amazing."

His grin stretched into a full-blown, blinding smile. "Ah, thanks. I appreciate it."

"I'm even more impressed that you did all of this yourself," she said, gesturing around the room with a sweeping motion.

Still grinning, Devan glanced down and gave a modest shrug, suddenly looking like a shy teenager.

Just when I thought he couldn't get any cuter, Josey thought.

"Okay, you gotta tell me," she said, cocking her head. "How did you end up with such great style?"

His eyes widened. "Huh? Uh... you really want to know about that?" he asked, sounding just a little nervous.

"Yup." Her answer was immediate and unwavering.

He folded his arms, then brought one hand up over his nose and mouth. He closed his eyes for a moment, like he was trying to talk himself out of something, then slowly let the breath go and dropped his hands to his sides again.

When he spoke, his voice pitched up a little. "Are you sure you want to know? It's kind of an embarrassing story... Even Lisa doesn't know about it."

"Then I *definitely* need to know."

He groaned and shook his head—this time in surrender.

"Okay," Devan said, letting out a slow breath before launching in. "It all started when I was twelve. I had to, uh..."—his voice sped up—"do a number two. And like all manly men, I needed a magazine to pass the time."

One of Josey's hands flew to her mouth while the other gripped her knee for support as she burst into laughter.

Devan sighed, his head dropping in mock defeat. "I *knew* this was coming."

"I'm sorry," she giggled, barely getting the words out. "I just... I didn't think your story would literally start with *shit*. But ain't that some shit?" She doubled over in a full-on laughing fit.

Even though the joke was on him, Devan smiled and waited it out. There was something about her laugh—free, full of joy, nonjudgmental. It made him feel safe and seen. Like with Josey, being himself wasn't just accepted—it was exactly what she wanted.

After a few stop-and-go waves of laughter, Josey finally managed to get it under control. She wiped a tear from the corner of her eye and looked up at him, still grinning. "I'm sorry, please continue."

Devan gave her a skeptical look, waiting a beat before continuing. "So... I go into the living room and grab what I *thought* was my dad's sports magazine. But once I was—well—*settled in*, I realized it was actually one of my mom's home decor magazines. And since I couldn't exactly get up at that point, I figured I'd just flip through it. I mean... how bad could it be, right?"

Josey nodded, her eyes sparkling mischievously.

"I started looking through it... and to my surprise, it was actually kinda cool. The designs were amazing. Then I hit this one page—the layout was stunning. The colors, the patterns, the vibe—it all just clicked. After that, I stopped taking my dad's magazines and started sneaking my mom's instead."

Josey tried to keep a straight face but stayed quiet, letting him continue.

"Two years later, I ended up in a Home Ec class. Most of the guys hated it, but I *loved* it. It gave me an excuse to explore all the stuff I'd been interested in—fashion, decorating—without being singled out or teased for it."

He smiled, his voice softening as he reflected. "For years, I had ideas I was too scared to share. Stuff I wanted to try, but

I didn't think my parents would get it. Then in Home Ec, we had this project where we had to sew something. My mom had just bought a new sofa, and I remembered her wishing she could afford the fancy pillows she saw in those magazines. So I decided to make her some."

Josey leaned in, her eyes wide with curiosity. "What grade did you get?"

Devan rubbed the back of his neck, grinning. "I got an A."

"Wow," she breathed, genuinely impressed. Sewing had never been her strong suit—she'd barely scraped by in that class.

"The teacher even pulled me aside. Thought I'd bought it or had someone from the fabric store help. I had to show her the leftover fabric and explain why I picked the design, how it tied in with our sofa at home. After we talked, she realized it was all me. And for the first time, I felt comfortable enough to tell someone about my ideas."

He paused, then looked her directly in the eyes.

"I'm not gay or anything. But you know how it is—people hear a guy likes design or fashion, and that's where their minds go."

Josey nodded. "That's true."

"When I got home, I told my mom I finished the pillows and wanted to give them to her." His voice brightened as he continued. "She gave me this smile that I could tell meant, '*no matter how bad they look, I'll use them because my baby worked so hard to make them.*'"

He giggled. "It probably didn't help that I'd stuffed them in a black garbage bag to bring them home. I didn't want anyone to see them and start asking questions. But when I pulled them out of the trash bag, she gasped. She couldn't believe how pretty they were. She kept going on about how the quality was impeccable—just smiling and telling me how proud she was." His smile widened.

There he goes with one of those earth-shattering smiles again, Josey thought. She could tell how much he loved his mom—and how much he loved making her happy.

He still had that smile, but his voice softened. "That's when I knew I could tell her. I said, 'Mom, there's something I need to tell you.' She turned to me and said, 'I'm listening.' That was the first time I felt like an adult. I was surprised at how she just smiled and quietly listened while I spoke. Once I was done, she said, 'Well, there's only one thing left to do.' I asked, 'What's that?' And she said, 'Go shopping for some fabric! What else is there to do?'"

Devan and Josey both laughed.

Devan walked over to the stove, lifting the lid off the gumbo pot and giving it a slow stir. The rich, savory aroma immediately filled the kitchen, making Josey's stomach rumble in anticipation. She closed her eyes for a second, savoring it, feeling like the warm, homey scent was wrapping itself around them just as tightly as the story Devan was sharing.

He replaced the lid and turned back to her, his smile lingering.

"From then on, whatever I wanted to do, my mom made it happen. The funny thing is, no one ever suspected a thing. When we'd go to the fabric store, the adults would always say what a good son I was to accompany her. She'd laugh and say, with a twinkle in her eye, 'I couldn't have a better son than him!' When my dad finally came home from the oil rig, he looked at everything I'd made and said, 'So you've been splurging on all these high-priced items while I've been gone?' My mom just smiled and said, 'Nope. These are all homemade.' Then he looked at her and said, 'Woman, why you been hidin' all this talent? I didn't know you could sew like this! Maybe we should start a business. We can name it after you—Victoria Rose Decor!' She just laughed it off. But I loved the name."

"Me too. Your mom has such a pretty name!" Josey beamed.

"After that, anything I made, I stitched 'Victoria Rose' on it, with each 'O' shaped like a rose."

"That's amazing!" Josey gasped in wonder.

"When I started college, I decided to major in criminology with a minor in interior decorating."

"You must've been the only guy in those classes," Josey teased as she pulled him into a hug.

"Let's just say, it didn't hurt to be in that situation," he chuckled.

Josey was sure he'd charmed plenty of girls, but oddly, she didn't feel jealous. Why would she? She was the one here in the present, while they were nothing but forgotten memories. What might stir a little jealousy, though, was if he'd given one of them one of his treasures. And they really were treasures. She could tell how much love and care he poured into them—how much they meant to his mom. Giving one away would mean putting another woman on the same level as her.

"I'm sure they were just as impressed with your skills as your mother was," she said, her tone casual but edged with curiosity. "I bet they asked you to make them something too."

"They did," he said, chuckling. "But by that time, my mom had a backlog of 'orders' for me to fill. So anything I made went straight back home."

Josey let out a quiet sigh of relief. "I'd love to have one of your pieces!" she replied dreamily.

"I'd be happy to oblige," he said, his voice quiet. "But to be honest, I haven't made anything since my mom passed away."

He held her tightly, nestling her head into the crook of his neck as they gently rocked back and forth.

Monica's soothing voice drifted through the room, smooth and steady:

*"When I first saw you I already knew
There was something inside of you
Something I thought that I would never find
Angel of mine..."*

Pulling back just enough to meet his gaze, Josey smiled softly. "It's okay," she said, pointing a finger at him, "so long as I get to have the very first Victoria Rose Original."

Looking deeply into her eyes, Devan smiled. In that moment, he realized there was nothing he wanted more than to be hers. He caressed her cheek, then leaned in and gently kissed her on the lips. "I'm pretty sure I can make that happen."

As Devan pulled back, something caught his attention from the corner of his eye. He glanced toward the stove and saw steam rising from the pot of gumbo.

"I think it's time to dig in," he said with a smile.

Josey nodded in agreement.

Devan went about filling their bowls with rice and gumbo while Josey sat patiently at the table, her mouth watering as she imagined how good it would taste.

As soon as Devan set her bowl in front of her, she scooped up a big helping onto her spoon and started to blow on it.

After a minute, she finally took a bite. The combination of onions, bell peppers, and celery mixed with the Creole seasoning, sausage, and okra set off a wave of savory goodness.

"Mmm," she moaned, rocking side to side with satisfaction. "This is really good," she mumbled, nodding as she pointed her spoon at her bowl. "You made your grandma proud with this one!"

"I'm glad you like it," Devan chuckled.

For a while, there was only the occasional clinking of metal against ceramic as they ate.

Devan smiled inwardly, thinking back on their conversation. He still couldn't believe how easily she had gotten that story out of him. But he had to admit, it felt really good to share something so personal—with her.

If this keeps up, I won't have any secrets left, he thought, amused.

But there was something he had always wanted to know about her, even before they officially met. He figured now was his chance.

With an inquisitive yet playful look, Devan broke the comfortable silence.

"Now that I've answered your 'gotta know' question, I have one of my own."

Josey's eyebrows lifted as she swallowed her latest spoonful of goodness. She hadn't expected him to have a question for her—and with the look he was giving her, she had no idea what it could be.

But fair was fair. Even though he'd been embarrassed, he had answered her question with complete honesty.

"Okay. What is it?" she asked.

Devan chose his words carefully. He didn't want to sound accusing or condescending. He just genuinely wanted to know.

"You're so caring, smart, and full of joy," he began, grinning nervously as he rubbed the back of his head. "So I've always been curious about why..."

"Why what?" Josey's voice rose a little.

His voice was full of sincerity, without a hint of judgment.

"Why do you feel men up at work?" he asked. He paused, then added, "It's been hard for me to reconcile the you I know with the one I've heard about."

With a gasp, Josey's spoon clattered into her bowl as her hands flew up to cover her face.

"Oh my God," she moaned.

She hadn't realized Lisa had told Devan about that. Now that she thought about it, how could he not know? He had to have known in order to pull off the prank they played on her.

All at once, heat radiated from her face—as if her shame was a geyser, shooting hot water and steam to the surface.

Devan laughed silently in surprise. He hadn't known exactly how she would react, but he definitely hadn't expected her to be so embarrassed.

It was another side of her he hadn't seen before—and he was glad he did.

Straightening his face before she dared to look at him, he waited, not wanting her to go from self-conscious to defensive.

After a few moments, he said in a lighthearted tone, "I'm listening. Or do you need me to come over there and pry your hands away from that pretty face of yours?"

She could tell by his tone that he was enjoying this—just a little—but in a good way.

The thought made some of the heat fade from her cheeks, and with that small reprieve came clarity.

He already knew.

He already knew and still told Lisa he liked her.

Still asked her out.

Still sat here, now, waiting patiently for her answer instead of running away.

In an instant, the realization blew away the embarrassment that had plagued her.

Slowly, she lowered her hands.

"No," she said shyly, glancing over at him.

Devan nodded in satisfaction, leaning forward and propping his arms on the table, settling in to listen.

It was easy talking about this with other women—because unfortunately, most had encountered something similar. But she'd never had a guy ask her about it before, let alone with such care for how she felt.

If it had been anyone else but Devan, she probably would have laughed it off without ever giving a real answer. But this was different.

She let out a deep sigh.

"Well, I guess you can call it get back."

Devan's eyebrows rose slightly, but he stayed silent.

Josey grabbed her spoon and started stirring what was left of her gumbo.

"When I was thirteen, I started filling out in all the womanly places. My mom had talked to us about puberty, so I understood what was happening to my body," she said, her voice lowering. "But what I wasn't ready for... was the men. At first, it was an uncomfortable stare or two when we were out in public.

Gradually, men started making comments like 'Damn, girl, you fine.'"

Her voice started to rise slightly. "One day, I was hanging out with my friends at the house. We had some change, so we decided to walk to the store around the corner to buy some candy. As we were leaving, my mom called me back and asked me to pick up something for her. My friends went ahead without me.

When I got to the store, a really old man with a cane was standing out front. As I was about to go in, he stopped me and held out a hundred-dollar bill. In my thirteen-year-old mind, I thought he needed help shopping. I felt sorry for him, so I said, 'Sir, you can hold onto your money. I'll help you shop for whatever you need.'"

She paused, her fingers tightening around her spoon.

"He looked me straight in the eyes and said, 'Oh, baby, I don't need help with shopping. This is for you. All you gotta do is come with me.'"

Devan's eyes widened in shock, then quickly narrowed with anger as he realized what the old man had meant. But he stayed silent, willing himself to let her finish.

Tears formed in Josey's eyes as she pressed on.

"I had no idea what he was really talking about... but I had this disgusting, scary feeling in the pit of my stomach. I just knew he wanted to do something *bad* to me. So I started screaming at the top of my lungs, 'Get away from me!'"

She wiped at her tears, her voice rising with anger.

"Even though he had a cane, he jumped into his car real quick and drove off."

She shook her head. "I didn't even know what sex was. I was only *thirteen years old*, for God's sake!"

Devan stood, slid his chair next to Josey's, and sat down beside her, gathering her carefully in a tender, protective side hug.

"I'm sorry you had to go through that," he said gently. "You did exactly what you were supposed to do in that situation."

"Thank you," she whispered, her voice trembling.

This was always a hard story to tell—even when she told it to other women—but she was glad she had the chance to tell Devan.

She wanted him to fully understand her why.

Wiping away her tears, she continued, her voice steadying.

"After the shock wore off, I got angry. I couldn't understand why some men would do something like that to a female. So when it happened again, I went off. After that... it just became easier to do it to someone else before they could do it to me. I wanted them to know what it felt like—to be harassed like that."

She turned to look up at him.

"I know, I know," she added with a self-aware smile. "It's wrong of me to take it out on men who never did anything to me. Lisa's been drilling that into me since we met."

Devan hugged her tighter. His voice was loving, full of understanding.

"That's true. But you've also been through a lot. You were dealing with it the best way you knew how. No one could ask for more than that."

In truth, he wished he had a time machine—so he could go back and beat the hell out of the old man and every other predator who had tried to take advantage of her.

As a police officer, he'd seen firsthand the aftermath of situations like that.

It always made his blood boil.

He simply couldn't understand how a man could even *think* it was okay to do something so vile.

Josey smiled as she sank deeper into Devan's embrace.

She couldn't fully explain it, but in a way Devan's actions and words were asking, no, *demanding* her to do more than what she had been doing.

She realized, for all the *get back* she had dished out over the years, it had never stopped the pain.

But this—

having a Victoria Rose Original—

was a game changer.

Chapter Sixteen

Underneath It All

Miriam moved about her apartment like a ghost. She had no real recollection of how she'd made it home. What she did remember was the overwhelming comfort of locking her front door behind her, the solid click of the deadbolt granting her a small sense of safety. She had slid to the floor in a heap, sobs wracking her body as waves of relief and fear shook her. She couldn't recall how long she stayed there. At some point, she had gathered enough strength to drag herself to bed, pulling the covers over her head as if she could shut out the world—Nathaniel, their father, all of it.

She had drifted into a fitful sleep, but it hadn't lasted long. She tossed and turned for most of the night. Even this morning, though she felt slightly steadier, the fear still clung to her. It crept up at the slightest sound or the fleeting glimpse of a shadow out of the corner of her eye.

As much as she wished she could forget, her mind wouldn't let her. It dragged her back to it over and over. She and Nathaniel had argued before—plenty of times. They had even gotten in each other's faces. But he had never laid a hand on her. Not until yesterday.

She never imagined he could go that far. That was something their father would have done without hesitation. A shudder ran through her as her mind dragged her back to the disturbing image—the one where their father had taken over Nathaniel's body like in some grotesque horror movie. Miriam quickly pushed the thought away again, along with the fear that threatened to rise when she remembered the way Nathaniel's hands had gripped her arms.

Forcing her mind back to the conversation itself, she sifted through his words. Most of what Nathaniel had said was paranoid and twisted. But one thing still cut deep.

You've never been there for me.

His words echoed in her mind. She could still see the look in his eyes, the bitterness in his voice. Now, with the heat of the moment behind her, she could see through the anger—to the hurt, the loneliness, the fear. He had been crying out for help. And she had missed it.

Her stomach twisted with guilt. She messed up. She had let her rage blind her, and everything spiraled out of control because of it.

As a psychologist, the signs should have been obvious. Picking up on a cue like that and using it to start the healing process should have been second nature. After all, the very reason she had chosen this path was because she had wanted to help Nathaniel and their mother heal from everything their father had done. She had poured years into her education with that hope burning inside her.

And now, when it truly mattered, she had failed them.

If I can't even help my own family, how can I possibly think I can help anyone else? I'm nothing but a useless failure, she thought bitterly.

Miriam groaned aloud, burying her face in her hands. As if that thought wasn't bad enough, it reminded her of yet another disaster in the making. With a grunt of exasperation, she slumped her shoulders and glanced at the clock.

Lisa would be there any moment.

Miriam tried to mentally brace herself for whatever was coming, but she couldn't summon the strength. She was drained—mentally, physically, emotionally. All she really wanted was to crawl back into bed and disappear under the covers.

Before she could even form her next thought, there was a knock at the door.

For a moment, she hesitated, wondering if she could just stay quiet until Lisa left—just like she used to do as a kid when Jehovah Witnesses came knocking. She almost smiled at the memory, but dismissed the idea. Whatever Lisa had come to say, it was better to face it here, within the safety of her locked apartment, rather than somewhere public.

Dragging herself to the door, Miriam peeked through the peephole to confirm it was Lisa. Lisa's figure appeared slightly distorted, stretched like a funhouse mirror. But there was nothing amusing about her face. Her jaw was tight, her lips pressed into a thin line.

Miriam inhaled sharply and opened the door.

"Good morning," Lisa said, her voice flat.

"Good morning," Miriam echoed dully as she closed the door behind her.

As soon as Miriam turned the deadbolt, a swell of fear rose in her chest. She couldn't shake the feeling that she had just, locked herself into a cage. Her body screamed at her to run, the same way it had yesterday. But today, there was nowhere to go. She was already in her safe place, or at least, what was supposed to be safe.

Spinning around, wanting to rip the band-aid off quickly, she asked, "What do you want to talk about?" The words came out more like a harsh demand than a genuine question.

Lisa's eyebrows lifted slightly, but she kept her tone even. "I want to talk about you and me."

"What about us?" Miriam couldn't hide the agitation creeping into her voice.

Lisa let out a scoff—short, humorless—and shook her head. "Okay. So that's how you want to play it," she muttered. She stared at Miriam for a beat longer before continuing, her voice tight with anger. "When my parents died, you weren't there for me. You left me all alone when I needed you the most." Her voice cracked slightly at the end, the anger edged with something rawer.

Miriam instinctively took a step back. Her chest constricted as a tidal wave of fear and humiliation slammed into her. Lisa's voice—the hurt, the rage—was almost identical to Nathaniel's the day before.

It wasn't as if Miriam hadn't already accused herself of the same thing earlier. But deep down, she still clung to the belief that it wasn't true. Nathaniel's accusation had stung, yes—but hearing it now, from Lisa's own mouth, felt catastrophic. Like a nuclear strike straight to her heart, leaving nothing behind but wreckage.

It was a reality she didn't want to accept. A truth too painful to acknowledge. She felt naked, cornered, exposed.

"That's not true. I *was* there," Miriam argued, forcing the words past the tightness in her throat. "Every time I asked you to come somewhere with me, you said no."

"That's because that's what *you* wanted!" Lisa shouted back, her voice shaking. "All you wanted to do was go to parties, laugh and joke around—like there wasn't a care in the world. Like my parents dying didn't matter. Like *I* didn't matter."

In truth, Lisa had been carrying far more than grief.

The nightmare had already been haunting her for years back then, though only once in a while.

Whenever she woke up shivering and drenched in sweat, her mother had been there—arms warm, voice soft—chasing the terror away.

But after her mother was gone, the nightmare returned almost every night, uninvited.

And Lisa was left to face it alone.

Every evening, she would curl up small beneath her covers, praying—praying the nightmare wouldn't come, praying Miriam would.

"I was hurt. I was afraid. I was lost," Lisa said, her voice trembling with the weight of the memory. "What I needed was my best friend to be there for me. To be my anchor when everything else was falling apart—even if it just meant sitting with me in silence."

Miriam's heart raced as another tidal wave—this time of shame and regret—crashed over her. She knew, deep down, that Lisa had needed her. She had seen the pain back then, recognized the silent pleas for comfort. And she had wanted to be there.

But the truth was, she hadn't been strong enough. Lisa—and everyone else—had no idea that Miriam was a coward. The parties, the jokes, the constant busyness—they had all been a facade to hide her own fear and anxiety.

She had been running, sprinting away from the darkness inside her for as long as she could remember. And when faced with Lisa's grief, Miriam simply didn't have the strength to carry both of their burdens. So she chose herself.

"I was a kid," Miriam said defensively, her voice sharp and brittle. "I was doing what normal teenagers do."

For a moment, Lisa felt herself yanked backward in time, standing once again in the ruins of her teenage years.

The same fear.

The same crushing rejection.

It hit her like it had back then, slamming into her chest before she could brace for it.

But this time, she refused to let it swallow her whole.

She deserved better from Miriam—then and now.

She wasn't going to back down.

Lisa's eyes narrowed, steady and unflinching.

"You say that like it's supposed to excuse everything," she said, her voice slicing through the tension.

"Like being a kid meant you couldn't hurt me."

She leaned forward slightly, her words landing hard.

"I was a kid too."

Miriam wanted to argue, to defend herself—but what was the point? She knew Lisa was right.

Still, the words shot out of her, bitter and sharp:

"It's not like I can go back and change it!"

She wished she could.

She would have given anything.

But wishes were useless now.

Frustration and guilt tangled inside her, spilling out as she snapped, "So you're mad because I didn't act like an adult? What do you want from me?"

Lisa thrust her hand toward her in a hard, jabbing motion. "What I'm mad about and what I want are exactly the same thing!" she shouted. "I'm upset because all these years you never even tried to make it right! You acted like you didn't care about me or our friendship. And now that I'm back, you're pretending like nothing happened—like you've been the perfect best friend all along!"

Miriam stood frozen, everything around her blurring at the edges.

Acknowledging the truth—that she had chosen not to be there for Lisa, deliberately avoided her after their bond fell apart and that she had willfully chosen not to fix it—would mean facing a brutal reality: this was all her fault.

Her eyes widened as a sickening realization hit her.

She had done exactly what she hated her father for. Maybe not physically, but emotionally—using people and then discarding them when they no longer served her needs.

Lisa shook her head, disgust etched into every line of her face.

"I see now... I was right to answer Angellica the way I did."

The mention of Angellica's name struck Miriam like a lightning bolt. Panic seized her.

When had Lisa even spoken to Angellica? What had she said? Would Angellica see her for who she really was—and walk away in disgust?

Desperate, Miriam grasped wildly for anything to defend herself. "Oh, so that's what this is about? You're jealous of a twelve-year-old!" she accused.

Lisa just stared at her, the disappointment in her eyes worse than any yelling could have been.

"Wow," she whispered, shaking her head.

Then lower, her voice almost vibrating with contempt: "For someone who calls herself a Psychologist, you have no fucking clue how to be there for the people who need you the most."

Miriam stood frozen, the words slicing into her.

Lisa had uncovered the last secret she had been trying to keep even from herself:

She had no idea what she was doing.

Lisa stared at her for a long moment—one last glance to seal the distance between them.

Then Lisa spoke, her voice flat and final. "But don't worry. You won't have to avoid me for much longer. After Mom gets out and settled, I'm gone."

And before Miriam could find a single word, Lisa brushed past her and was gone.

Victoria Rose

Lisa barely made it to the car before the tears came.

Gripping the steering wheel with both hands, she dropped her head against it, breathing in ragged gasps between sobs.

She had gone in with every intention of making things right with Miriam.

She missed their friendship—the late-night conversations, the whispered dreams and hopes they used to share.

They had survived so much together, more than most best friends ever faced.

And she had truly believed they could start rebuilding what they had lost.

She thought Miriam would be able to understand how she felt, now that she was a Psychologist. Someone dedicated to helping others heal, someone who went out of her way to be there for her clients, even taking extra after-hour shifts to make sure no one felt alone. She had even tucked the poem she wrote — *Supporting Cast* — carefully into her pocket before leaving, hoping she could find the right moment to give it to her. A way to explain everything she had carried inside for so long, without the words getting stuck in her throat.

Watching the way Miriam smiled and was so full of life with Angellica had convinced her even more. After seeing how protective and supportive she was with her, Lisa thought maybe—just maybe—Miriam would finally be able to give her the kind of support she needed.

But she had been wrong.

What she wanted and what Miriam wanted were two entirely different things.

Lisa had known the conversation wouldn't be easy.

Talks like this never were.

She thought she had prepared herself for the worst.

But nothing had prepared her for the callousness she faced—the flippant dismissal, the anger at even being confronted, the cold denial of any wrongdoing, and then, the final gut punch: the accusation of jealousy.

It was as if Miriam really was a stranger now—someone Lisa didn't recognize at all.

After a few minutes more, her tears had subsided. She felt drained.

Her hand drifted into her pocket and closed around the folded piece of paper. She had carried it with her, believing today might be the day she shared it. That maybe Miriam would listen, and understand.

But the poem remained unread, the words still sealed away, like so much else between them.

Slowly, Lisa pulled it from her pocket and let it fall onto the passenger seat, the crisp lines of the fold still perfect. Untouched.

Just like the part of herself she had once trusted Miriam to hold.

She wished she could talk to Sean, but he had been called to the hospital for an emergency with one of his patients.

She didn't dare text him; she didn't want him worrying about her on top of everything else.

Her best option was to head back to Devan's place.

He had taken Josey to church that morning, so she'd have the apartment to herself for a little while.

At least there would be some time to pull herself together.

She sighed sadly as she wiped the last of her tears away. There was no way to get out of being around Miriam tomorrow since Ma was being released. She just needed to make it through that day, and then it would all be over.

She could go back to Atlanta and act like none of this had ever happened — just like she knew Miriam would.

But underneath it all, some things could never be undone.

Chapter Seventeen

TODAY, IT ENDS

Nathaniel wove through the sluggish Monday morning traffic on I-10 West like an angry NASCAR driver determined to reclaim first place. He hated the forty-five-minute drive from Donaldsonville to Baton Rouge. It was always the same—frustrating, slow, and filled with other drivers who didn't seem to understand the urgency boiling beneath his skin.

After what felt like an eternity, he finally took his exit and followed the winding road until the skeletal frame of the new building came into view. Excavators, cranes, and bulldozers littered the site like sleeping giants. It didn't look like much yet, just a mass of steel bones and dirt, but eventually it would become a three-story office complex.

A cool morning mist clung to his skin as he stepped out of the car and headed toward the site. He knew it wouldn't last—by noon, the Louisiana humidity would wrap itself around him like a wet blanket, his clothes sticking to him like second skin.

At work, Nathaniel kept mostly to himself. Conversations were brief and only when necessary. It didn't matter what job site he was on—he always had the same uneasy feeling that someone was watching him. That constant pressure gnawed at his nerves. Keeping his distance made things easier. Safer.

He'd been with Harrison Construction Company for a year and a half now—longer than he usually lasted anywhere. Most times, once the job was done, the bosses would pat him on the back, tell him he'd done great work... then say there wasn't anything else available for now. They never called him back. No matter how hard he labored or how clean his work came out, it was never enough to stick. That old feeling would creep in again—the one that whispered he wasn't good enough, not worth keeping around.

The only exception was Mr. Jones, his foreman. The man was calm, no-nonsense, but fair. He always greeted Nathaniel with a warm smile and asked how he was doing. When he reviewed Nathaniel's work, he'd often give him a solid pat on the back and say, "Excellent job!" It reminded Nathaniel of the kind of relationship he imagined he would have had with his father—something steady, respectful, and earned. And maybe that was the problem.

The other guys noticed. They saw the way Mr. Jones treated him, and they didn't like it.

Most of them kept their distance, but two in particular—John and Herman—seemed determined to get under his skin. From the look of them, they were around his age, but were nothing like him. They were always loud, always laughing, always performing. To Nathaniel, it felt forced. Fake. No one could be that happy all the time. And somehow, they were always nearby, close enough for their booming voices to carry over in waves of exaggerated jokes and laughter. Nathaniel knew what they were doing—mocking him. Taunting him. They wanted a reaction.

He tried to ignore them. For Mr. Jones' sake, he stayed quiet, swallowed it down. Until the day they went too far.

As he packed up his tools to leave, Nathaniel noticed something was missing—his measuring tape. He looked everywhere but couldn't find it. Then he remembered how John had been especially loud that day. How his eyes had flickered with something smug when they'd briefly locked gazes.

Without another thought, Nathaniel marched across the site and stopped just inches from John.

"Where is it?" he demanded, voice tight and seething.

John jerked back. "Whoa." He held up a hand in mock defense, face tight with irritation despite the look of surprise. "What're you talkin' about?"

"You know what," Nathaniel growled. "You took my measuring tape."

"Man, I don't know where your damn tape is! Why would I take your shit when I got my own?" John snapped. "You better get outta my face with that bullshit." John gave a dismissive swipe in the air as he walked away.

Nathaniel took a few steps towards the direction John was heading, fists tightening.

Before he could go any further, Herman slid into his path, hands raised in a playful, mock-surrender gesture.

"Not tryna get in the middle or anything," he said casually, "but did you check over in the area you were measuring and cutting the lumber?" He pointed in the direction where Nathaniel had been working earlier in the day.

Nathaniel looked toward the spot. A small crowd had begun to gather. He could feel their stares, their anticipation. Part of him wanted to ignore Herman's suggestion and go after John anyway. But he clenched his jaw and turned away.

He stomped toward the lumber pile, this time moving pieces instead of just glancing around. On the second try, he saw it—the familiar orange glint of his tape measure peeking out from under a plank.

As he bent to grab it, Mr. Jones appeared, with John trailing close behind.

"What's going on, Nathaniel? John says you accused him of stealing your tape."

Nathaniel turned, locking eyes with John before facing Mr. Jones. "It was a misunderstanding," he said flatly, holding up the tape. "I misplaced it."

His expression stayed neutral, but inside, he was boiling. He could see John's smug look as he stood behind Mr. Jones. More than anything, he wanted to punch him in the face and wipe that conceited look right off. Instead, he clenched his teeth and held it in.

"I'm glad you found it," Mr. Jones said, then addressed the others. "Alright, folks—see y'all tomorrow."

The group dispersed, leaving Nathaniel to finish packing up. Only Mr. Jones remained, watching him with a quiet intensity that made Nathaniel shift uncomfortably.

"I... I didn't mean to cause any trouble," he said.

"I know," Mr. Jones replied with a sigh. "But you can't go around accusing people without proof. I get it—some of these guys aren't easy to get along with. Believe me, I know. But next time, come to me first, alright?"

"Yes, sir."

"Good." Mr. Jones patted him on the shoulder. "You should get going. Beat that traffic."

Nathaniel gave a faint nod and headed toward the parking area, the corners of his mouth twitching into something that could barely pass as a smile.

He hadn't lied—he truly didn't mean to cause trouble. He liked Mr. Jones. Respected him. But there was no denying the look on John's face earlier—it was filled with mocking laughter. Nathaniel had been set up. All someone had to do was slip his measuring tape back in a spot he'd already searched. Make it easy to find, just after he'd made a scene.

And he knew exactly who had done it—Herman.

The memory sharpened into focus now: how Herman had slithered into his path during the confrontation, casually suggesting he check near the lumber again. It had all been orchestrated—calculated to make him look foolish in front of the one person whose opinion actually mattered.

As Nathaniel neared the scaffold, the sky dimmed. A thick cloud drifted across the sun, casting a shadow over the job site. Darkness spilled across his face as he stepped beneath the unfinished structure. He narrowed his eyes and released a low, simmering grunt. His hand gripped the scaffold's middle rung tightly, and he drove his foot onto the bottom bar with deliberate force, beginning his climb to the second floor.

He hated being underestimated. Hated being made to look stupid.

He could see it in their eyes—John and Herman didn't just dislike him. They looked down on him. Thought he was dumb. A joke. Just like *her*—the Murderer. Sneaky. Conniving. Always waiting to twist the knife when no one was looking.

As he climbed, his movements grew more aggressive. His feet and hands beat against the metal with increasing force—as if he were battling a fierce opponent—one rung at a time.

But then his hand froze midair.

The memory of Miriam's ten year old frightened horrified face flashed in his mind.

That look had haunted him since Saturday. Over the years, she'd given him annoyed looks, worried looks, even hurt ones. But never fear. Never *that* look.

That look wasn't for brothers. It was meant for devious good for nothing scumbags - criminals - killers.

Like John and Herman. Like the Murderer.

Not him.

There was only one reason she'd see him that way.

"It's all that fucking Murderer's fault," Nathaniel snarled under his breath.

Then, just as the wind picked up, he caught it: laughter.

At first, faint. A whisper.

Then again—louder. Then again—louder still.

Wave after wave, it echoed in his ears, building to a climax that throbbed in his skull, stabbing at his eardrums. He squeezed the scaffold tightly, bent his head, and shut his eyes.

Suddenly, he wasn't on the scaffold anymore.

He was in his worst nightmare.

John. Herman. The Murderer.

All of them stood around him, laughing hysterically, pointing down with twisted, mocking grins. And he wasn't a man anymore—he was a child. Small. Helpless. Alone.

They took turns like a chorus of bullies:

"You're nothing but a stupid fool!"

"Dummy!"

"Who would believe an idiot like you?"

Nathaniel clutched his face, curling in on himself as the taunts pierced deeper.

Again.

The laughter. The pointing. The shame.

Just like growing up.

I'm not stupid! I'm not dumb! I'm not an idiot! SHUT UP! he screamed inside as he sprang upright.

Silence.

Then, just like that—he was back.

The scaffold trembled beneath him, his whole body radiated heat as if someone had doused him with gas and lit him on fire. He opened his eyes, and something new—something dark—settled there. Hatred. Cold and ruthless.

With a violent smack, his hand slammed down on the scaffold bar. The sound rang out like a warning shot.

He pulled himself upward, fueled by rage.

When he reached the top, his boots landed with a heavy thud. Jaw clenched. Fists curled tight. He stormed across the floor, weaving around loose equipment and scattered materials like a man on a mission.

As he rounded the corner toward his work area, the sound returned—laughter.

John and Herman.

Standing there, talking and grinning as if they hadn't done a damn thing wrong.

Then on cue, their laughter fell to silence as they noticed his presence.

They shifted awkwardly as John quickly folded the paper he'd been holding and tucked it into his back pocket.

"So, looks like it's gonna be another hot-ass day!" John said with exaggerated cheer, shooting a glance at Herman.

The moment he spoke, the laughter came back. Not from them—but from inside Nathaniel's head.

Louder this time.

Faster.

And it wasn't stopping.

The day's barely started, Nathaniel thought, *and already they're trying to screw with me. Smiling. Pretending. Like I don't see it. Like I'm too dumb to figure it out.*

They think they can keep embarrassing me.

Make me look like an idiot.

Mocking me. Laughing in my face.

And thinking they can fucking get away with it!

Nathaniel's glare burned into them like fire through glass. His nostrils flared, teeth bared, muscles coiling as his eyes locked on his target.

"AHHHHH!" he screamed as his body exploded into motion.

John and Herman turned just in time to see him charging. Confusion and shock painted their faces.

Before either could react, Nathaniel's fist connected with John's jaw.

John staggered back with a grunt of pain—but quickly steadied himself. He swung hard and caught Nathaniel across the face.

Nathaniel reeled, then lunged again.

They collided with a crash of limbs and fists.

"Nathaniel, what the fuck is wrong with you?!" Herman yelled, trying to wedge himself between them. "You need to stop this crazy ass shit!"

But Nathaniel didn't hear him.

Other workers came running, scrambling to pull the two apart. The shouts, the chaos—it all blurred together.

Then—

"What the hell is going on here?"

The roar of Mr. Jones' voice cut through everything. Nathaniel froze.

He blinked and saw Mr. Jones step into view, eyes wide with shock. The fight drained from Nathaniel's limbs as reality slammed back into him.

His coworkers released him, but kept a close eye on him.

John, still clutching his jaw, spat out, "We were just talking like always—and this motherfucker just attacked me!"

Mr. Jones turned toward Nathaniel, jaw tight. "Is that true?"

"They were whispering," Nathaniel said coldly. "Plotting. I saw John hide something in his back pocket the second I walked in."

"See that's the shit I'm talking about." John snapped. "He's outta his mind." John pointed a sharp finger at Nathaniel. "We weren't even thinking about you. You wasn't even on our radar!"

"If that's true," Nathaniel said, his voice like ice, "then show him what you hid."

John hesitated.

Nathaniel's lips curled into a smile. Finally. Proof.

Mr. Jones stepped forward. "If you have something in your pocket, I need to see it. Now."

Reluctantly, John pulled out a folded piece of paper. Mr. Jones took it, opened it, and read. His gaze moved from the page to John, then to Herman. Both stared at the floor.

"I told y'all—no gambling on my time."

Gambling? Nathaniel's heart thudded. That can't be right. He took a step forward, instinct flaring, but forced himself to stop. He didn't trust John, but he trusted Mr. Jones. Mostly. Still, he couldn't shake the doubt—maybe there was another paper, or something hidden.

John stammered, "It's not what it looks like. We were just talking about Final Four picks. March Madness, that's all. We weren't placing bets—we didn't want anyone to get the wrong idea, so I put the paper away."

Mr. Jones' jaw was tight. "I said no gambling. I meant no gambling. Do you understand me?"

"Yes, sir," they mumbled.

The group around them began to disperse. Everyone knew that tone.

Mr. Jones turned to Nathaniel. "Come with me." This time there was no warmth in his voice.

Nathaniel followed in silence, dread clenching his gut. Just like when he was a kid when he first got sent to the principal's office.

PEACE AMID THE CHAOS

Inside the jobsite trailer, Mr. Jones turned and looked him over—hands on hips, disappointment etched into every line of his face.

Nathaniel stared at the floor. He couldn't bear to meet his eyes.

"What was the one thing I asked you to do, Nathaniel?" Mr. Jones' voice cut like a blade.

"To come tell you if there was a problem." Nathaniel's voice cracked. "I know how it looks to you, but I swear the two of them are always messing with me. Every time I look around they're where I am. Following me, watching me, trying to get under my skin!" His voice rose as he pleaded his case.

Mr. Jones shook his head slowly. "That's because I told them to work near you."

Nathaniel blinked, stunned.

"I'm going to be honest with you. The other workers said they didn't feel safe around you," Mr. Jones continued. "They said you'd just stare, wouldn't speak. Or if you did, it was rude and clipped. I figured you just needed to adjust. I asked John and Herman—guys your age—to work with you. Thought it might help."

He paused. Then, his voice softened—not with sympathy, but with finality.

"After the first time, I thought we had a breakthrough. I thought we were both going to trust each other to do the right thing. But I see I was the only one. As the foreman, I'm responsible for everyone's safety. I can't let this happen again. Nathaniel... I have to let you go."

Panic shot through Nathaniel's chest. Sweat slicked his palms. He realized that Mr. Jones was trying to look out for him. That he was trying to believe in him. And he fucked it all up.

"I'm sorry." Nathaniel pleaded. "I can do better, I promise."

Mr. Jones shook his head. "There is no third chance. I pray—whatever's causing you so much pain—you find a way to let it go."

Nathaniel couldn't feel his body anymore.

This morning, his only worry had been getting off in time to make it to the hospital for his mother's release. He couldn't understand how it went from that to...this.

"I'll make sure you get paid for today. I'll walk you out."

The silence between them said everything.

One moment Nathaniel was in the trailer. The next, he was in his car, parked outside a gas station near the I-10 exit. He didn't even remember the drive.

He gripped the steering wheel, rocking slightly, teeth clenched.

He just couldn't wrap his mind around it. How the hell had it gotten to this point?

When he thought about it, the same thing happened with Miriam Saturday. Both times, everything was business as usual and then bam! People were looking at him with terror, disappointment and regret.

He barely noticed the laughter creeping in at the edge of his thoughts.

Then it clicked.

It was the Murderer.

If she hadn't turned Miriam against him, he never would've been this upset. Never would've snapped at John. It was all her. Always her.

The laughter rose, but this time it felt comforting.

Somehow, she always ended up taking everything from him. His father, his relationship with his sister, Mr. Jones, his job.

She was already trying to take his mother.

And one day, she'd take the only thing he had left—himself.

Now the laughter raged almost deafening in his ears.

But instead of bringing him pain, it brought power.

And then, somewhere beneath it all, he heard himself laughing too—quiet at first, out of place and unfamiliar, until it blended so seamlessly with the rest that he wasn't sure where their voices ended and his began.

The heat returned, searing through his skin, filling his eyes with something black and merciless.

She will not take one more thing from me.
Not today.
Today, it ends.

Chapter Eighteen

JUST DO

Miriam glanced at her watch, then scanned the neatly stacked rows of broccoli. Cooking wasn't one of her strengths, so picking out fresh vegetables felt like guesswork. It all looked the same to her. She tapped a finger against her chin, made another pass, then gave up and grabbed the biggest bunch she could find, tossing it into a thin plastic bag.

Her shoulders relaxed as she let out a sigh and crossed broccoli off her shopping list. That was the last thing she needed. Without wasting another second, she half-walked, half-jogged toward the nearest open checkout line. She was cutting it close—the shopping should have been done days ago. But too much had happened.

The weekend from hell had left her exhausted and afraid. She'd thought about going to her mother's house to clean up and toss out the junk food, but the fear of running into Nathaniel stopped her cold.

And then there was Lisa.

After Lisa left, Miriam's mind scrambled for excuses. But there was no place to hide. Lisa had cut straight through her lies like a lighthouse slicing through fog, exposing everything she'd tried to hide. She couldn't outrun it anymore.

It had left her beaten—exposed.

But most of all it left her full of guilt and regret... and no idea of what to do next.

It baffled her—how clearly she could see other people's problems, and yet how blind she was to her own. Her thoughts slid into the same worn-out loop: *I'm so useless.* But then a memory flared to life—something Josey told her the day they met:

"Don't forget, psychologists are people too."

A spark flickered in her mind like a light bulb blinking on. She hadn't considered it before—probably because she'd been too busy denying it.

"I need help... just like everyone else," she whispered, almost in awe.

"Okay. What do you need help with, ma'am?" a cheerful voice asked.

Miriam looked up, startled, to see the cashier smiling politely.

She burst into laughter. "Oh! I'm so sorry. That wasn't meant for you."

The cashier looked a little confused but nodded and began scanning her items.

Miriam couldn't stop smiling. She hadn't expected to laugh—not this soon after everything. Her chest swelled with a warmth she hadn't felt in a long time. At first, she couldn't place it... but then she knew.

Comfort.

There was peace in knowing what to do next. Reaching out to a psychologist wasn't weakness—it was a step toward healing. Toward clarity.

But her small victory dissolved the moment she turned into the hospital parking lot. A fresh wave of dread crashed over her. It felt like returning to the scene of a violent crime.

She parked in the first open space near the entrance. Before she could even turn the key, her hands started to shake. Cold sweat broke out across her skin. Not wanting to lose momentum, she forced herself not to think—just do.

She cut the engine, grabbed her purse, and jumped out of the car like a paratrooper landing in enemy territory. The sharp clack of her heels echoed as she sprinted for the hospital doors. Panic rose as she realized she hadn't slowed down.

The doors won't open in time! Maybe I should've thought a little before just doing.

She braced herself for impact—but then came the soft swoosh of the automatic doors, followed by a blast of cool air. She opened her eyes, stunned to find herself standing in the hospital lobby. A few people turned to stare.

Clearing her throat, she smoothed her hair and walked calmly toward her mother's room.

When she reached the hallway, she started to pause to gather herself—but then kept going. Just do, she reminded herself. So

PEACE AMID THE CHAOS

far, it was working. She didn't know if Nathaniel or Lisa were already there, but she needed to be ready for anything.

She began taking deep, focused breaths as she approached the door. Without hesitation, she turned the knob and marched inside.

Relief swept through her like a breeze.

The room was quiet. Her mother was alone.

Mary looked up, her eyes sparkling with mischief. "I was wonderin' when one o' y'all was gonna show up. I thought fo' sho' Nathaniel would be the first one here."

Miriam had to stop herself from cringing at the sound of her brother's name. She didn't want to dampen her mother's good mood.

"I thought I was gonna have to hitchhike home," Mary added with a wink.

"Wow, really?" Miriam replied with mock shock.

Mary giggled.

"My weekend was hectic, so I didn't get a chance to stop by the house. I'll toss the junk food and catch up on the chores when we get there."

"Don't worry 'bout it, bae. I know you be busy. It shouldn't take too long, especially with Lisa helpin' out. And I bet that sweet lil' friend of hers will lend a hand too," Mary said, beaming.

Lisa's parting words from Saturday echoed in Miriam's mind:

After Mom gets out and settled, I'm gone.

Miriam knew it was too much to hope for, not after everything she'd done. Still, she prayed—faintly, silently—that God had a different plan.

"Hello, hello, hello," Dr. Crane said brightly as the door slid open.

Following close behind were Lisa, Josey, and Devan.

Miriam's first instinct was to look away, weighed down by guilt—but then she remembered: *Just do.* She needed to keep her head up and eyes fixed on the light, to keep moving forward.

She softened her expression, aiming for a mix of calm and openness. Even a small shift mattered. She wanted Lisa to see she was trying—even if it was too little, too late.

Their eyes met for a brief second. Lisa's gaze was back to its usual guarded state—but even that was a relief. It was worlds better than the look of disappointment and disgust she'd worn on yesterday.

Josey's expression mirrored Dr. Crane's—warm and cheerful—but Miriam knew better. Josey missed nothing. Miriam had no doubt she'd already sensed the tension.

Devan, on the other hand, looked distracted. He made brief eye contact with her, then glanced around the room as if searching for something.

"Mrs. Butler," Dr. Crane began, turning his attention to the patient, "I've reviewed your test results and vitals from the weekend—everything looks great. I've submitted the paperwork for your release. A nurse will be in shortly to go over your discharge instructions and answer any questions."

"Wahoo!" Mary grinned.

Dr. Crane took a moment to meet each person's eyes with a warm smile before leaving. He saved Lisa for last, his gaze lingering a moment longer.

Despite everything, the look made Miriam smile. She was genuinely glad Lisa had found her special someone.

But as soon as the doctor left, an awkward silence settled over the room like dust.

Not wanting to raise her mother's suspicions—and hoping to give Lisa a quiet moment with her—Miriam decided it was time to leave.

The thought of facing the parking lot again twisted her stomach into knots, but she reminded herself: *Just do.*

She smiled at Mary. "I'll bring the car around."

"I'll walk with you, if you don't mind," Devan offered.

Miriam's heart leapt at the unexpected kindness.

"I'd appreciate that," she said, smiling.

Miriam grinned at Devan as she pulled the car around to the entrance. After their walk and talk, she felt better—safer, even. He hadn't walked the whole way with her, stopping just short of the parking lot, but he'd watched her until she made it. She'd forgotten that he was just as much as her big brother as he was Lisa's.

She hopped out and jogged around to the passenger side, just as the hospital doors slid open.

A nurse appeared, wheeling Mary toward the curb. Lisa and Josey walked beside her, one on each side.

Miriam stepped up to the nurse. "I'll take it from here."

Josey darted ahead and opened the car door.

As Miriam and Josey helped Mary settle in, Lisa glanced over at Devan. Something about his expression caught her off guard.

He was standing still, his face unusually focused but distant—like he was looking through something, not at it.

She approached slowly and tilted her head into his line of sight. "Why your face lookin' like that?"

Devan blinked, surprised. His features softened. "What face?"

"The *face* you had before you switched to your surprised *face* 'cause you didn't realize I was in your *face*," she said, that familiar smart-alecky tone only a little sister could get away with.

Devan chuckled. "Oh, *that* face. That's just my deep thought method. Top secret technique. Very advanced. Only a select few can pull it off."

Lisa slapped his arm. "Whatever."

His grin widened. "I still got some work to finish up. I'll catch up with y'all later, ok?"

"Aight," Lisa said with a smile as she turned toward the parking lot.

Josey gave Devan a big hug before hurrying after her.

As soon as they were out of sight, Devan's smile slowly faded. That faraway look returned.

Victoria Rose

Lisa parked behind Miriam. The moment the house came into view, a slow uneasiness crept over her, thick and murky like early morning fog. Her heart began to race as emotions stirred and jostled inside her chest, trapped with no way out. It reminded her of pulling the dreaded "Go to Jail" card in Monopoly—no choices, no breaks, just a steady march back to a place she never wanted to see again.

Without taking her eyes off the house, she stepped out of the car and stood still, one hand pressed to her chest as if that alone could steady her pulse.

"Hey, you alright?"

Josey's voice floated over from the porch, pulling Lisa out of her daze.

Only then did she realize Miriam and Mary had already gone inside.

"I'm okay," she called back, though her feet remained planted on the pavement.

Lisa could see the worry in Josey's eyes as she glided down the steps and over to her.

"You know you don't have to go in if you don't want to. I'm sure Mrs. Mary would understand."

Lisa knew that she would too, but that wouldn't stop her from being disappointed though.

She took in a deep breath and forced a smile. "I'm good. Everything's fine," she said, her voice too bright, as she set off towards the porch.

"There's nothing *fine* about any of this," Josey whispered under her breath as she followed suit.

As Lisa crossed the threshold, a heavy, invisible weight seemed to drop onto her shoulders. Her knees bent slightly under the pressure, and for a moment, she couldn't breathe. The air inside the house felt denser, older—thick with memories of the past.

She sensed Josey close, waiting but not hovering, ready to jump into action if needed.

Lisa closed her eyes. Inhale. Exhale. Again. Slowly—softening the tension in her shoulders, unclenching her jaw. She let the air steady her.

After a moment, she opened her eyes and looked around.

The room was nearly frozen in time. The same worn furniture. The same faint scent of lemon polish. The way the afternoon light spilled through the windows, cutting across the living room floor in long golden lines.

She looked to her right, where the living room opened into the kitchen, expecting to see more of the same—except the kitchen door was missing.

It shouldn't have meant much, but somehow it did. It was like Mary had removed it as a quiet reminder that the door would never open again and Nathaniel Sr. be on the other side.

Lisa stared at the empty doorway, something shifting inside her. The heaviness remained, but beneath it, a flicker of resolve began to rise.

She squared her shoulders. Her spine straightened. Her chin lifted just slightly, and her jaw set with quiet purpose.

With newfound determination in her step, Lisa moved toward the kitchen.

"There you two are!" Mary beamed as she spotted them. "I was wonderin' where y'all ran off to. Miriam went to put some clothes in the wash."

Then her smile melted into a dramatic pout. "Now she want y'all to violate my senior citizen right to eat whatever I want. Said go through the kitchen, find all my sweets and junk food, and toss 'em."

"Don't be like that, Ma," Lisa said with a grin. "You know it's for your own good."

"Don't mean I gotta like it," Mary grumbled playfully, folding her arms.

Lisa and Josey laughed and got to work. Cabinets were opened, boxes checked, and the pantry thoroughly raided. The simple task brought a strange but welcome sense of normalcy to it all—like slipping into a rhythm Lisa hadn't realized she missed.

By the time they were nearly done, Miriam stepped back into the kitchen from the laundry room. She paused, taking in the sight of the three of them crowded around the sink, laughing mid-debate.

"What's going on?" she asked, brow raised.

Before Lisa could really think, she turned around holding up a nearly full two-liter bottle of Mountain Dew. "Ma is trying to convince me to let her keep this."

It came out too easily—uncalculated, unguarded. Another crack in the armor. Working with Miriam like this—casual, familiar—it felt too easy. Too normal. Her guard had slipped before she even realized it, and she was certain Miriam had picked up on it too. But what could she do? There was no room for tension here, not while Mary was smiling and laughing, soaking in the joy of having them all together. Lisa reminded herself this was temporary. Just for today. Tomorrow, the distance would return—right where it belonged.

"Really, Mom?" Miriam said, crossing her arms.

Mary looked down like a guilty kid caught red-handed and gave a sheepish shrug.

The three women exchanged looks, then broke into laughter.

"This was the last of it," Lisa announced, pouring the soda down the sink with a flourish.

Josey wiped her hands on a paper towel and leaned against the counter. "What's next?"

Before anyone could answer, the screen door creaked open.

"Who's there?" Mary called out.

The air thickened, tension winding through the room like smoke. No reply.

"I said, who's there?" Mary asked again, her voice sharper now, laced with unease.

And then—footsteps. Heavy, deliberate, drawing closer.

All four women instinctively huddled in front of the sink, eyes fixed on the doorway as a foot, then a leg, came into view.

And then—Nathaniel.

A collective gasp broke the silence as he stepped fully into the kitchen.

He stood there for a moment before turning toward them, his grin wide and unhinged, his face twisted into something barely recognizable. And then he laughed—loud and maniacal—eyes locking on Lisa.

"Nathaniel, what's going on?" Mary asked, her voice mixed with concern and disbelief.

He didn't answer her. His focus never wavered from Lisa.

"I knew I'd find you here," he said, voice laced with venom. "Spinning your lies. Biding your time. Waiting to finish off Momma."

"That's not true," Mary cut in quickly, her voice shaking. "Nathaniel, you know that's not true."

Still, he stared at Lisa. Silent. Seething.

Lisa's heart thundered in her chest. She felt a chill crawl down her spine. Something about him was different. He still had that cold look of hate, but there was something...off. Unstable. Wrong.

She could feel Miriam trembling beside her. When they had huddled together, Miriam had ended up right beside Lisa, her body shuddering so hard Lisa could feel it with every breath.

Lisa tried to keep her voice as steady as possible. "I have never wanted or will ever want to kill Ma. I only came because she *wanted* me to. I don't have a reason to lie about that."

Nathaniel let out another eerie round of laughter. Just as it faded, he pulled a gun from behind his back and pointed it at Lisa.

"You sure about that?" he asked. His voice was flat, cold. Calculated. The smile never left his face.

Another gasp tore through the room—this time sharp, panicked.

Miriam clutched Lisa's arm and buried her face in her shoulder, sobbing uncontrollably.

She looks just like she did when we were little, Lisa thought. Broken. Terrified. Helpless. And just like before, the sight sparked something hot and fierce inside her. That same protective rage flared up now, dulling the edge of her fear.

"I sure am," she said, her voice hard.

Nathaniel's grin twitched. "You think you're so smart. Think you can fool everyone. How about you tell the truth about how you murdered my dad?"

"You don't want the truth," Lisa shot back. "You've already made up in your mind what you *think* happened."

Suddenly, a ringtone cut through the air like a blade. Everyone turned to look at Josey.

"It must be my mom. She calls me everyday to check on me." She stammered as she instinctively reached towards her back pocket.

"Don't you dare you fake green-eyed bitch!" Nathaniel shouted.

"These are my real eyes you creepy motherfucker!" Josey yelled, jerking her hand in the air. Fueled by pure adrenaline, the insult flew out before she could stop it.

Nathaniel growled and swung the gun toward her.

Josey squeezed her eyes shut and screamed.

"Nathaniel, no!" Mary cried, throwing her arms around Josey protectively.

Nathaniel laughed again—louder, wilder.

So that's what it is, Lisa thought. *He's enjoying himself. Our screams, frightened faces, tears—he's taking pleasure in all of this.*

As Lisa swallowed, the realization sank through her like an iron anchor, settling with crushing weight in the pit of her stomach. He was too far gone to reason with.

Lisa exhaled, steadying herself. There was only one thing she could think of that might get them out of this. She couldn't see any other options at this point. And even it was a long shot.

"Fine," she said, her tone cold. "You want to know what happened back then?"

Pleased at Lisa's question, he continued to grin as he turned the gun back on her, "Move over there." He nodded to the right where the back and side wall counter tops met. "I want the audience to get a good view of your performance."

"No!" Miriam cried in a helpless whisper, her sobs racking her body as Lisa tried to step away. But Miriam clung to her tighter.

Lisa's eyes met Mary's and Josey's—pleading.

Help me.

They understood immediately. Quietly, gently, they pulled Miriam over to them.

Lisa moved to the corner, her steps slow, deliberate.

Nathaniel laughed again—sharp like broken glass.

His eyes shined bright with excitement, but his voice was cold and hard. "Start talking."

Chapter Nineteen
WE HAVE TO DO THIS

It had rained earlier in the week, but now the sky was a bright canvas of blue, dotted with thick, puffy clouds. A warm spring breeze rustled the leaves overhead as Lisa and Miriam sat beneath the magnolia tree in Miriam's front yard—their favorite spot. It was where they always sat to eat snacks from the corner store and talk about their favorite TV shows.

"Did you see *The Cosby Show* last night?" Miriam asked excitedly, popping a green Now and Later into her mouth.

"Of course!" Lisa replied, crunching loudly on her Pringles.

"Theo and his friends went to prom. I can't wait until we get to go. I bet it's going to be so much fun," Miriam said dreamily.

Lisa held up her hand, fingers dusted with potato chip crumbs, and counted off. "We're in seventh grade, so we've got... one, two, three, four years before we can go."

Miriam let out a dramatic pout. "Four years is so long!"

"We're gonna be so old by then!" Lisa teased, exaggerating her voice.

"I know, right?"

"But those dresses their dates wore were so pretty. Especially the one with the pink top and green bottom. I wouldn't have thought to put those colors together, but it worked!"

"Mmm hmm" Miriam nodded energetically, still chewing.

"What colors would you wear?" Lisa asked.

Miriam smacked away on her candy. Her face tilted up to the sky as she thought. "Mmm. I think I'd wear blue. Just like the sky."

"That's a good choice." Lisa grinned. "We could wear matching blue dresses!"

Miriam scooted closer, her eyes bright as she waved her hand in the air like she was painting the sky. "I can see it now—us in beautiful matching blue dresses, fancy hairstyles, glittery nail polish, shiny jewelry and shoes!"

Lisa beamed. "Wow, we'd look so good!"

They both burst into laughter, their giggles echoing in the breeze.

But then came a sound—faint yelling from inside the house.

Lisa's smile faltered. "So... who would you want to go with to prom?"

Miriam smiled too, but there was something forced behind it. "I think AJ is really cute. It'd be nice to go with him." Her voice was softer now, hesitant.

The yelling inside grew louder—no longer distant, but sharp and clear.

Screams.

Their smiles vanished. Both girls froze, eyes locked on the screen door.

It was like their dreams had been sucked away, replaced by a rising dread.

Then came Mary's voice, shrill and desperate: "Miriam!"

They flinched. Miriam turned to Lisa, fear etched deep into her face. "You should go home."

"No," Lisa said, voice shaking. "Maybe if I stay... he'll stop."

Miriam grabbed Lisa's shoulders. Tears welled in her eyes. "Believe me—he won't. Please, just go. I don't want anything happening to you."

Lisa stood still, searching Miriam's face, silently asking if she truly wanted her to leave.

"Please," Miriam begged again. "If you stay... it'll probably make it worse."

That word—*worse*—hit Lisa like a punch. She didn't want to imagine what it meant.

She pulled Miriam into a hug, squeezing her as tight as she could. Then she pulled back, locking eyes with her best friend. "I'll see you at school tomorrow, right?"

Miriam gave a weak smile and nodded.

Another scream tore through the air.

Lisa grabbed her bike and took off. Her legs pumped as fast as they could, pedaling away as her heart pounded in her chest. Tears spilled down her cheeks, blurring her vision.

Please let them be okay, she prayed silently. *God, please protect them.*

The next morning, Lisa rushed to their usual meeting spot near the gym.

She spotted Miriam already waiting, dressed in a long-sleeve shirt and jeans. The weather was far too warm for that kind of outfit, and Lisa instantly knew why. As she got closer, her heart sank. A nasty bruise darkened Miriam's lower jawline.

Lisa's fists clenched. "Are you okay?"

Miriam gave a small nod, but her eyes said otherwise.

As they walked toward class, they felt the stares. Teachers. Staff. Other students. Some gave sympathetic looks. Others whispered openly as they passed, their glances lingering. Miriam kept her head down avoiding eye contact, while Lisa tried to stare holes into their souls.

Relief finally came when they reached their classroom door.

But just before they could step inside, a voice called out behind them. "Miriam, come here for a second."

They turned to see Mrs. Whitaker, one of the science teachers, motioning Miriam over with a smile.

Miriam hesitated, then slowly shuffled across the hallway. Her shoulders slumped, her face blank.

Mrs. Whitaker spoke a little too loudly. "I know life can be tough sometimes, sweetheart. But things will get better."

She pulled something from behind her back and pressed it into Miriam's hand. "Here's a little something to brighten your day."

Miriam looked down. It was a Hershey's chocolate bar. She didn't say a word, just turned and walked back to Lisa.

"What did she give you?" Lisa asked as they stepped inside the classroom.

Wordlessly, Miriam placed the bar in Lisa's hand.

Lisa stared at it, disgust curling her lip. "You don't even like chocolate."

The rest of the morning passed quietly. At lunch, they retreated to one of their secret spots—a bench near the library, just far enough away from the buzz of the cafeteria.

Lisa shook her head. "I don't get it. They know what's happening. Why doesn't anyone do anything?"

"I hate how they look at me," Miriam muttered. "Like I'm a stray dog that got hit by a car. They feel bad, but not enough to save it."

"I care," Lisa said softly.

Miriam gave a weak smile. "I know. It's just... if the grown-ups don't start caring soon, we're all going to die."

Her voice trembled as she tried to hold herself together. "Last night, I really thought he was going to kill us. He was hitting Momma so hard..." She choked back her tears. "Then he started hitting me. It hurt so bad. When Momma tried to protect me, he got even angrier. He just kept hitting her... and hitting her."

Her voice cracked as the memories overwhelmed her. Lisa reached over and pulled her into a hug, rubbing her shoulder gently.

"After a while," Miriam whispered through her sobs, "Momma stopped moving. I thought she was dead."

Lisa held her tighter, both of them sitting in silence while Miriam cried.

Eventually, her sobs faded into sniffles.

"There's gotta be someone who can help," Lisa whispered. "What about the police?"

Miriam wiped her eyes. "Whenever Momma calls them, they just talk to him until he calms down. Then they leave."

Lisa frowned. "What? So you're saying the cops are useless?"

"Basically."

Lisa's jaw tightened. "What about your relatives?"

Miriam shook her head. "Everyone's scared of him."

"I'll try talking to my dad," Lisa offered. "Maybe he can—"

"No." Miriam's voice was sharp with panic. "If your dad gets involved and it doesn't work... my dad might stop us from being friends."

They both shuddered at the thought.

Silence stretched between them as they searched for answers that didn't exist.

"I hate him so much," Miriam whispered through clenched teeth. "I wish *he* would die instead of us."

PEACE AMID THE CHAOS

As soon as the words left her mouth, they both froze—eyes meeting, a quiet understanding forming in the space between them.

Lisa leaned in, her voice barely a whisper. "If he *were* to die... how could it happen?"

Miriam sat up straighter, then leaned forward, hand over her mouth as she thought. Her eyes slowly widened. She stood and motioned for Lisa to follow.

They circled around the back of the library and out toward the fence behind the school. It was quiet there—secluded. On the other side of the fence stretched a marshy patch of woods.

Miriam lowered her voice. "My dad has a gun. He says it's to protect us from intruders. But *we're* the ones who need protecting from *him*."

She took a shaky breath. "I just have to sneak it out of its hiding place... and use it."

Lisa stared at her. "If you kill him, you'll go to jail. They won't care what he did. People always think parents can do whatever they want. It'll be easier if I do it."

Miriam gasped. "No way! I can't let you—"

"You're not *letting* me. I'm telling you." Lisa gripped Miriam's shoulders gently. "Think about it. If he attacks me, and I kill him, nobody will think we planned it. They'll think he's really gone off the deep end and tried to hurt someone else's kid."

Miriam hesitated, weighing the risk. "But how would I even let you know when it's happening? It's not like I can say, 'Hang on, let me call Lisa' while he's losing it."

"You said it takes him a few minutes to go fully crazy, right? He starts mumbling first?"

Miriam nodded. "Usually five to ten minutes before he... you know."

Lisa nodded back. "A couple Christmases ago, Devan got these expensive walkie-talkies that work over really long distances. He barely used them. We can use those."

Miriam blinked. "Really?"

"Yeah. As long as I already have the gun, I can get to your house fast."

"Are you sure about this? Do you even know how to *use* a gun?"

"What other choice do we have?" Lisa asked, her tone serious.

Miriam didn't have an answer for that.

Lisa gave her a grim smile. "My dad taught me. Every now and again, he takes me and Devan out to practice."

"Wow. I didn't know that."

"He says it's not something we should brag about."

Miriam took a deep breath and exhaled slowly.

"We just need to come up with a story. Something we both stick to. Then I get the walkie-talkies. You get the gun."

Miriam nodded slowly, as if steeling herself. "We can do this... We *have* to do this."

A few weeks later, school was out for the summer, and everything was almost in place. Lisa and Miriam had prepped every part of their plan—except for the most important piece: the gun. Miriam was waiting for a day when she could be sure both her parents would be gone, and that opportunity was supposed to come in just a few days.

It was a normal late morning. Lisa was in her room, curled up with a book—*Claudia and the Phantom Phone Calls*, one of her favorites from *The Baby-Sitters Club* series—when the walkie-talkie on her nightstand crackled to life.

She froze.

Then, slowly, she reached over and picked it up.

For a moment, there was only static. Then she heard it—Nathaniel Sr.'s voice, cold and sharp, like the bite of a knife.

Lisa's heart dropped.

No... no, no, no. This can't be happening. We're not ready. I don't have the gun yet!

Panic surged through her. She kicked off her blanket and scrambled for her sneakers, hopping on one foot as she yanked them on. Every second felt like an eternity.

She bolted from her room, careful not to make too much noise, her breath coming fast and shallow. Moving quickly but quietly, she slipped out the front door, jumped on her bike and took off.

She raced down familiar streets, past the white picket fence in front of Mrs. Blanchard's house. Normally, it was a peaceful detail, the kind you barely notice—today it felt like a landmark in a nightmare. The pedals spun beneath her feet, legs pumping like pistons as she willed her bike to go faster, faster, faster.

When she rounded the last corner into the yard, a sound tore through the air—raw, terrified screaming.

Lisa's heart stopped.

God, please... please don't let this be it.

She barely noticed when her bike tipped and crashed behind her. She was already running, feet pounding up the porch steps, chest heaving with shallow, frantic breaths. Even though the screen door's mesh distorted the view inside, she could feel it—danger, thick in the air, sharp and waiting.

Her hand reached for the handle. Her body locked up.

Muscles seized.

A breath stuck in her chest, frozen mid-inhale.

It was like her whole body had turned to stone—but her heart kept pounding.

Then came the sound that split the moment in two.

"What have you done to my child!"

Mary's voice—wild, broken, enraged.

Lisa flinched as though the scream had struck her physically.

She tried to breathe, to calm herself, but then—

His voice, low and venomous: "This is what I did, you dumb bitch."

Then the sound.

A sickening, solid crack.

Lisa had heard the pop of a baseball bat hitting a ball plenty of times. But this wasn't that. This wasn't play. This was final.

Her paralysis broke in an instant.

She ran.

Through the living room. Down the hall. Straight into the bedroom.

She dropped to her knees and scrambled beneath the bed. Her hand hit something metal. Cold. Heavy.

The gun.

Just like Miriam said it would be.

She yanked it free, the box scraping against the hardwood floor. Her hands were slick with sweat, but she didn't hesitate. The weight of the gun in her hands grounded her, but also terrified her.

She ran back, flying toward the kitchen.

The door swung open wildly as she shoved through, and for one sharp second the kitchen looked normal—sunlight pouring in, gleaming tiles, bright windows.

Then her eyes dropped.

Miriam.

Crumbled. Still. Too still.

Lisa's gaze lifted slowly. Past her friend's body.

To the scuffed boots.

To the monster towering above her.

Lisa hadn't seen him at first—she'd been so focused on Miriam. But now, standing just feet away, Nathaniel Sr. loomed, eyes blazing with rage, his lips twisted into a snarl.

Her heart stopped.

She froze, forgetting everything—why she was there, what she was supposed to do. Even the gun in her hand felt like it belonged to someone else. Her body acted on instinct, trying to call for help—but before she could draw in a breath to scream, his fist connected with her face.

The blow sent her flying backward into the kitchen cabinets.

Her body slammed hard against the wood. The gun flew from her grasp, clattering to the floor and sliding just beyond Nathaniel Sr.'s boots. He didn't notice. His fury had a singular focus: Lisa.

He stormed toward her, shouting words she couldn't hear over the piercing ring in her ears. Her entire face throbbed—burning, aching, like her skull might split in two. Her heart pounded behind her eyes, her vision smeared and unsteady. One eye was swelling shut.

She tried to move. Her body refused.

She whimpered, kicking weakly—feather-light strikes that barely touched him.

Then he dropped to his knees, one hand pressing down on her chest, pinning her like she was nothing.

"No, no, no!" she cried, voice cracking with terror as she squirmed beneath him.

He raised his hand again, preparing for another blow—no hesitation, no mercy. His eyes were empty.

She squeezed her eye shut.

Then—

CRACK.

A deafening sound split the room.

The weight lifted from her chest.

Something heavy collapsed beside her with a dull thud.

Lisa gasped, air rushing into her lungs in jagged bursts. Her whole body shook. Slowly, she turned her head toward the sound, dreading what she'd see.

Nathaniel Sr. lay motionless on the floor.

Blood pooled beneath his head, dark and spreading.

Chapter Twenty

A Way Out

The silence smothered the room as Lisa's final words echoed like gunfire.

Nathaniel's eyebrows pulled together, his whole face contorting as if trying to solve a problem too tangled to make sense. His twisted, unnatural grin remained frozen on his lips—twitching at the corners like it no longer belonged there. Slowly, he shook his head.

"Nah. Nah, that's not right," he muttered, voice breaking under the weight of disbelief, hurt, and confusion. "*You* killed him." His voice rose, shrill and shaky. "Even now..." He lifted the gun slightly, its glint catching the light. "You still refuse to tell the truth."

Lisa didn't flinch. Her eyes stayed steady, voice calm. "There is no other story I can tell. This is the truth."

Nathaniel began to sway. The anger returned—hot, ragged, and wild. His chest rose and fell in sharp bursts. The cold edge in his stare gave way to fire as he exploded.

"TELL THE FUCKING TRUTH!"

A voice cracked through the room like thunder.

"She's tellin' you the FUCKING TRUTH!"

All eyes turned toward Mary. She stood tall, only a few feet in front of Josey and Miriam, her arms out slightly as if shielding them both. Her stance was rigid, her presence immovable. Her eyes locked onto Nathaniel's, daring him to challenge what she was about to say.

Her voice softened, laced with memory. "When I first met ya daddy, he was the most fun-lovin', kind-hearted man I'd ever come across. We met at a backyard cookout—music playin', people laughin'... and there he was, watchin' me like I was the only person in the world. Every time our eyes met, he'd smile. Lord, it was a smile full of warmth. He finally came over and struck up a conversation, nervous but sweet. By the end of the night, he'd asked me out."

Her lips lifted slightly at the memory, the warmth real but fragile. "We had fun. So much fun. Talkin' for hours, goin' out, spendin' time with friends. He'd help anybody with anythin'—wouldn't even hesitate. That's the man I fell in love with. And when he said he was gonna enlist, I was proud of him. He wanted to serve, to do right."

Mary's voice thickened with emotion. "He had a cousin, Albert—more like a brother, really. Their mamas were sisters, their daddies were brothers, made 'em double cousins. They were thick as thieves. When your daddy said he was signin' up, he talked Albert into it too."

She paused, her hands clasping in front of her. "A couple weeks fore he left, he asked me to marry him. Said he needed somethin' good to come back to. Who could say no to somethin' like that? So, of course I said yes."

The glow in her expression faded as shadows clouded her features.

"But war... war changes people. When he came back, he wasn't the man I said yes to. I don't know everythin' that happened over there—he never really talked about it—but I *do* know he lost almost his entire platoon. And he lost Albert. That tore somethin' inside of him clean in two."

She stared past Nathaniel, as if seeing something far away. "He came home and barely spoke. I figured he was mournin', tryin' to make sense of what he'd seen. Maybe even blamin' himself. I tried to give him space. I thought time and love would help."

Mary's voice cracked, barely above a whisper now. "But then he started seein' things that weren't there. One day, I'd just come back from makin' groceries. I asked him to help bring in the bags. He took a few, but then he froze when a car passin' by backfired. Next thing I knew, he was yellin', 'Get down! The bomb's gonna blow!' Threw the groceries in the air and dove to the ground. I had to kneel beside him, hold his face in my hands and whisper, 'You're home. You're safe. There's no bomb here.' Took minutes for it to sink in."

Her jaw clenched. "Then he started accusin' me of sayin' things I hadn't said. Doin' things I hadn't done. Little things would set him off. If his toothbrush was on the wrong side of the sink, it'd be a fight. And then one day... one day, it wasn't words anymore."

Her hands trembled at her sides, but she didn't look away. "He hit me. Just once at first. Then again. And again."

She shuddered, her shoulders tightening as the memories played out behind her eyes. "I didn't know what else to do, so I got down on my knees and prayed—with all my might—day and night. I asked God to fix it, to fix *him*. But the beatins, the yellin', the screamin'... it all got worse. It went from happenin' every blue moon, to sometimes, to all the damn time. Before I knew it, *peace* was the exception, not the rule. It was like the devil had taken him over."

Her voice cracked as she bit her bottom lip, trying to steady herself. "I know what y'all must be thinkin'. 'Why didn't you leave?' Lord knows I've asked myself that same question a million times. But the truth is—I didn't think I *could*. I didn't understand back then that I had a right to leave. But the problem was the world had already made that choice for me. I was raised to believe that a woman stays with her man no matter what. And at first, that's what I tried to do."

Her tone sharpened, rising with a quiet fury. "But when I finally couldn't take it no mo, I went to the only place I thought might help—my family."

She inhaled shakily, her voice now bitter and tight. "I planned it all out. Packed my purse with just the basics so he wouldn't suspect nothin'. Told him my momma said she hadn't seen me in a while, and I was going to visit. He nodded, said okay. I coulda cried from relief right then. I thought—*finally*, this nightmare might be over."

She looked down briefly, shaking her head. "But the second I stepped into my momma's house, I broke. Tears just started fallin' like rain. I told her everythin'. *Everythin'*. I was shakin', sobbin', beggin' for help."

Her gaze turned hard, her jaw tight. "But instead of help... all I saw in her eyes was disappointment. She asked if I was sure I was doin' everything I was supposed to do as a wife. Told me to go back home and pray harder. Said maybe I wasn't submissive enough. Quoted Bible verses about wifely obedience like they were shackles."

She let out a bitter laugh that held no humor. "She made it sound like *I* was the problem. Like I deserved it. Like if I left, I'd be headed straight to hell."

Mary's voice dropped to a near whisper, raw with betrayal. "She patted me on the back... and sent me right back to him. Just like that."

She paused, swallowing hard. "My own momma—the woman who gave me life—didn't care that it was bein' slowly, painfully taken away. If your own momma won't fight for you... who will?"

Her bitterness gave way to quiet sorrow. "Still... I wasn't ready to give up. Somethin' in me kept whisperin' that *somebody* had to care. So the next time he hit me, I called the police."

She let the memory hang in the air a moment.

"They made him calm down. Told him to cool off. That's all they did. Then they left. And the second that door shut... he picked up right where he left off. Like nothin' had happened."

Her voice fell to a hush, drained and hollow. "That's when I knew. No one was comin' to save me. Not my family. Not the police. Not even God. I was in a prison I couldn't escape. Trapped. Sentenced to life for a crime I didn't commit."

She went still for a moment, her breath locked beneath the weight of it all—until she found the strength to continue.

"Then I had Miriam. And you." She looked at Nathaniel, her voice lifting with fragile hope. "My two beautiful lights in all that darkness. For the first time in so long, I felt... alive again. Like maybe God hadn't forgotten about me after all."

Her eyes shimmered, but her smile was soft. "Y'all gave me somethin' I hadn't felt in years—joy. Real joy. The kind that makes you believe in tomorrow. I thought maybe, just maybe, seein' y'all... feelin' your love... would open your daddy's heart. Even if just a little."

Her voice turned harsh, like stone cracking under pressure. "But the devil had different plans. It was like Lucifer took the love your daddy had for y'all and twisted it into somethin' vile. I did everythin' I could to protect you. Kept the house clean, meals cooked, made sure every little thing was just right. Every day before he got home from work, I'd run myself ragged straightenin' this and fixin' that, hopin'—prayin'—that maybe today he wouldn't get set off."

She shook her head slowly. "But none of it mattered. Nothin' ever did. It was like he fed off our fear. I'll never forget the first time he turned his rage on y'all. The way he looked at you... it wasn't right. His eyes lit up like a little boy with two new toys."

Her voice cracked as her tears finally fell. "All because he couldn't find that damn newspaper. Convinced himself one of y'all took it. He backed you into a corner in the livin' room, demandin' someone confess. And all y'all could do was stare up at him—wide-eyed and scared outta your minds. You were just babies. Helpless. I tried to shield you, but..."

She couldn't finish. Her voice faltered, the memory too painful to speak aloud.

After a moment, she inhaled sharply, rage creeping back in. "When it was over, he came to me *laughin'*. Laughin', like he'd just found somethin' funny. Said he'd left the newspaper on the porch the whole time. Didn't even glance at y'all. Didn't see the bruises. Didn't see your lil' bodies shakin' next to me."

She blinked slowly, her voice low and haunted. "That's when I realized—your daddy didn't come back from the war. *The devil* came back in his place. There's no other explanation. No man with a heart—*no human being*—could treat their own children that way."

She looked away, ashamed. "And the worst part? I was the one who let him back in. I opened the door. I invited the devil into our home. I spent every day tryin' to figure out how we could escape, how to give y'all the life you deserved. But the world had already condemned us to hell."

Her voice dropped to a whisper. "Until the day everything changed."

She lifted her chin, the weight of what was coming already tightening her chest.

"I was tired. So damn tired. His anger, his fists, the way he sucked the life outta us bit by bit. But when he hit Miriam so hard..." Her voice trembled with fury. "Somethin' inside me broke. I screamed at him. I *dared* to scream. And like I should've known, he turned on me. I didn't even have time to brace myself. His fist connected with my jaw—and then came the darkness."

She paused, breathing uneven. "I guess I wasn't out for too long, 'cause I could hear his ragged breathing when I came to. I didn't move. I stayed still, like I always did. Hopin' he'd think I was out cold so maybe I'd get a break. Sometimes that worked. Sometimes he'd just keep hittin' anyway. But that day... he stood still."

Her voice dropped to a whisper. "Then I heard the kitchen door open. And a little gasp."

Tears filled her eyes again. "I didn't need to look. I knew it was Lisa. My heart stopped. I didn't know she was in the house. I screamed inside for her to *run*, to get away. But I knew—he wouldn't let her."

Her body trembled, fists clenched. "And then I heard it. His fist. Her cry. The sound of her body hittin' the cabinets. That's when I opened my eyes."

Her gaze went distant, as if watching the scene all over again. "Somethin' slid across the floor. Right past him. Right to my feet. And there it was. Our way out."

Her voice softened, filled with wonder and realization. "I don't know how Lisa came to have it. Or why I hadn't thought of it before. But the moment I saw it, I knew. God hadn't forgotten us. He'd opened a door. *He'd given me a choice.* I just had to take it."

She looked up slowly, her eyes blazing with conviction.

"I sat up. Watched him stalk toward Lisa like a wild animal. The devil had already taken my husband, our marriage, our happiness. But now he wanted more. He wanted *everythin'*. But I had nothin' left to give. *I was done.*"

Her voice rose, fierce and clear.

"I made a decision—right then and there. If it had to be one of us, it was gonna be *him*. I wasn't gonna let that monster kill a child. Not while I still had breath in my body."

She straightened her spine, her voice now steady as steel.

"I got up. Took the gun in my hands. He was kneelin' over her, fist raised. And I fired."

Chapter Twenty-One
What Have You Done

Nathaniel's wild, frenzied grin had vanished. His jaw slack, his eyes wide and unfocused, he stared into nothing. The gun dangled uselessly from his hand, forgotten, his arms limp at his sides like a marionette with its strings cut. He blinked rapidly, as if trying to wake from a dream—or a nightmare.

Beside Miriam, Josey stood frozen. Her hands were pressed tightly over her mouth, and her eyes, round and glistening, stayed locked on Mary. She didn't speak, couldn't speak. Her breath ragged with each inhale.

Miriam felt like she was being pulled under water. Waves of shock, sorrow, and disbelief crashed through her. She looked back and forth between Lisa and her mother, trying to anchor herself, but the room kept spinning.

She had spent her whole life seeing her mother as a two sided coin – weak and helpless when her father was alive, strong and resilient after his death. The two sides never existing together. But now... now she saw the truth. Her mother hadn't just been one or the other. She was fragile, powerful, tough and powerless all at the same time. And all of those combined is what made her strong all along. Stronger than any of them knew.

Miriam's throat tightened as she stepped forward and gently placed a hand on her mother's shoulder. Her voice trembled but came out steady.

"Momma... I didn't know. I didn't know you went through all of that. I'm so sorry you had to. I'm glad you told us. I'm glad we finally know the truth."

Mary didn't turn around fully. She simply reached up, patted Miriam's hand, and gave a soft, silent nod.

Miriam let her hand fall away. She turned slowly toward Lisa, her chest rising and falling with uneven breaths. Her voice was barely above a whisper, as if the truth might shatter if spoken too loud.

"All this time... I thought our plan had worked. That you'd pulled the trigger. You never told me he almost *killed* you. That momma had done it. Why didn't you tell me?"

She already knew the answer—or part of it. Deep down, she'd known for years but hadn't let herself face it. Because facing it meant acknowledging just how much Lisa had sacrificed. How much she'd endured. And how much Miriam had taken for granted.

Lisa had been her peace amid the chaos. Her anchor. And still, Miriam had turned away. She'd treated her like a temporary fixture—disposable. All while Lisa had carried this burden silently, almost lost her life. On top of that, she neglected Lisa when she had needed her the most.

Tears streamed down Lisa's face. Her voice came out low and raw. "After I saw your dad on the floor, I looked over and saw Ma standing there... and she just collapsed. Her face was covered in tears, and she looked so small. So tired. I ran over, asking if she was okay, and when she tried to speak... she couldn't. Her jaw was broken."

Lisa wiped her cheek but the tears kept coming.

"I called the police. We sat there, quiet, waiting for them to come. When they got there, I told them I was the one who shot him. Women were in the same boat as children back then. If you're caught killing your abuser, you get punished. There's no way I could let Ma go to prison. After everything he did to her... to y'all... I couldn't let that happen."

Lisa's gaze dropped for a moment, then slowly lifted to meet Miriam's again.

"I didn't tell you because you were already dealing with a lot. All you would have done was worry. You didn't need me adding anything else to your plate."

Miriam couldn't hold back the sob that rose in her throat. Her heart cracked wide open.

She saw it clearly now—how Lisa had carried the weight alone, quietly suffering while holding everything together. While Miriam had run.

"I'm sorry," she whispered. Her voice broke as the tears came harder. "I'm so sorry."

She stepped forward, arms reaching out, but before she could reach Lisa—

"Don't!"

The word cracked through the room like lightning.

Nathaniel's voice was wild and filled with rage. He had the gun pointed at Lisa again, his hands trembling, but his aim steady. His face—twisted with hatred and confusion as a storm raged inside him.

His breath came in harsh bursts as he tried to make sense of what he'd just heard.

His mother.

A killer?

It couldn't be true.

His thoughts spun into chaos, crashing into one another like waves during a hurricane. Nothing made sense. His dad couldn't have been that bad—he couldn't. His mom would never do something like that. Would she?

But every time he tried to reach for a good memory, something warm to anchor him—his mind went blank. No smiling father tossing him in the air, no proud hand on his shoulder. Just fragments. Just silence. And then—

The memories hit him one after the other.

Miriam's frightened little face as their father closed in on her. Their mother moving frantically, nervously, tidying things that didn't need tidying. Him and Miriam huddled in the corner in fear.

And finally.

His father's face. Twisted in an evil grin, looking down. Pointing and laughing at *him*.

He staggered backward a step.

If this was real—if all of it was true—then everything he went through, the teasing, the fights, the loneliness, the pain and suffering, was all his own doing. His life had been built on a lie, and now it was crumbling. He really was the *dummy*, the *fool*.

No.

He clenched his jaw. Before the guilt could settle in his chest, something dark, defiant, pushed back.

"This is all lies!" he screamed, the gun unwavering as he aimed it directly at Lisa.

Mary stepped forward, her voice sharp, fierce, and full of fire.

"You want to blame someone so bad for what happened?" she snapped. "Then blame me."

Nathaniel's eyes flicked to her, startled by the force of her words.

"Instead of leavin' your daddy, I stayed and let fear reign over me. Like a fool, I stayed and not only let him beat me day in and day out, but my own precious babies too. And if that wasn't enough," Mary's arm shot out, trembling as she pointed at Lisa, her voice breaking. "I let this poor innocent baby get hurt and TAKE the fall for me!

Ooh, but I don't stop there. when it was over, when I should've told you the truth—I let you build up this fantasy of your daddy. A dream so big, so blinding, you can't see the truth even when it's staring you in the face.

But see, I'm tired of not fightin' back, I'm tired of hidin', I'm tired of making mistakes and not ownin' up to 'em. You lookin' to pass judgment on somebody?" She pounded her chest with her fist, once, twice, three times—her voice rising with each word. "Here I am!"

The room was silent except for Mary's ragged breathing. Nathaniel stood frozen, the gun slightly lowered, still pointed at Lisa—but his hands were shaking now.

His mother's words had sliced through the darkness, splitting him open. His thoughts raced. Could this really be true?

Could his mother really have done those things and still be the woman he remembered tucking him in at night? The woman who cooked his favorite meals? Who kissed his forehead and prayed over him?

He knew those memories were real.

But to believe that meant accepting everything else—that she was a lying, ruthless conniving, murderer—that deserved to die.

His grip on the gun faltered as he grit his teeth. His mind couldn't make the two conflicting images coexist. It was too painful to think of pointing the gun at his own mother, and pulling the trigger.

His gaze drifted to Lisa—and in his mind, the darkness roared back like a tide. His thoughts twisted, reshaping into something easier. Something familiar.

Blame.

"It's all your fault!" he shouted, his voice breaking as the rage overtook him. His eyes burned with fury. "Look at what you've done!"

He raised the gun, finger trembling on the trigger.

Victoria Rose

Nathaniel's last words echoed in Lisa's mind as the world around her shifted—and suddenly, she knew.

She was back in the dream.

But this time, she was fully herself—an adult, conscious, aware. She wasn't caught in the chaos of it; she was an observer now, standing in the center of a scene that had haunted her for years.

She turned and walked toward the child version of herself, whose face was twisted with rage, hatred carved into every inch of her young features. Lisa watched, enthralled, as the girl screamed, "What have you done!"

She followed the scream, her gaze moving to the figure on the receiving end. Her heart stopped.

It was her. Another young version of herself—smaller, softer, confused. Innocent. Unaware of what was happening.

In that moment, the dream's meaning clicked into place with perfect clarity.

She wasn't angry at someone else. She had been angry at *herself* all along—because she hadn't protected everyone like she was supposed to. She had nearly gotten them all killed.

It finally made sense.

Subconsciously, she had believed she didn't deserve to be surrounded by people who loved her. Friends. Family. Support. Because she was a failure. She had kept everyone at arm's length, not out of pride—but out of guilt. And she hadn't wanted anyone to rely on her, because deep down, she believed that when it really mattered... she'd just screw it up again.

A wave of emotion washed over her—grief, yes, but also relief. Sadness that even now, in this very moment, she still felt like she was falling short. But relief that she finally understood the dream. Her body had spoken to her, just like Sean had said it would.

The image shifted. The younger Lisa with the gun faded, replaced by Nathaniel—raising the weapon toward her, but moving impossibly slow.

Everything around her was in slow motion.

She saw Josey in the corner, crouched behind Mary and Miriam, sobbing, her hands still covering her mouth. Lisa's chest tightened. She had never meant for her to get caught in this. Josey was just an innocent bystander. If Lisa had known it would come to this, she never would've brought her. Now all she could do was pray Nathaniel wouldn't hurt anyone else.

Then she saw Mary—mouth open, hand stretched toward her son in a desperate plea. Pain pierced through Lisa's heart. Mary had already gone through so much. She was the one who saved them all that day, and now—after everything—she was trying to save her again.

Lisa froze, breath faltering as her gaze landed on Miriam.

Miriam's eyes were locked on her, fierce and determined. Her body had fallen into a running stance, every muscle coiled with purpose. Her lips pressed into a firm line, her expression laser-focused—like a runner in a race, determined to win first place.

Then, something extraordinary happened.

Lisa heard Miriam's voice—not aloud, but clearly, undeniably. Like a response whispered through time and memory. It was as if she were answering Lisa's poem... even though she had never shared it.

At first, I didn't show up
I ended up making you last
But now I'm giving you the leading role
And assigned myself to supporting cast

From now on, I'm going to show up every day
My focus only on you
I diligently learned my lines
No need to tell me what to do

I understand now, how to perform
I come into the scenes right on cue
Nail every detail flawlessly
I give a strong performance for you

The importance of my role
I've finally grasped
Never again will you have to be
Your own supporting cast

Warmth spread through Lisa like sunlight breaking through storm clouds.

That look in Miriam's eyes—pure, unflinching—told her everything.

They had never stopped being best friends.

Despite the pain. Despite the distance. Despite everything.

Lisa wished she had more time. Wished she could apologize for telling Miriam she wasn't a good psychologist. Wished she could take back the moments where her hurt had bled onto the people she loved.

Damn, she thought, *this must be how Neo felt in The Matrix.*

A small smile tugged at the corner of her lips.

That's the weirdest shit you can think of before dying.

And for the second time, the kitchen filled with the deafening sound of a gunshot.

Chapter Twenty-Two

I Won't Go Back

As the gunshot rang out, a searing pain tore through Nathaniel's outstretched arm.

He screamed, the gun slipping from his grasp and clattering to the floor. Staggering, he looked down at his bloodied arm, stunned. His wide eyes blinked in confusion. *How could he be the one shot when he was the one holding the gun?*

Before he could process it, a powerful force slammed into him, knocking him sideways. He crashed onto the cold kitchen floor with a howl, pain radiating from his wounded arm.

He heard the muffled sound of feet as he gasped for air, his vision going in and out of focus. He tried to sit up, but the force shoved him back down again. He heard a grunt as he was violently flipped onto his stomach, something heavy pinning him in place.

Panicked, he pressed his good hand to the ground, trying to push up, to fight back, to breathe.

But it was no use.

A strong hand grabbed his wrist and twisted his good arm behind his back. He squirmed back and forth, trying everything in his power to break free. His face twisting in agony, he shrieked as a jolt of pain surged through his wounded arm as it was harshly placed behind his back.

Cold metal snapped around his wrists—click. The sound echoed through the kitchen like a final sentence.

The weight on his back shifted as he was quickly pulled to his feet and spun around.

The sudden movement sent blood rushing to his head, blurring his vision.

A tight grip pulled him in close. His skin crawled as he felt puffs of hot forceful breaths against his face as the sound of uneven breathing filled his ears.

He trembled, blinking and squinting as he struggled to bring his eyes into focus.

As his vision cleared, a face emerged before him. Lips curled tight, nostrils flared, eyebrows knitted together—a murderous pair of angry eyes glared back at him.

He gasped, instinctively stepping backward, desperate to create distance between them.

Before he could plant his foot backwards, Devan yanked him forward with a growl, his eyes fierce and unflinching.

Nathaniel whimpered. His shoulders sagged. His eyes dropped to the floor.

In the silence that followed, only the sound of weeping filled the room.

Devan scanned the kitchen. Josey and Mary clung to each other in the corner. Miriam held Lisa protectively in her arms. His chest loosened slightly—everyone looked shaken, but safe.

He turned back to Nathaniel. No one moved. The air was thick with shock.

Then—faintly—the sound of car engines outside. Doors slamming. More footsteps.

Without looking away, Devan shouted, "All clear!"

Moments later, officers rushed in. Two came straight to Devan as he handed Nathaniel over and gave a quick rundown. The other officers spread out, checking on the others.

As soon as the handoff was done, Devan turned to Lisa.

She let out a small cry as she collapsed into her brother's embrace. He held her tightly rocking her back and forth. Her breath skipping between sobs.

"It's ok," he whispered, tears falling freely down his own face. "I got you."

After a long moment, he looked up and saw Josey, Miriam and Mary huddled together. Still trembling, still crying.

He silently held his hand out, beckoning them over.

Lisa shifted, making room as they joined the embrace. All five of them swayed together, enveloped in a collective sense of warmth, love, safety, and peace.

After a while, Lisa looked up at Devan, her brow lifted in tired wonder.

He met her gaze and gently wiped away a tear.

"How did you know what was going on?" she asked softly.

A faint smile pulled at his lips. "My deep thought method."

Lisa let out an exhausted chuckle.

Victoria Rose

Earlier...

Devan and Miriam stepped out into the hallway, the door to Room 98 clicking shut behind them.

Over the weekend, a couple had reported witnessing a disturbing altercation in the hospital parking lot. A man and woman had been arguing. Then, without warning, the man grabbed the woman forcefully by the shoulders. He only let go when he noticed the couple watching. They made sure he entered the hospital—and noted he'd walked down this very hallway.

From the description they gave, Devan had a strong suspicion about who the man might've been—especially since Nathaniel hadn't shown up today, not even for Mary's release. The thought sat heavy in his chest, stirring a growing sense of unease.

As they walked in step, Devan glanced sideways. "I was wondering... have you seen your brother today? Heard from him at all?"

At the mention of Nathaniel, Miriam flinched. Her eyes darted away as she shook her head.

That was all Devan needed to see.

"Did something happen between you two over the weekend?"

Miriam's eyes snapped back to his, wide with surprise. "How... how did you know?"

"Couple said they saw something in the parking lot. The way they described it... I thought it might've been you and Nathaniel."

"Oh." Her voice was small now.

"You want to tell me what happened?" Devan asked gently.

Her expression grew distant. Her voice flattened as she spoke.

"Saturday. I was leaving the hospital when Nathaniel stopped me in the lot. He had just seen Lisa and Dr. Crane together. He was furious—ranting that Lisa was cozying up to Dr. Crane so she could... so she could *murder* Momma." Her voice spiked with emotion. "I told him he was being paranoid. That Lisa would *never* hurt Momma. That she and Dr. Crane liked each other and that was all."

Her tone dropped to a whisper as they turned the corner into the hospital lobby.

"That only made him angrier. He started going on about how I was never there for him, how I always took Lisa's side. The whole thing escalated."

She stopped walking. Her hands trembled slightly as she spoke.

"Then he got up in my face... and grabbed me hard by the shoulders." Her voice shook. "He said he'd rather drag *both* of them to hell before letting Lisa be happy."

Devan's jaw clenched. His shoulders tensed as Miriam's words echoed between them, the unease he'd felt earlier now spreading through him like wildfire.

Outside, they stepped through the automatic doors, pausing at the edge of the parking lot. Miriam lingered, staring ahead.

She hesitated for a moment, as if contemplating whether or not to say more. Then her furrowed brow smoothed, her chin lifted slightly, and her eyes narrowed with resolve. Her voice was still barely above a whisper, but this time it was steady.

"He scared me, Devan. The look on his face, the tone of his voice... it was like he was our father. And I think he meant what he said—about dragging Lisa to hell."

Devan's fingers curled into fists, tendons taut beneath his skin as his eyes burned with a protective fire, sharp and unwavering.

"Don't worry. I'd never let that happen. Do you know where he might be?"

Miriam paused, thinking.

"He might be at work. He's been on a construction site in Baton Rouge—with Harrison Construction Company. They're based here in town."

"Got it. I know the company," Devan said with a short nod. "I'll check it out. Thanks."

As he looked at Miriam, still shaken, his heart ached. He hated seeing that kind of fear on her face—especially caused by someone who was supposed to protect her. He couldn't fathom Lisa ever being afraid of him, and the thought of Nathaniel becoming more and more like their father filled him with silent fury. How could he not see what he was doing to them? To their mother? Hadn't they endured enough already? Or maybe that was the problem—maybe Nathaniel didn't think about the damage he caused at all.

Devan's voice softened, the weight of emotion settling behind it. "You know I've always seen you as my little sister, right? I care about you. I want you safe and happy. You don't have to deal with Nathaniel alone. If anything like that ever happens again—you call me."

Miriam's mouth fell open slightly, her eyes widening before crinkling at the corners as a smile spread across her face. They'd never said it out loud before, but it was true—Devan was like a big brother to her. And hearing him say it meant more than she expected.

"Thanks," she said. "I appreciate it... big bro."

Devan grinned and pulled her into a hug, wrapping her up tight. "And that goes for anything. I know things between you and Lisa have been rough since high school, but I believe in y'all. I think you can work it out."

"I'll try my best," she said, her voice tinged with quiet determination.

"That's all you've gotta do." He gave her one last squeeze before stepping back. "We don't want your mom coming out and the car's not ready. Go ahead—I'll watch while you head to the parking lot and pull it around."

Once Mary was settled in the car, Devan watched everyone leave.

Then he immediately turned and strode to his squad car. Miriam's words still echoed in his ears. The uneasiness he'd been carrying had sharpened into a clear sense of urgency the moment she told him what Nathaniel had said about Lisa. But he kept calm—he didn't want to worry Miriam or the others. Especially without proof.

There was a chance he was wrong, that Nathaniel simply hadn't been able to get off work. In fact, he hoped he was wrong. But something deep down inside said otherwise.

Nathaniel's apartment was on the way to Harrison Construction, so he made that his first stop. When he pulled into the complex, there was no sign of Nathaniel's car. He didn't bother getting out to knock. Instead, he threw the car in reverse. He hadn't expected him to be there—but still, a jittery current hummed through him like static just beneath the skin.

He took one last glance around before pulling away.

Several minutes later, he arrived at Harrison Construction. The static hadn't gone away—instead, it had intensified. As he stepped out of the car, he shook his arms and legs one at a time, as though trying to physically rid himself of the building tension.

PEACE AMID THE CHAOS

Cool air hit his skin as he stepped into the lobby.

The receptionist smiled brightly. "Hello! What can I help you with today?"

Devan's face remained impassive. His tone was flat. "I need to speak to one of your employees. It's urgent."

The receptionist's expression shifted as she straightened in her seat. "Oh, okay. What's the name?"

"Nathaniel Butler."

Her hands froze above the keyboard. She gasped and looked up, her face tightening with concern. "He was terminated today—for starting a fight with another employee."

The words hit like a surge of electricity—short-circuiting the static and replacing it with a roaring current.

Devan didn't say a word. He turned on his heel and bolted outside, cold sweat breaking across his skin. His pulse pounded in his ears as he raced to his squad car.

His breaths came in ragged gulps. He gripped the steering wheel as panic tried to overtake him, reminding him of how helpless, powerless he was the last time Lisa was in trouble. How her frightened, tear-stained face, black eye and bruises, looked up at him—and there was nothing he could do to stop her pain.

But before it could swallow him up, his father's voice echoed in his memory:

"Take real good care of your sister, ya hear?"

His father's words cut through the chaos like a lightning rod, grounding him. The fear and adrenaline were still there, but they were reshaped—honed into focus.

He wiped the sweat from his face and steadied his breathing.

First, he needed to check Mary's house.

If Nathaniel was already there, Lisa couldn't risk answering a call. But Devan knew how to get around that. He pulled out his phone and called Josey. Nathaniel wouldn't suspect a call from someone local—and Josey would never miss his call unless something was wrong.

The phone rang. Then rang again. And went to voicemail.

His stomach dropped.

He started the car, turned on the lights, and sped off toward Mary's. He kept the sirens off. Just in case.

Over the radio, he called for backup. "Approach quietly. No lights, no sirens," he instructed. "Cut everything before turning onto the street."

He did the same—killing his lights just before turning onto Mary's block. He parked a few houses down and stepped out silently, crouching low as he ran down the sidewalk, gun drawn.

The neighborhood was quiet. No one outside. Good.

He crossed Mary's yard quickly and crept up the porch. Voices drifted from inside—coming from the right of the front door. The kitchen, if he remembered correctly.

Step by step, he climbed the porch.

As his hand reached for the screen door, Nathaniel's voice boomed: "Don't!"

In that instant, Devan moved—opening the screen and slipping into the living room. But he didn't have time to shut it behind him.

Silence followed.

His heart thudded as he debated rushing in or staying hidden.

Nathaniel made the decision for him.

"This is all lies!" he screamed.

Devan shut the screen door softly, Nathaniel's voice still echoing through the house.

He pressed against the wall and crept forward, covering the short distance to the kitchen. Peeking through the doorway, he froze—Nathaniel stood directly in his line of sight.

Devan raised his gun, steady and ready.

Mary started to speak, but Nathaniel was too focused to notice Devan's approach.

Her words were shocking. But they barely registered.

Devan's entire focus was on Nathaniel.

He saw the hesitation flicker in Nathaniel's face. Maybe the weight of his mother's words were finally sinking in. Maybe he was backing down.

But then something in him snapped—and the rage returned. His eyes locked on Lisa.

The moment Nathaniel raised the gun, Devan didn't think.

He pulled the trigger.

Victoria Rose

Lisa, Miriam, Josey, and Mary listened in silence, hanging on Devan's every word as he finished recounting what had happened from his side.

"I'm really, really glad you're my big brother," Lisa said softly, tightening her arms around him.

"Me too," he murmured, hugging her back just as tightly.

Josey reached into her back pocket and pulled out her phone. Everyone leaned in as she checked her missed calls—not because they doubted him, but because the whole ordeal felt unreal now that it was over. Seeing Devan's name in her call log was a confirmation, something tangible. Proof that they had survived something terrifying—and that it hadn't just been a bad dream.

As his name popped up on the screen, they all let out a collective breath. Quiet nods followed, a shared moment of relief and recognition.

Mary looked up at Devan, her voice calm, thoughtful. "Thank you, *babae*. For holdin' back on Nathaniel—even though he gave you every reason not to."

Devan nodded, saying nothing.

"You already done so much for me," she continued. "And I'm truly grateful. But I need to ask one more ting from you."

"What's that?" His eyebrows lifted slightly.

Mary straightened. "I want to go on record sayin' I shot and killed my husband."

Miriam and Lisa gasped at the same time.

Lisa gently grabbed Mary's hand. "Ma... you don't have to do that."

"I agree," Miriam added, her voice quiet but firm.

"Yes, I do." Mary's tone didn't waver.

Lisa shook her head. "But everything's fine now. It's over."

"No, babae. Everythin's not fine—not inside a me."

Mary's tired eyes moved between Miriam and Lisa. Her voice was soft, but filled with unwavering resolve.

"I'm tired of livin' this lie. Tired of carryin' this weight. I want to move on, but I can't."

Her eyes swept across the kitchen before settling back on their faces.

"Not with this holdin' me back. I've been chained here, to this place, for so long without realizin' it. Today, I finally tasted what real freedom was when I told y'all the truth. And now that I have, I won't go back."

Lisa and Miriam exchanged a long glance, then slowly nodded in resignation.

Mary gave each of their hands a gentle squeeze before letting go. Then she turned to Devan.

He held her gaze for a moment, then nodded silently.

Without another word, he turned around to find an officer to take Mary's statement.

Mary stood still, her hands resting at her sides, eyes closed.

In her mind, she saw an open field filled with purple and yellow flowers.

She raised her hand to block the bright sunlight as a warm breeze touched her skin.

After a moment, she noticed something in her other hand.

It was a chain—heavy at first, but then it began to break apart and fall away.

For the first time in a long while, she felt free.

Chapter Twenty-Three
Why Not Start Here

Miriam had slept longer than expected—and for once, she welcomed the rest. The last three days had been brutal. Nothing about them felt real, and yet, every moment had reshaped her in ways she couldn't quite explain. Somehow, in the midst of all the chaos, she felt closer to her true self than ever before.

As she got dressed, her thoughts drifted to what she hoped to accomplish today. She'd decided to start something new—a "just do" list. Not a wish list or a maybe list. Just the things that mattered. Necessary things. Hard things. And after everything that happened yesterday, today's list almost felt easy by comparison.

She took a deep breath before stepping into the living room to tackle her first task.

Mary was already there, sitting on the couch and looking up at her expectantly. Miriam had half expected her mother to be taken away in handcuffs yesterday. But to her surprise, the police had only taken Mary's statement and promised to follow up. Maybe Devan had something to do with that—Miriam wasn't sure. Either way, she was grateful to have this time with her. They'd agreed Mary would stay at Miriam's place for a while.

Miriam eased onto the couch beside her mother. "Good morning. How did you sleep?"

"Good mornin'. I slept pretty good," Mary answered, her voice light.

"Same." Miriam smiled.

It was hard to believe her mother had confessed to killing her father just yesterday. Her demeanor now was so peaceful, almost radiant. In a way, it gave Miriam the courage she needed to open a door between them—one she hoped would lead to a new kind of relationship.

"Momma, I'm really glad we have this chance to talk. A lot happened in the past week. I learned things I didn't know... about you, Lisa, Nathaniel—even myself. I'm still trying to process most of it. But some things became clear right away." She paused, her expression serious. "That's what I want to talk about today."

Mary nodded, attentive. "Okay, babae. I'm listenin'."

Miriam inhaled deeply, then let the air out slowly. "First, I want to be honest with you. I've been angry with you for a long time." Her voice trembled. "I couldn't understand how you stayed with him. How you let him hurt you—and us. I thought it was because you were afraid. I thought you were weak. And why you never confronted Nathaniel."

She blinked back tears. "But then you told us what really happened. How no one helped you, how you suffered alone, how you tried to protect us. You felt guilty and ashamed for staying. You hated what he became. And when it finally ended, you were relieved."

Her voice cracked. "I didn't know, Momma. I didn't know any of that. And I'm so sorry I judged you."

Mary gently pulled her into an embrace, cradling Miriam's head on her shoulder. "It's okay, babae. If anythin', I owe you an apology. It's my own damn fault. I shoulda talked to you and ya brother about it. I could feel how upset you were, but I thought I deserved it. I didn't think I was worthy of forgiveness."

She tilted Miriam's chin, so their eyes met. "But all I did was make things worse. I know I didn't act like it, but I love you. With all my heart. I'm sorry I wasn't a better mom. But I promise I'll try to do better. Okay?"

Miriam nodded, wiping away a few lingering tears. "Okay, Momma. I love you too."

Mary smiled and brushed away a tear from Miriam's cheek. "What else you wanna talk about?"

Miriam sat up straighter, steadying herself. "I want to talk about... Nathaniel."

Mary exhaled, bracing herself. "Okay."

"I'm angry about what he did. I think he should be held accountable. I know he was a victim too, just like you and me—but that doesn't excuse what he tried to do."

Her voice lowered. "And I'm scared of him. The way he was this weekend... it's made it hard for me to separate him from our father."

She clenched her fists. "But I don't want to see him like that. That's not what I want our relationship to be. Looking back, I can see now there were times that he tried to reach out to me, but I turned a blind eye to it because I was still hurting and lost myself."

She drew a shaky breath. "I couldn't understand our father. But Nathaniel... I still might have a chance. So I'm going to try. I'm going to write to him. Slowly, build something. And I want all three of us to start going to family counseling."

She looked at Mary. "I was hoping you'd be open to that."

Mary's face softened. "I'd like that very much. I'm part of the reason he turned out the way he did."

She placed her hand over Miriam's. "You know, for a second, I thought you were gon' say you didn't want anythin' to do with him. I was scared of that."

She smiled faintly. "I was actually gon' ask what you thought I should do to make things right between me and him."

Miriam blinked. "Really? You were going to ask me for advice?"

"Well, of course," Mary grinned. "You the expert, ain't ya?"

Victoria Rose

Miriam knocked on Devan's apartment door. A few seconds passed before she heard the familiar click of the lock. When the door opened, Lisa stood in the frame. Her expression was solemn—softer than usual. It was a stark contrast to the distant, cool look she typically gave Miriam.

Miriam took a breath and consciously relaxed her shoulders. She softened her expression, her voice gentle. "How are you doing?"

The question was sincere. After everything that had happened the day before, Miriam had been worried—worried that Lisa might be holding it all in, quietly unraveling.

Lisa met her gaze, reading the concern written across Miriam's face. Something about it touched her more than she expected. She didn't let it show, not entirely, but her voice was calm and honest. "I can't say I'm the best I've ever been," she said, "but I'm okay... considering."

Miriam let out a slow, quiet sigh—part relief, part sorrow. "I wish there was something I could have done to stop him before it got to that point."

"I don't think there was anything *any* of us could have done. I'm just glad no one else got hurt."

"Me too." Miriam looked away briefly, then turned back. Her voice dropped. "But there is something I *can* do—that I *want* to do now. Something I should have done a long time ago."

Lisa's heart skipped. She braced herself, unsure where this was headed. So much had happened in so little time that she couldn't begin to guess. Was it about Ma? About Nathaniel? Or was Miriam gearing up to revisit Sunday's argument? Her thoughts raced, but she stayed quiet, lifting her eyebrows in invitation.

Miriam's eyes found hers again.

"You were right... about everything you said," she began. "I knew you needed me, but I was a coward. I never dealt with what happened when we were kids—the abuse, the fear, the silence. It haunted me. Every single day."

Her voice quivered. "I felt like I was drowning. Like I was stuck in the middle of the ocean during a storm, barely able to keep my head above water. And when your parents died... I was terrified. I knew if I stopped moving, that storm would swallow me whole."

She drew in a shaky breath. "I didn't think I was strong enough to face it—and be there for you. So I chose myself. I left you alone when you needed me most. And I'm sorry. I should've been there for you when your parents died."

Lisa's eyes widened. Her chest ached as tears spilled freely down her cheeks. She opened her mouth but couldn't speak. In all these years, through all the hurt, this was what she had longed for: acknowledgment. And now that it was here, the weight of it hit her all at once.

Miriam continued, her own tears blurring her vision. "After that, everything spiraled. I felt so guilty. I couldn't bear to be reminded of what I'd done, so I stayed away. I told myself I didn't need you anymore, but that was a lie I clung to out of fear."

She paused, her voice lower now. "When Momma wanted you to visit, I knew I couldn't avoid it anymore. So I faked it—pretended like I hadn't abandoned you. And when you finally called me out... I snapped. Not because you were wrong, but because you were right."

She shook her head. "I didn't want to admit what I'd done. Because then I'd have to face the truth... that I treated you like he treated us. That I used you—and discarded you when I felt like I didn't need you anymore."

Lisa's sobs came like a wave, sudden and sharp. The pain in her chest was unbearable, as if years of grief and abandonment had been waiting for this very moment to break loose. She bent forward, clutching her chest as the tears poured out.

Miriam winced. Watching Lisa break down, knowing she had caused that pain, was almost too much to bear—but she didn't look away. She couldn't. The time had come to stop running and just do.

Her voice rose through her tears, raw and unwavering. "But the biggest lie I told myself was that I didn't need you."

She swallowed hard, the words spilling out like truth finally set free. "You brought so much warmth, so much color and laughter into my life back then. You were always there—to hold me when I cried, to listen when I needed to talk. And somehow, even on the worst days, you'd slip in a joke just to make me smile."

Miriam's gaze stayed locked on Lisa, her voice steady despite the emotion in it. "Without question, I knew you had my back. Despite all the chaos around me, you never stopped being there for me. You were my peace. I wouldn't have survived if it weren't for you."

Lisa felt the weight in her chest begin to lift, just enough to breathe again. She wiped her tears, then straightened up and looked at Miriam. Miriam's eyes met hers—clear, steady, and open. There was no deflection, no fear. Just honesty. Care. Confidence. Lisa blinked, overcome by a strange and unexpected sensation. It felt like she was seeing Miriam for the first time in a long, long while.

"Yesterday," Miriam began softly, "when I found out I had almost lost you back then—and nearly lost you again—I was terrified. I realized how much time I wasted, running from someone who loved me deeply, someone I love just as much. The one person I can't imagine living without."

Her voice grew quiet, almost childlike, but her eyes never wavered. "I know I can't undo the pain I caused. I can't change the past. I haven't earned the right to ask you to be my best friend again. I haven't earned your forgiveness. But... I was hoping you'd let me try. Let me be there for you—like you were always there for me. Starting right now."

Hearing those words—words she had dreamed of for years—made Lisa want to jump for joy, throw her arms around

Miriam, shout yes, and forget all the hurt. But the ache was still there, quieter now, but present. That old voice whispered doubts: *What if things go back to how they were? What if this doesn't last?*

But Lisa was tired—tired of the distance that had grown so familiar between them. She wanted more. She knew their relationship wouldn't be what it once was, but it could be better than what it had become. Maybe, with time, it could even grow into something stronger. If that was the future she wanted, she had to put in some work too. That meant letting go of the fear, stepping beyond the walls she'd grown used to, and meeting Miriam halfway.

So why not start here.

Lisa wiped the last of her tears as a small, quiet smile formed.

"I'd like that very much."

EPILOGUE

Lisa felt like a bundle of nerves as she surveyed the restaurant. The dim chandeliers cast a soft golden glow across the room, while a live band filled the air with smooth, soulful jazz. Waiters moved in sync, weaving between tables as customers enjoyed their meals.

She and Devan had swapped places for the weekend—Lisa to visit Sean, and Devan to spend time with Josey. It was a meet-the-parents kind of moment, a milestone in any relationship, and one Lisa had never quite reached before. The thought stirred equal parts joy and apprehension. She was happy with where things were going, but this was unfamiliar ground. Vulnerable ground.

Sean had tried his best to calm her nerves. Sensing her unease, he'd said gently, "You don't have to worry. My dad already adores you."

Still, her mind whispered doubts: *What if he doesn't like me?*

Just as the question resurfaced, she spotted Sean waving enthusiastically across the room. Lisa took a deep breath, gave her outfit a quick once-over, and made her way to their table.

Mr. Crane's back was to her as he and Sean stood to greet her. But the moment he turned around, all of Lisa's fears began to melt. His face was open and warm, his eyes kind, his smile stretching ear to ear.

With a polite, slightly nervous smile, she extended her hand. "Hello, it's so nice to meet you."

Instead of shaking it, he pulled her into a gentle, fatherly hug. "Family don't shake hands—we hug," he said with a laugh. "It's nice to finally meet you too, young lady."

As he stepped back, his hands rested warmly on her shoulders, his expression beaming like he'd just unwrapped the best gift in the world.

"Come, let's sit," he said, gesturing to the table. "Speaking of family, I'm sorry I missed your brother, Devan, this time around. I was hoping maybe you and Sean—and Devan and Josey—could fly up to Chicago for a visit soon."

Then he leaned in a little, lowering his voice with a conspiratorial smile. "What do you think?"

Lisa blinked, stunned. Her mind raced.

Did he just call me family? Did Devan and Josey's names roll off his tongue like he's known them forever? Did he really just invite us like some kid excited to bring new friends home after school?

Sean chuckled beside her. "Dad, she just got here."

Mr. Crane gave him a playful look, murmuring like a scolded child, "What? It's not like it's a demand."

Then, brightening again, he added, "You told me Devan's a big Saints fan. Bears and Saints play in a couple months—we've got home field advantage. I could get us some great seats, but we'll need to act fast. And I know how much she wants to see Oprah," he said, turning back to Lisa with a mischievous sparkle in his eye. "I know some people. I could pull some strings, get you behind-the-scenes access."

"Dad!" Sean exclaimed, though his tone was more amused than annoyed.

Mr. Crane held up his hands innocently. "What? I'm just saying..."

A wave of mixed emotions suddenly swept over Lisa. She wished her parents could have been here. She imagined how her mother's eyes would've lit up at the mention of Oprah—how she'd leap at the chance to meet her, no hesitation. Her father, quieter and more composed, probably would've worn the same stunned expression she had now. She could almost see the two of them: her mom grinning, nudging her dad; her dad looking like he was about to make a break for the door.

The image made her laugh out loud.

She had a feeling that, given the chance, her parents and Mr. Crane would've gotten along great. Eventually, they would've been really close.

Both Sean and Mr. Crane turned to her, smiling with raised eyebrows.

"It's fine," she said with a smile, her voice light. "It's a great idea. And I think Devan and Josey will think so too."

Victoria Rose

As Josey chatted animatedly with her mother and sisters, Devan sat back, quietly reflecting on the weekend. He couldn't have asked for a better visit.

Josey had picked him up from the airport on Friday, and they'd spent that evening together, just the two of them. Saturday was the big day—he finally got to meet her family. But thanks to all the stories Josey had shared beforehand, he felt at ease the moment he walked in the door.

Apparently, the feeling was mutual.

As soon as Josey introduced him, her mother pulled him into a hug and rocked him gently—but with surprising strength—murmuring, "I finally get to meet my baby's knight in shining armor!"

Normally, that kind of greeting would've thrown him off, but Josey had warned him ahead of time. Since then, they hadn't stopped complimenting him on how kind and gentlemanly he was. He felt a bit embarrassed by the attention, but also deeply grateful. It felt good to be seen and appreciated.

He especially loved how eager they were to share stories about Josey growing up. He'd chuckled to himself watching her try to hide her face, begging her mom to stop talking about how quiet, shy, and innocent she used to be. It was obvious they were close. The love they shared as a family shined through in their laughter, their teasing, and the way they simply enjoyed being together.

They'd spent Saturday sightseeing, hitting up the King Center, the Botanical Gardens, and the Underground. Sunday had been just as packed—church in the morning, then dinner at her mother's house. Ms. Duncan had insisted on cooking, claiming she couldn't let Devan leave without a proper home-cooked meal. He didn't want to be a burden, but his stomach wasn't about to argue.

Now, full and content, everyone sat around enjoying the afterglow of good food and company.

Devan cleared his throat gently. "It's about time for me to head out."

Josey's lip jutted into a pout, and her mother and sisters let out a chorus of disappointed sighs.

"You gotta go already?" Amelia, asked sadly.

He nodded. "Unfortunately, I've got a 5AM flight. But I want to thank you all for showing me such incredible hospitality. I've really enjoyed my time here."

He turned to Josey's mom. "Ms. Duncan, before I go—I'd like to give you something."

He handed her a rectangular box wrapped in pink and gold. Josey had helped him sneak it in earlier while her mom was busy in the kitchen.

"Ooh, what's this?" Ms. Duncan asked, her eyes sparkling.

"I made it for you. I hope you like it."

She tore off the wrapping and opened the box. Her eyes widened as she lifted out a light pink shawl.

"Oh my Lord," she gasped. "I was just telling the girls I needed something like this for when the weather cools!" She ran her fingers along the fabric in awe. "It's so soft... so beautiful..."

As she opened the shawl fully, her fingers brushed over the inside, where an emblem was stitched near the hem.

"There's a tag..." she murmured. "'Victoria Rose.' I've never heard of that brand before."

She looked from the shawl to Devan, her brow furrowed as realization set in.

"Wait a minute. You said you made this. Did you really?"

Devan gave a sheepish smile. "I did."

All at once, the room filled with gasps.

Clara blinked at him. "Uhm, you sure you don't have any other single brothers?"

Before Devan could answer, Josey jumped in with a smirk. "Sorry, there's only one Victoria Rose Original."

Early the next morning, Devan stood bleary-eyed in the security line at Hartsfield. He stifled a yawn as the queue crawled forward, silently cursing his decision to book such an early flight. At the time, flying home Monday morning and heading straight to work had seemed like a smart way to stretch out his time with Josey. Now, running on fumes, he wasn't so sure.

At least the line was moving quickly. He stepped forward again, almost at the front.

Just as the security guard motioned him forward, a firm voice rang out from behind.

"Excuse me, sir. You've been selected for a random security search. Please step this way."

Devan froze—then smiled. He'd know that voice anywhere.

He turned around slowly, grinning from ear to ear.

"This is gonna be fun," he whispered.

Victoria Rose

Miriam shaded her eyes from the sun, keeping a close watch on Angellica. A gentle breeze swept across the beach, carrying the sounds of laughter from families, couples, and friends savoring the last days of summer. It felt good against her skin—a welcome reprieve from the heat. The rhythmic crash of waves against the shore soothed her, lulling her into thought. Her mind drifted to the not-so-distant past.

She still couldn't believe what had happened after her mother's confession. Miriam had contacted a lawyer immediately, bracing for the long legal battle ahead. But instead of charging her with murder, the prosecutor declined to press charges at all. Their lawyer explained it was likely due to the numerous police reports filed over the years, the eyewitnesses to her father's abuse, and the fact that he had been attacking Lisa when it happened. To Miriam, it felt nothing short of a miracle.

Her thoughts shifted to Nathaniel. She wondered if he'd ever received the letter she'd sent. She had spent an entire week trying to write it—scribbling out paragraph after paragraph, only to ball up the paper and start again. She wanted to get the words just right, to say something that would reach him. Something honest. Something that might make a difference. More than anything, she hoped it would be the beginning of something new between them—a chance to build a relationship where they both felt seen and heard.

A small voice broke through her thoughts.

"Miriam!"

She turned to see Angellica running toward her, waving excitedly. She plopped down on a beach chair beneath their canopy, panting and grinning from ear to ear.

"Looks like someone's having fun," Miriam said, smiling.

"The ocean is so big! This is the best vacation ever!" Angellica shouted, breathless with joy.

"I'm glad you're having a good time."

"I really am. It's like a dream come true," Angellica said with a sigh of wonder.

But then, her smile faded. She hesitated, opening her mouth as if to speak—but then closed it again. Miriam recognized the look. There was something on her mind, and she wasn't sure if she should say it.

"What's up?" Miriam asked gently.

"Remember when you told me I should find something that reminds me things will get better, even when they're bad?"

PEACE AMID THE CHAOS

Miriam blinked, surprised. She hadn't expected Angellica to remember that conversation. To her, it felt like it had happened ages ago. She nodded.

"I know what it is for me," Angellica said quietly.

A surge of pride welled up in Miriam's chest. She smiled, her voice light with curiosity. "That's great. What is it?"

Angellica glanced away. "Well... it's not a what. It's a who."

Miriam laughed. "Okay, Alex Trebek. I'll rephrase—who is it?"

Angellica smiled shyly, then turned back to Miriam. "It's you."

Miriam's hand flew to her chest, her jaw dropping as she gasped. It had never occurred to her that she could be someone else's peace—that she could give someone hope. Her eyes welled with tears as a wave of warmth washed over her. She scooped Angellica up into a hug and spun her around, laughing through her emotion.

"That's the best thing anyone's ever said to me," she whispered.

Angellica squealed with delight as Miriam held her tighter.

"What did I miss?" came a cheerful voice.

They looked up to see Lisa standing in front of them, her smile radiant, holding three cones of ice cream out in front of her.

"You too!" Angellica giggled.

Lisa's brow rose. "Me too what?"

"Definitely her too!" Miriam echoed, grinning.

Lisa's voice shot up an octave. "Definitely her too what?"

Without another word, Miriam and Angellica rushed forward, wrapping Lisa in a playful, half-tackle, half-hug.

"Whoa—ice cream!" Lisa laughed, stepping back carefully, trying not to drop the cones as the two clung to her tighter.

She looked between them, confused but smiling. She wasn't sure what was going on, but something in her chest fluttered as lightness spread through her.

Then came the sound—Miriam's laugh.

Lisa had almost forgotten how it used to light up the darkest rooms, how it made her feel like everything was right in the world. It filled the air now—bright, unburdened, and free.

Then, through the joy and noise, another laugh rose up—so soft, so familiar, it made her pause.

For a heartbeat, she didn't recognize it.

But then she did.

It was her own.

About the Author

Shannon Singleton has been captivated by books for as long as she can remember. That early fascination turned into a passion for writing when she took Mrs. Tureau's creative writing class in 7th grade—and she's been writing ever since.

She is the proud mother of two sons, Jaylen and Ty. From a young age, Jaylen shared her love of reading, often finishing books in just a day or two. But as he read more, Shannon noticed a troubling pattern: very few of those books featured African American protagonists—or any Black characters at all. Jaylen didn't see himself reflected in the stories he loved.

It was a realization that mirrored Shannon's own childhood experience. Determined to help change that narrative, she launched her nonfiction children's book series in 2024: *Jaylen & Ty's Adventures Based on True Stories*.

Now expanding her storytelling to a wider audience, *Peace Amid the Chaos* marks Shannon's debut into adult fiction.

Through her work, she hopes to help shift the landscape of minority representation in literature—one story at a time.

Want to keep up with Shannon's writing journey, get behind-the-scenes peeks, or read her monthly "Reflections and Other Shit" (yes, that's really what it's called)? Scan the QR code or visit https://www.irisepublishing.com/meet-our-authors/shannon-c-singleton to sign up for her newsletter. It's just once a month—no inbox flooding, only good vibes, book updates, life musings, and where you can find Shannon's latest releases.

A NOTE FROM THE AUTHOR

Thank you so much for joining me on this journey. It truly means the world that you took the time to read Peace Amid the Chaos and spend time with these characters.

I hope at least one of them found a way into your heart—whether through their strength, their flaws, or the emotions they stirred.

If this story moved you in any way, I'd be so grateful if you shared your thoughts in a review. Hearing how the book connected with you is one of the most meaningful parts of this process for me.

Thank you again—and I hope this is just the beginning of our story together.

With gratitude,

Shannon Singleton

Made in the USA
Monee, IL
25 August 2025